"You're trembling, Mrs. Robey,"

Riley said softly as his arms came around her and his hand pressed warm and strong against her back. "Why is that?"

Summer tried to laugh. "It's been a long time since I danced."

"I was sure it had been," Riley replied.

There was a strange timbre in his voice that made her shiver even more, and her voice was bumpy as she said, "What if I've forgotten how?"

He smiled. "Would you like to stand on my feet?"

"I'm wearing heels," Summer said with a husky chortle. "You'd be crippled for life."

He laughed and said, "I doubt that."

And she thought, No, I'm the one who will be crippled. After this, when we leave here, how will I ever forget you?

After you, Riley Grogan, what man can there ever be…for *me?*

Dear Reader,

It's summer, the perfect time to sit in the shade (or the air conditioning!) and read the latest from Silhouette Intimate Moments. Start off with Marie Ferrarella's newest CHILDFINDERS, INC. title, *A Forever Kind of Hero*. You'll find yourself turning pages at a furious rate, hoping Garrett Wichita and Megan Andreini will not only find the child they're searching for, but will also figure out how right they are for each other.

We've got more miniseries in store for you this month, too. Doreen Roberts offers the last of her RODEO MEN in *The Maverick's Bride*, a fitting conclusion to a wonderful trilogy. And don't miss the next of THE SISTERS WASKOWITZ, in Kathleen Creighton's fabulous *One Summer's Knight*. Don't forget, there's still one sister to go. Judith Duncan makes a welcome return with *Murphy's Child*, a FAMILIES ARE FOREVER title that will capture your emotions and your heart. Lindsay Longford, one of the most unique voices in romance today, is back with *No Surrender*, an EXPECTANTLY YOURS title. And finally, there's Maggie Price's *Most Wanted*, a MEN IN BLUE title that once again allows her to demonstrate her understanding of romance and relationships.

Six marvelous books to brighten your summer—don't miss a single one. And then come back next month, when six more of the most exciting romance novels around will be waiting for you—only in Silhouette Intimate Moments.

Enjoy!

Yours,

Leslie J. Wainger
Executive Senior Editor

Please address questions and book requests to:
Silhouette Reader Service
U.S.: 3010 Walden Ave., P.O. Box 1325, Buffalo, NY 14269
Canadian: P.O. Box 609, Fort Erie, Ont. L2A 5X3

ONE SUMMER'S KNIGHT

KATHLEEN CREIGHTON

Published by Silhouette Books

America's Publisher of Contemporary Romance

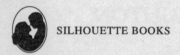 SILHOUETTE BOOKS

ISBN 0-373-07944-3

ONE SUMMER'S KNIGHT

Visit us at www.romance.net

Printed in U.S.A.

KATHLEEN CREIGHTON

has roots deep in the California soil but has relocated to South Carolina. As a child, she enjoyed listening to old-timers' tales and her fascination with the past only deepened as she grew older. Today, she says she is interested in everything—art, music, gardening, zoology, anthropology and history, but people are at the top of her list. She also has a lifelong passion for writing, and now combines her two loves in romance novels.

For the sisters Modrovich,
my daughters;
Gorgeous, talented, brilliant and utterly adored,
My constant source of worry, admiration,
inspiration, amusement and pride.

Chapter 1

It had never entered Summer Robey's mind that she might go to jail. Primarily because it was unthinkable.

Jail. The word, spoken in the judge's stern, Southern voice, rumbled inside her head like far-off thunder, ominous and threatening. Impossible, she thought. There were the children. The animals. She couldn't possibly go to jail.

Summer, she ordered herself, take a deep breath. They didn't really put people in jail for owing money anymore, did they? Hadn't there been wars fought over that sort of thing? Hadn't debtors' prisons been banished long ago?

Deep in her heart she knew she wouldn't *really* go to jail. For one thing, her family would never let it happen. It was the injustice of it all that was so overwhelming. And the humiliation. *Oh, Lord, the humiliation.*

Sitting in that overheated courtroom, hearing the judge's rebuke echo in her ears, Summer felt exactly as if she'd been slapped. Her cheeks burned with it! All right, she'd never actually been slapped in the face in her life, but she was sure this must be what it would feel like. To be scolded like a child, publicly chastised in front of all those people…those strangers, the clerks and bailiffs, the spectators and lawyers.

Especially *that* lawyer, the opposing counsel, her enemy, the hospital's high-priced ace. *What was his name?*

Two last names. Riley…Grogan—that was it. A strange name, she'd thought, for a man so polished, so elegant, so immaculately groomed—so utterly heartless!—with his soft, Southern aristocrat's voice and his cold blue eyes. A street fighter's name. Oh, how she wished she'd had someone as ruthless fighting on *her* side!

She should have hired a lawyer, no matter what the cost. Charly had told her so, and now that it was too late, Summer knew that she was right. Charly was Summer's sister Mirabella's best friend, as well as the family's attorney, but at the moment she was off in the South Seas honeymooning with her husband Troy, who also happened to be the big brother of Mirabella's husband Jimmy Joe. Which, as Jimmy Joe would have put it, was a whole 'nother story.

"First thing you do is get yourself a lawyer and declare bankruptcy," Charly had yelled over a bad satellite phone connection from somewhere in Tahiti. But Summer had cringed at the thought. It would have been bad enough having to ask Bella and Jimmy Joe for the money to hire an attorney. Horrible enough having to take her humiliating family problems— her miserable failures—to a stranger. But bankruptcy? Never. Summer Robey might be all but penniless and backed into a corner, but she did have her pride.

And what had all that pride got her? Simply the worst, the most humiliating day of her life.

How could this have happened? How could *she* be held liable for her ex-husband's hospital bill when it was *he* who had deserted her, deserted his kids, leaving them virtually penniless and with the bank foreclosing on their home?

But unbelievably, none of that had mattered to this Southern judge. Immaterial, he'd called it, even if she'd had proof of her allegations. Which she didn't. How could she have known Hal would become so desperate as to do such a thing? He'd seemed better, those last few months. She'd even allowed herself to hope.... Stupid. Stupid. She should have known.

But it had never once occurred to her that she might not be believed. It was Hal Robey who was the compulsive gambler and congenital liar, Summer who was the responsible parent and respected veterinarian—didn't that prove something?

Too bad. As the judge had coldly pointed out, there'd already been a ruling in this case, and the deadline for appeal had long since passed. The case could not be retried. Meanwhile, there was a judgment against her. She had been ordered by a California court to pay the rehab hospital's bill. An order that she had chosen to ignore. Therefore, the judge had no option but to find her in contempt.

Contempt. Oh, yes, she'd seen it in the judge's eyes when he'd scolded her as if she were a child—or an irresponsible nitwit. Of course, she knew that's what he thought, that she was just another California bimbo, a dumb little beach bunny. And who could blame him? Because, unfortunately, that was exactly what she looked like.

For most of Summer's life her looks had been her greatest trial. For while she realized she looked very much like her name—golden and breezy, carefree and sunny—that was not who she really was. For one thing, she knew she looked much younger than her thirty-five years—when she wasn't gaunt and hollow-eyed with worry—young enough to still get carded every time she ordered wine with dinner or bought a six-pack of beer at the supermarket, young enough that she could have fit right in with the crowds of gum-popping teenagers who hung out at the mall near her clinic, making conversation that seemed to consist mostly of ''I mean, like, totally awesome, y'know?'' No one would ever guess to look at her that she was a practicing vet with two kids and a truly frightening house payment.

And beach bunny? Well, she *was* blond—thanks to genetics, not choice—with a healthy glow to her skin that had little to do with exposure to the sun. But with the demands of her clinic, not to mention the hectic schedule set for her by the children's activities, she had precious little time for the beach. If it wasn't some school project, it was David's swim practice or one of Helen's gymnastics meets—for which Summer would almost invariably show up late, still wearing a smock smeared with heaven-knows-what and reeking of nervous animal. At least the children would forgive her for that, since it was what they'd grown up with and were pretty much used to. As co-custodians of an elderly and vile-tempered Persian cat, a timid but adorable Chihuahua, and an African gray parrot with an IQ surpassing that of some college students of her acquaintance, they often wore those telltale smears and scents themselves.

Theirs had been a lively household at times. Interesting, to say the least. *Had been.*

Summer sat quietly, her shoulders slumping with defeat. As she gazed out the courtroom's high, multipaned windows at a January sky the dingy gray of old dishwater, she thought about the blue of January skies in California, and the roses that would still be blooming in the front yard of her ranch-style house, nestled in its securely affluent suburb at the foot of the San Gabriel Mountains.

And she thought about the rented mobile home she and the children and the animals lived in now—an ugly brown shoe box set down in a patch of dusty, weedy grass, with a gravel driveway and a single oak tree for shade. *But* conveniently located only a mile from the terminus of the mobile vet service where she'd found employment as a vet-tech, traveling around to local communities, helping to dispense rabies shots and heartworm pills. Her own clinic—yes, perhaps she missed that most of all.

Lively, chaotic…interesting. Oddly enough, she realized as she pulled her gaze away from the windows and began to gather up her coat, her purse, notebook and pen, those words she'd used to describe her former life did still apply to this one. But, oh, how different. Thanks to Hal, that charming scoundrel she'd married right out of vet school with everyone's blessing, something else had been added. *Fear.* Of all the things she had to forgive her former husband for, that was the hardest.

Forgive you, Hal?

As much as she wanted to, she really couldn't blame Hal; she knew compulsive gambling was a sickness, like alcoholism or any other addiction. She knew her husband needed help, more help than she'd been able to give him, and that he'd tried, truly tried, more times than she could count, to straighten himself out.

But this…this time it's too much, Hal. Even for you. Yes, I'm angry, damn you. I'm angry with you for taking away the life we knew, but especially for putting that look of fear in your children's eyes.

The cold of the January sky came to settle around Summer's heart. No way around it, she would have to borrow the money to pay the judgment. Her sisters would help out—Bella, and Evie, if she could track her down in whatever desert or jungle she was filming at the moment. And Mom and Dad probably would, too, if she asked them. Oh, she did hope it wouldn't come to that. Their retirement income was stretched thin enough as it was.

Slowly she rose, lifted the strap of her handbag to her shoulder, folded her coat over her arm. She took a deep breath, pleased that her legs no longer felt as though they might buckle, and began the short walk up the aisle between the rows of spectators' seats to the double doors at the back of the courtroom.

"Would you excuse me for a minute?" Riley touched the sleeve of his client's expensively tailored suit and moved around him on a course intended to intercept the woman who was just emerging from the courtroom. She hadn't seen him yet. He had an idea that when she did she'd take pains to avoid him, and he meant to see that she didn't, if he could.

He saw that she still wore a dazed look, along with a slight flush—residual effects, he was sure, from the humiliation of the public dressing-down she'd just endured. Riley did regret that, especially since he knew it was mostly his fault the way Judge Stoner had lit into her. Well, hell, it was his job to bring judges and juries around to seeing things the way he wanted them to, and he was good at it. He could have had that judge convinced Summer Robey was Joan of Arc or Lizzie Borden, if he'd wanted to, but it had suited his purposes to make sure she came across as merely arrogant and irresponsible instead. The fact that she had a body that'd look right at home loping across a California beach in one of those red lifeguard's bathing suits they wore on that popular TV show hadn't made his job any more difficult, either. But while he hadn't wanted to risk her appearing even the slightest bit sympathetic, he really hadn't intended the judge to come down on her quite so hard.

He watched her come toward him, still unaware that she was on a collision course with the man responsible for her degradation, busy digging through her pocketbook for something—car keys, probably—a frown of distraction making a tidy pleat between her brows. In addition to the sun-streaked hair and a body that wouldn't quit, she had a certain coltishness, he decided, that made her seem much younger than she was. This in spite of the rather dowdy way she wore her hair, pulled back in a nondescript ponytail, and the unbecoming army-green shade of her slacks and turtleneck pullover. Pastels, he thought. She should wear sunny yellows, pale pinks, soft silvery blue....

His regret became a physical pressure inside his chest, demanding that he try to ease it with a breath...almost a sigh. Dammit, he knew this woman. Knew her kind, at least. Had seen them sitting bewildered and drained across the table from him, all too often still wearing the black-and-blue marks that came of too much love and too much trust coupled with too much pride. Neither saint nor bimbo, this woman. She was, for want of a better name, what Riley liked to call a Giver. The kind of woman Takers homed in on like bees to a blossom. A sucker for every underdog, a magnet for every weak and needy creature to come down the road. But when she needed help? Her kind of woman inevitably had way too much pride to ask for it. She'd try to go it alone even if it killed her. Sometimes, it did.

"Mrs. Robey? May I speak to you for a minute?"

The frown disappeared as her eyes widened and her head came up, reminding him of a wild doe when she hears a twig crack.

This is a mistake, Riley thought. He could feel the client's eyes on him, too, and knew the man was going to be wondering what the hell this crafty Southern lawyer of his was up to. In Riley's experience, Californians and northerners just naturally assumed Southern lawyers were all a bunch of good ol' boys and crooked as a dog's hind leg.

The woman had stopped directly in front of him. She was taller than he'd thought, with rather thin, sharply honed features and eyes the clear, pale blue of sapphires. On a level with his chin, they regarded him steadily, telegraphing her resentment, bitterness and hurt. But she didn't say a word. A little too polite, he thought, to tell him to go to hell.

Still mindful of the watchful client, he spoke softly, choosing his words carefully. "Mrs. Robey, I'd just like to offer you a word of advice. Next time you find yourself in court, you need to do yourself a favor...." She waited, cocked and wary, for him to finish. "Hire yourself a good attorney."

She caught her breath then, and made a soft sound that might have been a laugh. Her lips tugged themselves into a half smile, stiffly, no doubt against her will. "Yeah, I'll keep that in mind," she said as she stepped around him.

Riley watched her make her way down the marble stairs, one hand gripping the rail as if she really needed the support. Dammit, he thought as he turned back to his waiting client. *Dammit all to hell.*

Summer sat on her hands and stared through the windshield without really seeing the bleakness of the January sky while she waited for the smelly and rust-pocked sedan to warm up. The Olds had been all she could afford after selling everything she owned to pay off Hal's bills—an attempt to salvage her good credit that now appeared to have been an exercise in futility—and she hated it with a passion. It was transportation, nothing more, and she was never, ever, going to call it *hers*. In her mind there was a certain symbolism in the acknowledgment of the wretched junker that would be like conceding defeat.

I thought his eyes were cold, cold as that sky, but they aren't. Not at all.

The thought came out of nowhere, as the image in her mind's eye merged and blended with the winter scene before her until she could no longer distinguish one from the other. Perhaps she'd only imagined it, just now, but could it possibly have been *compassion* she'd seen in that coldhearted lawyer's eyes?

The Starr family's big old-fashioned kitchen was crowded that morning, noisy with laughter and the clatter of pots and the tinkle of metal jar lids. It smelled of burned blackberry jam, which wasn't as bad a smell as Mirabella would have supposed, mixed with the scent of new-mown grass carried in through the open door on a sweet June breeze.

The same breeze brought the sound of her stepson J.J.'s squabbles with his cousin Sammi June over baby-sitting rights to eighteen-month-old Amy Jo, who was gleefully in pursuit of the kittens a stray calico mama cat had hidden out in the garden shed sometime in April. The sound of that laughter, Mirabella decided as she watched her daughter through the screen porch door, had to be one of the sweetest in all the world, sweeter than the music of a thousand wind chimes…choirs of angels. Well, maybe she was a *little* besotted.

At the thought, her gaze shifted automatically to the man she could just see beyond the doorway to the hall, trying to talk on the phone. He had his head down and a finger stuck in his free ear in a futile effort to dampen down the noise all around him. And as so often happened when she caught a glimpse of her husband—little things, like the glint of light on

his dark blond hair or the flash of his slow, sweet smile—
something bumped up under her ribs and made her catch her
breath. Something composed of varying parts happiness, awe
and fear. A year and a half later, Mirabella still hadn't quite
gotten used to the wonder of Jimmy Joe Starr.

A year and a half. Could it really have been that long ago
that they'd shared the Christmas miracle of Amy's birth in the
sleeper of Jimmy Joe's eighteen-wheeler on an ice-bound
Texas interstate? Had a year—yes, to the day—gone by since
she'd gazed into his brown eyes and pledged through a shimmer of tears to love him for all the days of her life?

It was true, though—today was her anniversary. The family
was even now gathering for the celebration; tonight the whole
Starr clan would be here for barbecue and black-eyed beans
and corn bread, and plenty of fresh blackberries to go with the
homemade ice cream. But where in the world had the year
gone? It had passed in a moment, a snap of the fingers, the
blink of an eye. And yet, so much had happened in that time.

To begin with, there'd been the amazing and hectic week
leading up to the wedding, when Mirabella's best friend and
maid of honor, Charly Phelps, having flown out from Los
Angeles a week early, had somehow managed to get herself
thrown in jail in the tiny Alabama hill town of Mourning
Spring. And when Troy, Jimmy Joe's oldest brother and best
man, had gone to see what he could do about bailing her out,
in spite of the fact that Charly had once pledged to loathe and
despise all things Southern until her dying day, they'd wound
up falling in love. Speaking of miracles! They'd gotten married, themselves, just last fall. Now, to top it all off, Charly
was pregnant and, at this very minute, upstairs in the guest
bathroom suffering through a horrendous bout of morning
sickness.

As if that hadn't been enough excitement, just two days
before Mirabella's wedding, her sister Summer had arrived in
a U-Haul truck packed with all her worldly goods, including
her two kids and a motley assortment of animals, having just
filed for a divorce from her husband of ten years, that irre-

sponsible bum, Hal. And *that* was just the beginning! It
seemed that Hal—

"Hey, Marybell, how's it goin'?" Jimmy Joe's whisper in
her ear spilled a cascade of shivers down her spine.

"Fine," she whispered back. "Who was that on the
phone?"

"Ah, that was just my brother Calvin."

"Customer problems?"

"Nothin' he can't handle." He leaned down to kiss the top
of her head. "Take more'n that to pull me away on our anniversary, darlin'." He straightened and gave her shoulder a
squeeze. "Got to run over to the house, though. Cal's needin'
some numbers. Be right back."

Mirabella nodded and replied with a brisk "See you later."
But her brow furrowed as she watched her husband squeeze
past Troy and Charly's huge yellow-eyed chocolate Lab, who
had parked himself in front of the screen door. Poor Bubba
was suffering divided loyalties, what with Charly throwing up
in the bathroom and Troy gone off to the store to find her
some saltines and cola for her nausea.

Out on the lawn, Jimmy Joe had paused to swing Amy up
in a quick hug before handing her over to J.J. and Sammi
June. Mirabella watched him with a familiar lump in her throat
until he'd driven away in their silver-gray Lexus. But when
she turned back to the panful of dusty blackberries in front of
her, her gaze was snared instead by another pair of wise brown
eyes with a golden gleam of fire lurking in their depths.

It's the fire, Mirabella thought suddenly. That's what's missing from Jimmy Joe's eyes these days.

"Problems?" Jimmy Joe's mama, Betty Starr, asked softly.

Mirabella shook her head. "He just needs to get some information for Cal. He'll be right back." Her gaze dropped to
her berry-stained fingers as she quirked a wan half smile and
muttered, "Paperwork. Always something." But she knew the
evasion was useless; when it came to her kids, Jimmy Joe's
mama didn't miss much, and it was a pretty safe bet that she
hadn't missed the worry in Mirabella's eyes.

Okay, maybe worry was too strong a word, but concern, at least. And she didn't even know if she was justified in that. After all, in the last eighteen months, her husband's trucking business had grown beyond anyone's hopes and dreams, thanks to the hoopla over Amy's birth. All the major networks had carried the story of the gallant trucker delivering a baby on a snowbound interstate on Christmas Day. Jimmy Joe had been an overnight sensation, a hero, albeit a reluctant one. Job offers had begun pouring in almost immediately and hadn't slowed down since. As a result, instead of the one Kenworth Jimmy Joe had nicknamed "The Big Blue Star," Blue Star Transport now owned a fleet of six trucks and counted two of the Starr brothers, Calvin and Roy, among its drivers. Jimmy Joe still had more business than he could handle and was looking for a piece of property on which to build Blue Star Transport's new terminal. Mirabella just wished she could be certain all this success was making the man she loved *happy*.

From over at the sink, where she was up to her elbows in jam jars and soapsuds, Jimmy Joe's sister Jess, mother of Sammi June, gave a cackle of laughter. "Paperwork—now, there's something I just can't picture. I sure never did figure Jimmy Joe for a businessman, did you, Mama?"

Betty said, "Oh, I think he can be anything he sets his mind to." And she smiled at Mirabella and winked as if to say, *Don't worry about that one, hon—he knows what he's doing. Life is always goin' to have its little ups and downs....*

Mirabella nodded as the sounds of running water and banging doors came once again from overhead. All four women—Betty and Jess, Granny Calhoun and Mirabella—glanced upward and exchanged empathetic glances and sighs. They'd all been through it before.

When it got quiet upstairs again, Granny Calhoun, her twig-like fingers nimbly stemming blackberries, aimed a sly, sideways look at Mirabella and croaked, "You're lookin' broody, y'sef. Got those dark circles und'neath your eyes. You keepin' secrets, baby girl?"

"Secrets?" Mirabella frowned. "No, I just haven't been

sleeping very well the last few days for some reason, that's all.'' Suddenly aware of the listening stillness, she looked up and encountered three pairs of avid eyes. Heat flooded her cheeks. She laughed. ''What? Oh, no—not me. I'm not pregnant, if that's what you're thinking. No way.'' *At least, I hope not. Please, God. Jimmy Joe sure doesn't need anything else to worry about. Please God, not now…* She brushed back her hair with a careless hand, leaving smears of purple juice. ''I think I've just been worried about Summer and Evie.''

''Your sisters?'' Betty lifted a kettle off of a burner before she turned, eyebrows raised in concern. ''What's the trouble, hon? Summer doin' okay? I know she's had a pretty tough time, startin' all over and all.''

''She's doing okay, as far as I know.'' Inspired, Mirabella gave another laugh and embellished it with a touch of embarrassment, hoping it would be enough to account for the blush. ''I've just been…well, I've been dreaming about her lately. Evie, too. A lot.''

Granny Calhoun cried, ''Hah!'' Betty smiled and picked up a wooden spoon and went back to skimming.

Relieved at the success of her diversion, Mirabella let out a breath and muttered, ''Not that I'm superstitious.'' Well, she never had been in her life, before. Since coming to live in the South, and the way things had worked out with her and Jimmy Joe, and then Troy and Charly, she'd had to rethink some of her former convictions.

Granny Calhoun gave a little jerk and laughed suddenly, a sound like a twig scratching on a windowpane. She pointed a crooked finger at Jess and said, ''My sister Effie—that's your great-aunt Eufemia—thought she had the second sight, you know. You ask me, she just liked the attention it got her. All that stuff is just a bunch of hooey, anyway.'' She gave a snort and went back to stemming berries. After a moment she peered up at Mirabella, turtlelike, from her osteoporotic crouch. ''Dreams, now. Just means you can be expectin' a visit sometime soon. That's all that is.''

Over at the sink, Jess nudged her mother with an elbow and

said slyly, "Hey, Granny, I thought all that was just a bunch of hooey." Mirabella hid her smile.

Granny Calhoun said nothing, taking her time picking out a particularly nice ripe berry and putting it in her mouth. She ate it with soft, sucking noises, then delicately spat out the husk into her hand. "There's hooey," she said, "and then there's fact. You dream about somebody, they'll be a'visitin' soon, and that's a fact."

"Summer's coming for the party," said Mirabella. "Does that count?"

But Granny Calhoun had lost interest and was searching through the berries for another that looked good enough to eat.

"You ever get ahold of Evie?" Betty asked as she tossed the wooden spoon into the sink and reached for a clean, scalded jar.

Mirabella shook her head. "I've left messages on her machine. She'll get around to me when she gets back from wherever she's gone off to, I guess."

"She'll be comin'," Granny Calhoun croaked suddenly. "You can bet on it. Mark my words."

"Who's comin'?" Troy asked as he and Jimmy Joe clomped into the kitchen, leaving a disappointed Bubba whining outside the screen door. Jimmy Joe came to lean on the back of Mirabella's chair and drop a kiss onto the top of her head while Troy carried his plastic grocery sack over to the counter.

Granny Calhoun lifted one frail arm to point at Troy and instructed, "Pour some'a that cola in a bowl and let it go flat. You want it flat to settle the stomach."

Troy said, "I will, Granny," and then asked his mother in a soft aside, "Where is she? Still throwin' up?"

"Umm-hmm." Her hands full, Betty used her head to point the way. Troy gave a worried sigh and headed for the stairs.

"Who's comin'?" Jimmy Joe softly inquired of the back of Mirabella's neck.

Breathless and prickly, she had opened her mouth to reply when Granny's gnarled, blue-veined hand suddenly clamped onto her forearm. "Don't you fret," the old lady chirped, berry-stained lips curving in a smile of innocence belied by the crafty gleam in her sharp old eyes. "I'm gon' keep your secret for you, don't you worry."

Mirabella's breath exploded in a gust. Jimmy Joe straightened up and said, "What secret?"

Over at the sink, Jess sang out, "Hah—I *knew* it. Granny's never been wrong yet."

Betty made an exasperated noise and muttered, "Mama, for Lord's sake."

Jimmy Joe said, "What secret's she talkin' about?"

Granny Calhoun cast her eyes demurely downward and turned her fingers at her lips, pantomiming turning a key in a lock.

"Marybell?" Jimmy Joe's hands were gentle but insistent on her shoulders.

Trapped.

But fate must have been on her side, because at that moment, Bubba rose up from his post beside the screen door and launched himself down the porch steps in full cry. Out on the lawn, the excited yells of children blended with the clatter and thump of a badly tuned engine. The unmistakable smell of burning petroleum products drifted into the kitchen.

Mirabella gulped out a laugh and sprang to her feet. "Summer's here!" she cried, and brushing a kiss across her husband's perplexed half smile, she went out to greet her youngest sister, her heart pounding with relief and a certain guilty excitement.

Chapter 2

"Happy anniversary!" Summer sang as Mirabella hugged her. "I can't believe it's been a year."

"Yeah, I know, I was just thinking the same thing. Mmm, it's good to see you. I'm glad you were able to get away."

"Me, too." Summer broke the hug and held her older sister, tinier by at least a head, at arm's length. "You look great." *She looks tired,* she thought. *I hope everything's all right.*

"And how are the little darlings?"

Summer winced and bit back a defensive retort. Sure, the kids had been a bit difficult, and with everything they'd gone through, who could blame them? But—she took a deep breath—Bella was Bella. Yes, she could be judgmental at times, especially when it came to other people's kids, and Summer couldn't deny the twinges of hurt. But it was her sister's anniversary, and the last thing she wanted was to quarrel. She owed Bella and her family so much, and not just the money for the judgment, either. Without their help and acceptance...

She took a breath and said evenly, "They're doing okay.

David internalizes, Helen vents—that's about normal for them.''

Her sister made a little grimace, using her fingers to rake a wave of hair back from her face. ''Sumz, I'm sorry.''

So easily the pain was erased. Summer laughed and touched the smear of purple on her sister's temple. ''Hey, look—I know they're monsters, okay? Forget it—help me bring stuff in from the car.''

''Car? That's using the term loosely,'' Mirabella muttered as they approached the old clunker. Already back in form, she had her nose wrinkled up and was looking alarmed, as if she thought the oxidation and blotches of rust on the Oldsmobile's greenish-blue paint job was some sort of disease that might be caught by her shiny silver Lexus.

''Hey, I'm just glad it runs.'' Summer had wrenched open the back door and was gathering up the detritus of a three-hour car trip with a nine-year-old and a five-year-old—coloring books and broken crayons, David's tattered gray ''bunny'' blankie, Helen's fearsome-looking rubber lizard, and assorted pillows, Gameboy cartridges, shoes and socks.

She reached between the front seat backs and took a paper grocery sack from the passenger seat and peered anxiously into it. The African violet had survived the trip, she saw with relief. She handed it to Mirabella with a careless ''Here, this is for you and Jimmy Joe. Happy anniversary.'' But her chest was tight and her cheeks burned with shame. Her sister's first wedding anniversary, and all she had to give her was a two-dollar plant from the flower department at Winn Dixie.

But Bella was cradling the paper bag as if it contained the crown jewels. ''Oh, Sumz, you didn't have to do this.''

Summer couldn't look at her. ''The kids have something for you, too. Refrigerator magnets with their pictures on them. They made a card.'' Keeping her back turned. Keeping her distance. *Don't hug me, Bella, please don't hug me. If you make me cry, I'll never forgive you.*

From behind her she heard a huffed-out breath, a small

laugh, quivery with unexpected emotion. Bella? Sentimental? Oh, God, what did *that* mean?

But all her sister said was "Well. This is so nice. My very first anniversary present. Thank you." And after a moment she added, "You didn't bring the beasts?"

Blinking away the tickle of tears, Summer straightened with her arms full and said lightly, "I assume you mean the furred-and-feathered kind? The vet I work for was kind enough to keep them for the weekend."

"Nice of him," said Mirabella, her voice carefully neutral. There was a pause, filled with the hum of a June afternoon, punctuated with the nearby yips and cries of romping children. And then her voice came softly, oddly tentative for Bella. "Sumz? You okay?"

Caught off guard, Summer threw her a look of genuine surprise. The Bella she knew from childhood had never been so sensitive to the moods of others. "Yeah, sure. Why?"

"You *sure?* This is your sister talking—The Sisters Waskowitz, remember?"

Just for a heartbeat, Summer's resolve wavered. The old childhood nickname along with her sister's tone of unwonted concern had almost thrown her for a minute; it was going to take a while to get used to this kinder, gentler Mirabella.

She felt a sudden wave of emotion—nostalgia, but with sadness in it, and regret, too. *The Sisters Waskowitz.* That was how they'd been known in the small California desert town where they'd spent their growing-up years. The police chief's kids—two tall blondes and one short, spunky redhead. Evie, with her venturesome spirit and flair for the dramatic, always into something new and outrageous, like as not making the local papers, setting the standard of infamy for her sisters to live up to and the town on its ear in the bargain. Mirabella, the redhead, the brain, the feisty, pint-size dynamo with the king-size chip on her shoulder. And finally, Summer, quieter than her sisters, the one everyone depended on, the one people came to with their troubles. Summer, who could fix things—

and animals. Summer, who would always find a way to make it better.

The Sisters Waskowitz. The three of them, so different, and yet so close. As children, anyway. What had happened to them? How was it that as adults they'd grown so far apart? Until Bella's wedding last summer, it had been years since they'd been in close and frequent touch.

Suddenly, as if her thoughts had been wandering along similar paths, Mirabella said, "Have you heard from Evie?"

"Not for a while." Summer nudged the car door closed with her hip. "Last I heard, I think she was in Vegas."

"Here, let me take something… Vegas? That's not so bad."

Summer gave a short laugh as she relinquished a pillow and a plastic grocery sack full of fast-food trash; compared to some of the places their sister's career as a documentary filmmaker had taken her, Las Vegas did seem reasonably tame.

They were walking slowly toward the house when Mirabella frowned and added, "So, you'd think she'd call."

This time, Summer's one-note laugh said, Evie? Our Evie? You've got to be kidding! "Oh, you know," she said, smiling at the ground, "Evie immerses herself in her work." Neither would ever think to call their sister selfish—it was just her way. She let a beat or two go by, then slanted a look at her sister. "Are Charly and Troy here?" It was the right timing and she kept it casual, but under her ribs she could feel her heart quicken as she waited for the answer. If anyone could help her now, Troy and Charly could. Not only was Charly a lawyer, but Troy was a private investigator. And hadn't she heard someone say that he'd once been a navy SEAL?

Mirabella's smile tilted wryly. "They're upstairs. Charly's lying down. She hasn't been feeling too well."

Summer's heart gave a lurch. She could feel it now, tap-tapping away at the base of her throat. "Oh? What's the matter? She's not sick, is she?" *Please don't let her be sick. Not now. Not when I need her so badly.*

Mirabella gave a little gasp of chagrin. "Oh, God, that's right, I haven't told you the news—Charly's pregnant!"

"Pregnant…" Summer's heart sank into her stomach, where it continued to pulse away, now a dismal little drumbeat. "That's…wonderful."

"Well, I'm not sure she thinks it's so wonderful at the moment. From what I understand, she had a pretty lousy couple of months with her first, and that was more than twenty years ago. Anyway, the doctors have told her to take it easy, at least for the first trimester."

Charly's pregnant.… Well, that's it, then, Summer thought. *I can't possibly ask her. I can't.* She felt curiously numb. Almost relieved.

"It's no picnic, being pregnant at thirty-seven. Believe me, I know," Mirabella was saying in a tone half vexed, half musing, almost as if she were talking to herself.

Summer, finding herself in the lead all of a sudden, paused to look back at her sister. Mirabella had halted and was holding her hair back from her face with one hand clamped to the top of her head, something she'd always done, Summer remembered, when she was agitated. And there was that dewy flush on her forehead, and the purple smudges under her eyes that were not berry stains. One thing about Bella's skin—it was so fair and fine, when anything troubled her, physical or emotional, it showed up on her skin like a video on a screen.

They were almost to the porch steps. Summer took a breath to bolster her courage; confronting Mirabella could be a daunting prospect. "Bella?" she said in a low voice. "Is everything okay?"

Mirabella's shoulders rose with a gusty and impatient sigh. "Of course it is. I told you." And she would have plowed on in her typical steamroller fashion if Summer's hand on her arm hadn't kept her from it. Having no choice then, she paused, looking much put-upon. Looking up, looking down, looking anywhere but at her "little" sister.

Summer almost smiled; this was familiar territory, a familiar role to her in spite of their relative ages, that of confidant and sometimes surrogate mother. Their parents, loving and devoted in their own way, had been firm believers in the "benign neglect'' school of child-rearing; always there when it really counted, they'd never hovered or coddled, most of the time leaving their daughters to deal with minor problems on their own. Which had undoubtedly contributed to the degree of confidence and success with which all three had eventually launched themselves into the adult world. And which also, it suddenly occurred to Summer, may have been the key to the sisters' closeness, all those years ago. They'd learned very early two important truths: that three heads really were better than one, and that there had sometimes been safety in numbers. How had they all forgotten that?

"Bella? Come on, now, this is Summer talking. Tell me what's wrong."

Mirabella gave one more sigh, threw a guilty look over her shoulder in the direction of the open kitchen door, then lowered her voice and snapped in her typical machine-gun fashion, "Nothing's *wrong*. I'm just worried about Jimmy Joe, is all. I mean, you know, his business is growing so fast, and he's stuck behind a desk most of the time, and he has so much on his mind, and I don't know if he's happy—'' she gulped a breath ''—and I'm afraid I might be pregnant, too."

That almost got by Summer. Almost, but not quite. A beat late, she gasped and said, "You *what?* My God—Bella—"

"Shh! Not so loud!"

"You mean you haven't—"

"Of course not. I'm not even sure myself."

"For God's sake! Why don't you take one of those home tests?"

"I'm afraid to," Mirabella muttered furiously. Typical— there was nothing Bella hated more, Summer remembered, than being vulnerable.

"But at least you'd know for sure," she said in a coaxing tone. "Maybe you're worrying about nothing."

Mirabella was quiet for a moment, but her eyes had gone soft and misty. And when Summer looked to see what it was that had turned her sister's gaze so sappy with adoration, there was baby Amy, over on the lawn with her diapered bottom in the air, trying her clumsy best, with the help of her cousin Helen and big brother J.J., to negotiate a somersault. Mirabella drew a quivering breath and murmured, "It's not that I wouldn't love another baby. But…Jimmy Joe's got so much on his mind, and Charly's having such a hard time, and I'm not so young…"

"Oh, Bella, it'll be okay," Summer said softly, in the tone she might have used to calm a nervous animal. "You know what Pop always said: things have a way of working out the way they're supposed to."

"Yeah," Mirabella said with a shaky laugh. "Jimmy Joe says that, too."

"Well, then," Summer said, taking a deep breath, "you see? Everything's going to be fine."

It wasn't that she had forgotten her own problems—far from it. But as her own words settled almost gently into her consciousness, she felt a curious sense of peace. Of acceptance. She couldn't possibly tell them. Any of them. They would worry so. So it seemed she had come once more to the place that was most familiar and, perhaps, most comfortable to her after all. She was on her own.

"Please—sit down. Nice seein' you again."

The woman sat somewhat gingerly in the upholstered chair Riley had indicated, a faint, rosy flush across her cheeks. "I'm surprised you remember me."

"Of course I remember you." Riley Grogan seldom forgot a name or a face; it was one of his gifts. "I have to tell you, though, I'm a little bit surprised myself—to see you, that is." He settled back in his big swivel chair, adopting an attitude of relaxed attention. "What can I do for you, Mrs. Robey?"

She didn't pick up on his cue but sat ramrod straight, which he knew wasn't an easy thing to do in that big old chair, clutching her pocketbook in her lap as if she thought someone was about to take it away from her. He noticed that her hands looked as if they might be capable of stopping anybody who tried it, too. She had hands that could be either gentle or strong, with long bones and short, uncolored nails. No-nonsense hands. Nurturing hands.

She lifted one to cover her mouth while she gave a soft, voice-testing cough, then said, "The last time we met, you gave me a piece of advice."

"Yes, ma'am, I did." He didn't have to ask, or stop to think about it; he remembered that day all too well. It hadn't been one of his proudest victories.

"Yes, well…" She had the look of someone who'd taken a bite that tasted nasty but was too polite to spit it out. No choice but to swallow it. "I've decided to take it."

"I see," Riley murmured, keeping both expression and tone neutral. "So…I'm to assume you are once again in need of an attorney?"

A smile quivered across her lips and was gone. "A *good* attorney. Isn't that what you said?"

He allowed himself a chuckle at that. "Yes, ma'am, I believe I did. So. You are in need of a *good* attorney. Well." He leaned forward, inviting confidence. "That sounds serious. What sort of problem are you havin', Mrs. Robey? You do know, if it's anything related to that other matter—"

"It isn't. At least…I don't think it is. I don't know very much about how these things work—legally. Just because you were against me in one case, that doesn't mean I can't hire you for something else?" A little crease of determination lodged itself between blue eyes that had suddenly gone bright and fierce.

A tiny shiver of anticipation worked its way down Riley's spine. "Why don't you tell me a little bit about the nature of your problem," he said soothingly, "and then maybe I can tell you whether or not I'm goin' to be able to help you out."

She drew a deep breath and nodded. He leaned back again, giving her the full force of an attentiveness so focused as to be almost hypnotic—another of Riley Grogan's gifts. He would listen to and hear every word she said, along with every inflection and nuance, every hesitation and stammer; at the same time he would study her gestures and expressions, every twitch and quiver and blink. And he would forget nothing.

Her face, he decided, was interesting rather than beautiful, which he readily admitted was a subjective assessment, and dependent more on the current standards of beauty as set forth in television sitcoms, movies and fashion magazines than his own personal taste. No doubt her face would be considered too thin, the bones too sharply defined, her eyes too intense. And her mouth…ah, her mouth fascinated him, though not in the usual way, not the way of the lush, ripe-fruit, bee-stung lips that could just about be counted on to make his mouth water and his blood head south. Thin-lipped and intelligent, her mouth seemed never to be still, corners turning up in amusement or down in dismay, quirking sideways in irony, pursing in distaste, quivering and twitching, coiling around each word, molding and shaping it like a sculptor before revealing it to him with a caress of breath….

Astonished to find that his mouth *had* begun to water and his blood to head south, he gave his head a quick, hard shake.

She stopped instantly, looking nonplussed. "I'm sorry, was there something…?"

"No, I do apologize. I just had a thought. Nothing important—please, go on."

"Well, you probably know some of this, anyway," she said with the barely perceptible twitchiness characteristic of those who don't much like talking about themselves. "About Hal—my husband—cleaning me out financially and then disappearing, and the divorce, and my moving to Georgia. Because of—" she coughed and colored slightly "—the other case."

It was yet another reminder to him of the way her cheeks had burned with humiliation at their last meeting, and he shifted uncomfortably in his chair. "You said he has a gambling problem, as I recall."

He watched her lips as they curled briefly into a smile, then softened with sadness. "Hal was—is—a compulsive gambler, Mr. Grogan. That's an illness, you know, like alcoholism or drug addiction. Living with a compulsive gambler is like living with a heroin addict. You can't trust them or depend on them for anything, except to let you down. You learn to live with lies and uncertainty, violent mood swings and unexplained absences. You learn to live with worry and fear. You learn to live with the knowledge that the person you love will steal you blind, if you give him the chance, sell you and everything you own, plus his children and his mother, in order to get just one…more…stake.'' She stopped there and looked away, her mouth restless.

Riley propped an elbow on the arm of his chair and leaned his chin on his hand, supporting it in a cradle made of his extended fingers. ''And yet,'' he said softly, ''you stayed with him…for how long?''

''Ten years. He was—is—my children's father,'' she said on an exhalation, still not looking at him. ''And as lousy a husband and, in most ways, a human being he was, he *was* a good father. He couldn't hold a job, so more often than not he was the one who was home with the kids. They adored—they *adore* him. And he did try to get help. Especially toward the end. He'd joined Gamblers Anonymous and seemed to be doing better. That's why it was so unexpected—'' Her mouth quirked awry. ''No—I should have expected it. I just said that, didn't I? That's what compulsive gamblers do—let you down. I *still* should have seen it coming.''

Riley tapped his lips thoughtfully with his little finger. ''You keep referring to your husband—''

''Ex,'' she corrected him with a bitter smile. ''Please.''

He acknowledged that with a nod. ''Your ex-husband…in the past tense. Do I assume that to mean you still haven't heard from him?''

She sat forward, the frown-pleat deep between her eyes, focused and intent once more. ''No, nothing. It's been over a year.''

''I assume you've been to the police?''

Her lips curved, a tight little smile that left the frown intact. ''Yes, well, they seem to think the most likely scenario is, Hal's gambling finally got him way over his head with some dangerous people and he decided to take an extended leave for the sake of his health, and that he's probably laid up on some tropical island somewhere, living off what he stole from me and the kids.''

"Well, I'd have to say I pretty much agree with that," said Riley, moving the hand that had been supporting his chin in such a way that he could glance at his watch without being obvious about it. Fifteen minutes until his next appointment. "You have any reason to think otherwise?"

She shook her head. "Oh, I'm sure that's what happened. It's the only thing that makes sense. It seems to me it would take a great deal of money to make yourself disappear without a trace. And that's what he took…everything I had, anyway." She looked away again, but not before he saw the telltale movement in her throat that told of emotions ruthlessly suppressed.

Selfish bastard. Riley picked up a pen and began to manipulate it with quick and angry movements, venting with his fingers what he dared not say in words while he waited for her to continue. When she did not, he smiled and said gently, "Mrs. Robey, I'm sorry as I can be about what happened, but you still haven't told me why it is you think you need a *good* attorney."

"I'm coming to that." For the first time, her voice took on a hard edge.

But she wasn't there yet, not quite. First she had to take a deep breath, and then another, while she shifted around in her chair as if she was going to need a good solid support from which to launch this tale of hers. Riley felt a pulse begin to beat behind his belt buckle, an annoying little tick-tock of impatience.

"Anyway, I got the divorce and moved here—or rather, to Georgia, to be near my sister," she said finally. "I just wanted to put it all behind me, start over, for the children's sake as well as mine. And we'd been doing okay in spite of…one or two setbacks." Resentment flared in her eyes and then was veiled when she closed them briefly. After a moment she went on. "Then, about…three months ago, I started getting phone calls."

"Phone calls?" Now it was Riley who frowned. "You mean, from your husband?"

"No, no—I don't know who it was. A man. Some men, actually. Different ones. At first, you know, they'd call late at night, when the children were asleep. They said they were friends of Hal's and that they needed to find him. But there was something…I don't know, just sort of scary about it. I told them I didn't know where Hal was, but the calls kept coming, and they kept getting more and more threatening."

"Threatening? How?"

"Oh, you know—vague things. 'Tell us where your husband is, or you'll regret it.' Stuff like that. I didn't take it too seriously, but still, it was…upsetting."

Riley murmured, "I'll bet."

"But *then*…one day someone called when my kids were home. David—my nine-year-old son—answered the phone. I don't know exactly what the man said to him—David won't tell me—but I do know he was terrified. First he wouldn't go to sleep at all. It was like he thought he needed to stand guard, or something. He's been sort of like that since his father left, anyway—trying to be the man of the house, you know. Then when he did finally crash, he had nightmares." She shifted in the chair, edgy with anger. "That was it—the last straw. So I went to the police."

Riley nodded; it had been on the tip of his tongue to ask. "Good move. And?"

Again that tight, joyless smile. "They suggested I change my number. So I did. The calls stopped—for about a week. When they started up again, they were even more vicious than before. They—" her voice quivered unexpectedly; she shut it down and began again, this time in a lower tone "—they said they would take my children, and…hurt them…if that's what it took to force Hal out of hiding."

Pain reminded Riley to unclench his jaw. Tearing his gaze away from the woman's mouth, from lips that were taut and vibrant as bowstrings, he forced them to focus on the terror in her eyes instead. "Mrs. Robey, I don't know whether you need a lawyer or not, but I know you should be talkin' to the police."

"Oh, yes." She dipped her head in a quick, angry nod. "I did. They didn't seem to think there was very much they could do for me, not unless they had more to go on. They suggested I could change my number again, get caller ID, things like that. Oh—and they told me I might consider hiring a security guard—for my peace of mind. As if I could afford such a thing." Her voice had climbed the scale; now it was high and incredulous. "It was almost as if they didn't believe me, as if they thought I was *lying*."

"All cops sound like that," said Riley with an impatient wave of his hand. "I think they teach it at the police academy. Do you mean to tell me—"

"No, wait," she said grimly, "there's more." She spoke rapidly, and her eyes had a glow now that he could have sworn had as much anger in it as fear. "So, anyway, I had to drive back from the police station to where I was working that day— I work for a mobile vet, so we're at a different location every day, usually two or three in a day—which was about ten miles, with quite a few turnoffs. And I started noticing this car, this tan sedan, following me. Now, naturally, after those phone calls, I thought the worst, you know? I mean, I was *scared*. So I stepped on it. What else could I do? I was out in the middle of nowhere! And I'm driving like a bat outta hell— mind you, my car isn't capable of a whole lot, but it was doing its best—and this tan sedan is staying right with me. By this time, I'm terrified, shaking like a leaf. Finally, I make it to the parking lot where the mobile vet is set up, I go screeching up to the van, and before I can do a thing, the tan sedan pulls right up beside me, this man jumps out and yanks my door open, flashes a badge and says—" she lowered her voice at least an octave "—'Mrs. Robey, I'm gonna have to ask you to come with me, please.'"

Riley didn't know when he'd been so completely captivated.

His heart was actually pounding, and he could feel the quiver of terror in his own legs—empathy, unfortunately, being another of Riley's gifts, one he took great pains to keep secret. "You mean to say they *arrested* you?"

She shook her head almost gleefully; her lips parted. "They weren't cops."

"Then who…?"

"You're never going to guess…."

"FBI, ma'am, Special Agent Jake Redfield."

FBI? Summer felt a sudden and very brief impulse to laugh. Still on an adrenaline high, she spoke in a clipped, breathless voice. "May I see that ID again, please?"

"Of course." The man took his ID case from his inside jacket pocket as he settled into the seat beside her. He gave the driver's shoulder a tap and the car moved silently forward.

Summer studied the photo ID carefully, glancing up several times to compare it with the man sitting next to her. He returned her gaze obligingly with somber brown eyes. Not a bad-looking guy, she decided, handing the ID back to him with a sniff. A long, rather melancholy face, dark brown hair with a tendency to disobey orders, a perpetual case of five-o'clock shadow…somehow not exactly what she'd have imagined an FBI agent would look like.

"Is this about the phone calls?" Her voice trembled; the adrenaline was ebbing, leaving her jangly and cold.

Special Agent Redfield didn't seem to think he needed to answer that. He looked out the window as he tucked away the ID and said in a policeman's monotone, "We just want to ask you a few questions, Mrs. Robey. About your husband."

"I don't have a husband," Summer snapped, anger finally reaching her now that the fear had ebbed. "And if you wanted to talk to me about my *ex*-husband, why couldn't you just call and ask me? You people scared me to death, you know that? It's a miracle I didn't have an accident.''

The FBI man turned doleful eyes back to her. "Yes, well, I'm sorry about that. It's just that we'd rather not have it known that we've spoken with you. That's for your sake as well as ours. We wanted to be sure you weren't being followed."

Summer snorted. "Well, I was, obviously—by you."

Agent Redfield regarded her for a long moment, without even the hint of a smile. "Mrs. Robey," he said softly, "we know about the phone calls. I have to tell you, we believe these people mean business. They want your husband, and they want him badly. So do we. And it is vital that we find him before they do. Do you understand?"

"Of course I understand," Summer said, almost in a wail. "Do you? I'll tell you the same thing I told those guys on the phone. Hal is not my husband anymore, and I do not—repeat, do not—know where he is! If I did, do you think I'd be in this mess? That man took every penny I had and a considerable amount more. I'm in debt up to my eyeballs. It's going to take me years to climb out of the hole he put me in. If he owes those people money—"

"I'm afraid," Redfield said, "this isn't about money."

"If it's not money they're after your husband for," Riley said, "then what is it?"

She gave an impatient little jerk. "I asked Agent Redfield that. He acted as though I'd asked him to sell nuclear secrets to the Iranians. Then they took me to some sort of headquarters and questioned me for *three hours*. I never did get back to work. It's a good thing I have an understanding boss. But—" she held up a hand to forestall interruptions, though he hadn't planned any "—from the questions they asked me, and everything that's happened, I've sort of been putting two and two together. I know this all has something to do with some huge illegal gambling syndicate—the mob, I guess—do they still have that?''

Riley nodded. "Oh, yeah. Which explains the FBI's interest.''

"Right. Anyway, what I think is, that *they* think—both the FBI and the syndicate people—that Hal has something on the syndicate. I don't know what—some sort of information that could bring them down, I suppose. My guess is, the syndicate guys didn't even know Hal had...whatever it is...until he ran out of the money he'd stolen from me, and then, knowing him, he probably tried to blackmail them. That's when they started with the phone calls to me.'' She sat back, elbows on the arms of the chair, fingers clasped at her waist. Her breathing was quick and audible, and a muscle worked at the hinge of her jaw.

Riley regarded her for a moment, wondering why such a fantastic story should sound even remotely believable to him. Just something about her face, he decided; something he could only call *character,* for want of a better word. But there were things that bothered him. He frowned. "My question would be, how would your husband come by this...information? Why would a gambler have access—''

She made a soft, derisive sound. "Hal is a gambler, but he's far from stupid. In fact, in his own field, he's probably brilliant.''

"And that is...?''

"Math. Hal is—or was, when he could keep a job—an accountant...a bookkeeper. And while he's no hacker, he's very good with computers. When he was out of work and at home, that's what he did with his time—play with the computer. In fact, that's how he did most of his gambling—you know, on the Internet. I think that's how he did it. I think he must have somehow managed to tap into the syndicate's financial records, or something like that. That's why the FBI wants him so badly.''

Riley sat back, exhaling through his nose. "Shades of Al Capone.''

Her eyes turned silvery. "Oh, yeah. This Agent Redfield was practically drooling. He wants whatever it is Hal's got so badly he can taste it, and that's what scares me. I get the feeling this is some sort of crusade with him, bringing down this syndicate. You know—like Captain Ahab and Moby Dick. I think he wants to get them so badly and he's so focused on it, that he might not care who he has to hurt in the process. And *that*—" she let out a breath "—is why I think I need a good lawyer." She paused, her gaze holding Riley's as she added evenly, "I've been held accountable for my ex-husband's actions before. I don't intend for it to happen again."

Chapter 3

"The thing is, I can't afford to pay you." She said that in a raspy, embarrassed voice, sitting on the edge of her chair and staring at him, almost, it seemed to Riley, in defiance.

She reminded him of a wild rabbit he'd once caught in a snare he'd set in the woods. He could still remember the way it had felt in his hands, trembling but not struggling, resigned to the inevitable but wanting so desperately to be somewhere—anywhere—other than where she was. He'd let the rabbit go that day, knowing it meant he'd go hungry to bed again.

She swallowed and went on; he thought it seemed easier for her now that she'd gotten the worst out. "I don't have any money and my credit is shot. I can't go to my family for help...."

Of course not, thought Riley. *Pride. Way too much pride.*

"I already owe them so much for that hospital bill. I do have a lawyer, sort of—she's a family friend and her husband's a private investigator, too—but they have...things going on in their own lives right now. Personal stuff." She shifted in her chair. Her fingers curled over the top of her handbag; her knuckles whitened. "I just can't burden them with my problems—I won't. But—" she took a breath "—I'm not asking for charity."

Of course not, Riley thought, regarding her with half-closed eyes, his face once more cradled on his hand, index finger pointing at the corner of his eyes, little finger across his lower lip. *God forbid, Summer Robey, that you should ask anybody for anything.*

"I mean, if you will take me on as your client, I *will* pay for your services—I just can't pay you with money. What I thought was…I'd offer something in exchange—you know, like the barter system? They used to do that back in the old days—like, a farmer would pay with a pig, a miller with a sack of flour.…"

Riley was hard-pressed not to smile. His chest tingled with a strange anticipation as he murmured, "Well…now that's an interesting idea. What in particular did you have in mind?"

Her cheeks were bright with embarrassment, but he'd expected that. What touched him more was the determined light in her eyes, a little glow of courage that was like a candle held high in a dark and lonely woods.

"Obviously, I don't have anything to give you, except for myself. Oh, Lord." She abruptly closed her eyes. "I didn't mean that like it sounded. Please don't think—"

"Mrs. Robey, I never did for a moment, " Riley said kindly. He was grateful for the excuse to smile.

"What I meant was, I thought I could offer my *services.*…" She stopped again, put a hand over her eyes and muttered, "Oh, God, that wasn't much better, was it?" Riley was openly, if silently, laughing. She uncovered her eyes and glared at him. "What I *mean* is, I could *work* for you."

"Uh-huh." It took a gallant effort, but he managed to straighten his face. "Well, now, that sounds interesting. Doin' what, exactly?"

She looked desperately around her. "Well, like I could do your filing for you, you know, answer the phone.…"

"I have both a part-time law clerk and a full-time secretary-slash-receptionist to take care of that for me," Riley said gently. The truth was, Danell, his secretary, *did* have a vacation coming up. He'd been putting off calling the temp agency; he dreaded it so. But something in him—the devil, most likely—was entertained by the situation, and he couldn't bring himself to let Summer Robey off the hook. Not that easily.

Her brows had drawn together as she racked her brain for another offering. "Well, I am a veterinarian. How about—"

"Sorry. No animals. Pets or otherwise."

"Ah-hah." She drew a shallow breath and he could see her relax, as though she'd already accepted defeat and was just spinning her wheels. "I could clean your house…mow your lawn…."

"I have a cleaning service. And a gardener."

"Wax your car, carry your golf clubs…"

Riley stood, rounded the corner of his desk and put a firm hand under her elbow. The look of dismay on her face as he raised her to her feet was like a high-powered lamp; he didn't have to see it to know it was there.

"I'm sure we'll think of *something* you can do for me, Mrs. Robey," he drawled. The muscles in her arm jerked beneath his fingers. As it had with that bunny rabbit all those years ago, pity overcame him and he let her go. "And I mean something even your dear old gray-haired mama would approve of."

She surprised him with a breathless laugh. "I don't know if that's all that reassuring." She was clutching her pocketbook in front of her like a weapon, as if a street mugger had her by the elbow. "Last I heard, my mother had dyed her hair marigold and was into massage therapy."

Now, there was a thought. Riley allowed himself to dwell on it just a little bit while he eased her toward the door. But not for long; he did have a client waiting. He reached past her for the doorknob. "Now, first thing we're gonna want you—"

She spun around suddenly, putting her back up against the door so he couldn't open it, and at the same time trapping herself there between it and him. Her eyes, on a level with his chin, were silver as summer rain. "Does this mean…?"

Riley nodded, enjoying himself a lot more than he should have. "Well, sure. You've got yourself a lawyer." He smiled down at her, a big wide one that showed his teeth. "A *good* lawyer."

"Oh, thank you." The words were a whisper, borne on a breath.

And he suddenly felt the need of one himself, his brain, for some reason, having become oxygen-deprived. He gulped for air before he said, "Mrs. Robey—"

"Please—it's Summer."

Summer? And he thought, Oh yeah, it is. Hazy, hot and humid, and charged with electricity.

He got the door open and ushered her into the cool of the hallway. "Summer, what I'm gonna want from you is all the information you can come up with on your ex-husband—social security number, driver's license number, credit cards, any aliases he's used in the past, friends, relatives, habits and haunts—okay? I'm gonna want to get my investigator goin' on this as soon as possible. And I'm gonna see if I can get the police to put some surveillance on your house and your phone, if that's okay with you." While he waited for her nod, he slipped around her and got to the waiting room door first. He opened and held it for her but kept her there with a touch on her elbow as he said in a low, private voice, "In the meantime, next time you hear from the FBI, I want you to give me a call, okay? And don't say a word until I get there. Not one word."

"I won't," she whispered. "Mr. Grogan…thank you. Thank you *so much.*"

He nodded and watched her walk across the waiting room and out of his office. Then he hauled in a discreet breath of oxygen-rich, lemon-furniture-polish-scented air and smiled encouragingly at the client who was pacing a path in the Persian rug. Muttering, "Be right with you," he closed the door, then ducked into his secretary's office.

"Danell," he said briskly, "we're gonna want to open up a file for Mrs. Robey. And would you see if you can get Tom Denby on the phone? If you can't, leave him a message, tell him I've got a job for him. Oh—and let's see, who do we know over in Augusta that might be able to get us a favor outta their police department? Look into it for me, would you?"

Danell slanted him one of her looks. "You got a billing address?"

Riley stopped short. *Damn.* He'd been hoping he could make it out of the office before the subject came up. He gave a blithe little wave without turning around. "Just bill it to the firm for now."

"You *said* no more pro bonos. You told me to shoot you in the legs if you even looked like you were gonna take on another one."

He hitched up his shoulders and peeked winningly at his secretary over one of them. For a girl not out of her twenties, Danell did have a look that could make him feel like he was twelve and trying to sneak by with a copy of *Playboy* under his shirt. "Who said anything about pro bono?"

She stared him down. "We're way over quota for the month, you know we are."

He hesitated for a moment, then walked back to Danell's desk, put his hands on the edge of it and leaned on them. "Find a way to fit this one in," he said softly, meeting her eyes. "Just this one more. Okay? I have a feeling it's gonna be important."

It had turned hot and muggy since the weekend, and since the Oldsmobile's air conditioner didn't work, the first thing Summer did when she got into the car after seeing Riley was roll down all the windows. Backtracking the way she'd come, she drove through downtown Charleston and found her way to the interstate. When she hit freeway speed, she rolled the windows back up partway so the wind wouldn't whip her hair into a frizz during the long haul back to Georgia. By the time she'd done all that, more or less on autopilot, her brain had begun to function again.

Oh, Lord, I did it. She had herself a lawyer. A *good* lawyer. She felt confident of that. She'd done some research on this Riley Grogan, and from what she'd been able to gather, he was one of the best in Charleston, South Carolina. Relatively young—not much more than forty—but already highly respected…and rich, which was maybe a better measure of his effectiveness. He was also single, which she gathered was somewhat of an uncommon state for a respectable Southern male past twenty-five years of age to be in. Coupled with the fact that the man was handsome as sin, was known to dress as impeccably as any blue-blooded aristocrat, and had a reputation for being suave as the devil himself, that might have raised a few eyebrows and more than a few slyly phrased questions, were it not for his regular appearances at Charleston social functions with one marginally famous beauty or another draped on his arm. Hostesses known for their elegance and sophistication, it was said, were often reduced to stammers and blushes in his presence. If Riley Grogan still reigned at the top of a short list of the South's most eligible bachelors, then the consensus of opinion—especially among mothers of Charleston debutantes—was that it must be because he simply hadn't found the woman who could live up to his standards of beauty and style, wit and intelligence.

All of which impressed Summer not the slightest bit. She cared nothing for the man's looks, pedigree or sexual orientation. There was one thing she cared about, and one thing only: what kind of lawyer was he? The Riley Grogan she'd run up against that day in court, *that* was the man she wanted working on her side. She had no use for charm and elegance. What she wanted was the street fighter—someone cold, calculating, ruthless and manipulative, tough as nails and mean as a snake. After all, her children's lives were at stake.

Oh, but there was no use denying it—he *had* made her knees go weak just now. What was it about the man that made her blush and stammer like a hillbilly in her first town dress?

What was it about Riley Grogan that ate away at her confidence so? She'd never suffered from a lack of poise and self-assurance before, not since she'd learned the hard way that a handsome face and winning personality were foolish ways to measure the worth of a man. Hal Robey'd had a smile so sweet it'd fool bees into thinking it was honey, as her dad used to say.

But Riley, now...what he had was something different than your ordinary, garden-variety charm. Something more. What he had was an elegance so effortless that it could make even duchesses feel inadequate and prima ballerinas trip over their feet. And by the time she'd reached the Highway 78 turnoff to Augusta, Summer had decided that she knew what it was that gave the man that elegance. It was the very same quality that made him so intimidating in a courtroom—*quietness.* Riley Grogan was quiet the way a big cat is quiet, like a leopard draped along a limb or a lion lounging in the shade of a banyan tree, somnolent and relaxed, in the absolute certainty that he is undisputed lord of all he surveys.

A sudden shiver ran through her, a joyous little energy surge. Oh, but it felt good to be plugged into such awesome power and massive self-confidence after so many months of fear and uncertainty. Everything was going to be all right now.

At a stoplight in Augusta, Summer checked her watch and decided there wasn't going to be time to stop at the Winn Dixie before she picked up the kids. The church day camp she'd found for them allowed for some flexibility in pickup times, but she was running late as it was and she didn't like to push it. The day camp had been a lifesaver. She'd found out about it from Debbie Mott, her boss's wife, who was sending her kids there as well.

The children were waiting for her outside in the heat instead of in the air-conditioned building as they usually did. From halfway down the block, Summer could see them sitting on the brick planter that ran along the walk in front of the church. Both had the same pose—elbows on knees, chins propped on hands—but somehow David's attitude managed to convey dejection, while Helen's had the ominous look of a small black storm cloud.

Uh-oh, Summer thought as she pulled up to the curb, her recent euphoria only a memory. *What now?*

"Hi, babes," she sang out with cheerful optimism, wincing as David wrenched open the car door and clambered across the back seat without answering, followed by Helen, who flounced in after him and gave the door a mighty tug that latched it on the first try. Her heart sank farther as she beheld their flushed faces; the Waskowitz skin couldn't keep a secret if lives depended on it. She turned to smile at her offspring over the back of the seat. Two pairs of eyes flicked at her like beacons, but neither was smiling. Her son's eyes shimmered with embarrassed tears; her daughter's were bright with fury. "Did you have a good day?" Summer asked with faint hope.

The only reply was a click, as David fastened his seat belt and turned to gaze steadily out the window. Helen scooted forward and pushed an envelope over the back of the seat, then fanny-walked herself back into place.

Summer caught the envelope and said brightly, "Oh, what's this?"

"It's a note from Mrs. Hamburger," said Helen in a disgusted tone. "She wants to *speak* to you."

"It's Mrs. *Hammacher*," Summer automatically corrected her, then sighed with foreboding. "Oh, honey, what did you do?"

Helen stared at her shoes and was stubbornly silent.

"David?"

He turned from the window with a look of reproach, as if, Summer thought, whatever it was was somehow all *her* fault. "She filled up a water pistol with grape juice," he said in a hollow tone. "During morning snack time."

"Oh, Helen." Summer closed her eyes. "Please tell me you didn't actually squirt anybody with it. *Grape juice?*"

"Well, I *did*," Helen muttered defiantly, watching her Marvin the Martian sneakers bob up and down. "I squirted Jason."

"*Jason?* Jason *Mott?*"

"You should have seen him," David put in eagerly. "He had on one of those neat T-shirts, you know, with the red-and-navy-blue designs on them, the ones that cost about fifty bucks and you said I couldn't have one? It was *all* purple, Mom."

"Oh, Helen. Why?"

Helen's chin, fragile-looking as a blossom and an infallible barometer of her intractability, jutted upward. "Because he was being mean to me."

"Mean to you?" Summer's hopes flared; here, at least, was the possibility of some mitigation. "How?"

"Well…" The shoes bobbed furiously. "He said I talk funny."

"You do talk funny," said her brother.

"Do not!"

"David…"

"*He* talks funny. And he called me a name."

"What name?" Summer braced herself. "Come on, honey, tell me what Jason called you."

"He…he called me a *yankee,*" Helen huffed. "I don't even know what that is. Mom, what's a yankee? It sounds *nasty.*" Her nose wrinkled in disgust.

All Summer could do was shake her head; she had a hand clamped tight across her mouth to hold back a gust of laughter.

"Plus, Jason told Keisha her hair looked ugly and hurt her feelings. She was crying."

"Who's Keisha?" Aha, this sounded better. Definitely grounds for justification.

"Keisha's my friend, and her hair's *not* ugly," said Helen. "She has millions and millions of little tiny braids. Mom, can you do my hair like that?"

"I doubt it." Summer looked at her daughter's rather sparse blond curls. Both of her children had inherited the Waskowitz coloring, like their aunt Mirabella—fine red-gold hair and fair, tell-all complexions. "And don't try and change the subject, little girl. Jason was wrong to make Keisha cry, but you still shouldn't have squirted him with grape juice, of all things." A delayed realization struck her. "And where did you get a water pistol, anyway? You know how we feel about toy guns of *any* kind.''

The two children exchanged guilty looks.

''David?''

''Don't look at me, Mom.''

''Helen? Answer me this minute. Where did you get the water gun?''

Helen stared at the toes of her sneakers, which were no longer bobbing. Her chin sank onto her chest. ''I took it.''

Oh, God. It was worse than she'd thought. This was serious stuff, in the world of childhood, a class-A felony. ''Helen,'' said Summer in a voice low with dread, ''do you mean to tell me you *stole* it?'' Helen's head moved slowly up and down. Her brother made a disgusted noise. ''*Where?* Who did you steal it from, Helen? Tell me right now.''

Helen's voice was barely audible, and seemed to come from the vicinity of her belly button. ''From Jason.''

''From *Jason?* You mean, you…'' *Shot him with his own gun?*

Summer put a hand over her eyes. Silence reigned in the back seat as she counted slowly to ten, then turned back around and put the car in gear. ''Buckle up,'' she said briskly. *''Now.''* There was a subdued and dutiful click from Helen's side. Summer had just put on her blinker and was starting to pull away from the curb when she had to hit the brakes and wait for a fire engine to roar by, siren screaming. Right behind it came another one. Then another.

''Wow,'' David breathed, following their progress with avid eyes, ''it must be a really big fire. Can we follow them and see, Mom? Can we?''

''Don't be silly,'' said Summer, who in adulthood had developed a city-dweller's indifference to emergency vehicles. ''Hey, what do you guys want for dinner? I didn't have time to stop at the store. You feel like pizza?''

''Aren't we going to get Beatle and Cleo and Peggy Sue?'' David asked in a worried vice. ''They've been at Jason's four whole days, Mom. First you said it was just for the weekend while we were at Aunt Bella's, and then you said just till you got back from Charleston, and now—''

"I know, I know," Summer interrupted him with a sigh. She met her son's accusing frown in the rearview mirror. "But I'm not sure it's such a good idea to go over to Dr. Mott's right now, do you? After what Helen just did to Jason? Maybe we could let things cool off a little bit first?"

"Things" meaning Jason's mother, Debbie. Debbie Mott was a former high school cheerleader and beauty queen who'd given up on getting her figure back after her third child and made up for it in the self-esteem department by being somewhat of a snob. Summer was well aware that she wasn't Debbie's favorite person—she had good instincts for things like that—and suspected it had something to do with the fact that she spent most of every day sharing the intimacy of a motor home with Debbie's lean, lanky and still reasonably good-looking husband. Summer didn't really think Debbie had enough influence in such matters to get her fired over this grape juice incident, but the next meeting between them didn't promise to be a pleasant one, and it definitely wasn't something she felt like tackling on an empty stomach. She'd call first, she told herself. This evening, when Dr. Mott was likely to be home to referee.

She watched David's eyes spark with understanding, then flick resentfully toward his sister. "I guess," he said unhappily. "It's just, I hope they don't think we abandoned them, or something. Jason said his mom made Cleo stay on the porch because she was making so much noise. He said she says bad words. Does she, Mom? How come I never heard her say any bad words?" He sounded disappointed.

"Maybe she never felt the need to," Summer muttered. She sought her son's eyes in the mirror once more. "Honey, I miss the animals, too, but they'll be fine at Dr. Mott's for one more night, okay? I promise we'll go get them tomorrow. Right now, let's have something to eat—I'm starving. So how about it? Pizza sound okay to you guys?"

"Can we have tacos?" Helen piped up. "We haven't had tacos for a million years."

"Then we're definitely due. What about it, Davie? Tacos okay with you?"

"Sure." In the mirror, Summer watched him shrug and go back to staring out the window, his face somber, a vaguely depressed slope to his shoulders.

Sadness tightened her throat and lay heavy in her chest. *Oh, sweetheart, these burdens of mine are way too big for your shoulders. Please don't try to bear them for me. You're only nine years old.* I'll make it up to you, she promised her son silently. We're going to come through this all right.

Since tacos were way too messy to eat in the car, even one as decrepit as the Olds, Summer parked it and they went inside. She wasn't particularly eager to get home, anyway, and with the animals at Dr. Mott's, she could think of no reason to rush. It hadn't always been so. Once, "home" had meant her nest, her haven, her place of belonging. These days, "home" was the soul-sapping bleakness of a cramped mobile home, where every rust streak and shriveled blade of grass was a reproach and a reminder of her failures. And where, more recently, the ringing of the telephone carried with it the electric shock of fear.

But, she reminded herself, at least now I have a lawyer. A *good* lawyer. Riley Grogan. His confidence and quietness filled her. In her mind, his eyes regarded her—cool, blue and appraising. Unexpected warmth flooded her cheeks and spread into her chest.

I'll find a way to pay him, she vowed. I know he doesn't believe that, but I will.

Though it would be difficult, she acknowledged, since he lived so far away. Well, of course, she had no idea where he actually *lived,* but his law offices were in Charleston, so she had to assume he lived somewhere nearby. What must his home be like, a single man, a wealthy man, with no kids and no pets? It was hard for her to imagine. As elegant and imposing as the man himself was, probably. But godawful lonely. Maybe.

"Mom?"

She started and focused guiltily on her son, who had obviously just asked her a question of some importance. The children had been bickering over the movie monster action figures that had come in their kids' meals when she'd tuned them out and given her mind permission to wander. But how had she gotten so far off the mommy-track?

"Yes, hon—I'm sorry. What?"

"I said, do you think Jason's mom will still let us swim in their pool?" His red-gold hair hung slack, waving a little, as he tilted his head sideways to accommodate a bite of taco. His blue eyes regarded her somberly as he chewed, then swallowed with an audible gulp. "Mom, what am I gonna do if I can't practice? I'll be so out of shape, I'll never be able to make the swim team again. And it's all because *dodo,* here—" he gave his sister a fierce nudge in the side with his elbow "—just had to go and squirt grape juice all over dumb old *Jason.*"

"Quit it," Helen whispered, nudging him back and fixing him with a narrow-eyed glare. "Or I'll have my Godzilla *chomp* you to pieces."

"Big deal," said David with a shrug. "Your Godzilla is six inches tall. He couldn't chomp a bug."

"Yeah, well, you just wait. When I grow up I'm gonna have a *real* Godzilla, and he's gonna eat your *head.*"

"Ooh, I'm shaking."

"Well, you *better* be. Because—"

"Hey, guys," said Summer. "You know what I think?" Two pairs of eyes regarded her, one expectant, one wary. "I think we're going to have to do some apologizing to Jason and his mom. How 'bout you?"

"Not me, I didn't do anything," said David. Helen made a hideous face. "And," he added spitefully, "I hope your face freezes like that. How'd you like that, huh?"

"It won't!"

"Sure it will. If you don't believe me, just ask Granny Calhoun."

"Will *not!*"

"Ok-ay, time to go home," said Summer firmly. She gathered up their trash and deposited it in the receptacle and herded the children, still nudging each other and whispering dire threats they thought she couldn't hear, out to the car.

The sun was still high and hot at that hour of the evening in late June, and once they were in the car the children's quarrel died of heat exhaustion. Summer drove with the windows down, since there was no one to see her who was going to give a rip what shape her hair was in. Beyond the city's outskirts, strip malls, fast-food restaurants and gas stations quickly gave way to scattered businesses housed in metal or cinderblock buildings set far back from the road. Freestanding yellow signboards on the grass along the highway advertised used-tire specials, live nudes and the redeeming power of faith in identical black-and-red block letters. Sickly petunias bloomed beside driveways in planters made from old tires, and kudzu encroached on vacant lots littered with trash and old campaign signs. Normally the sight of all that lush squalor filled Summer with a contradiction of feelings, a kind of depressed restlessness that was similar to the way she felt when she walked into her rented mobile home—a futile urge to tidy something she knew no amount of tidying was ever going to make beautiful. But this evening she saw the yellow polka dots of dandelions in the grassy verges and felt an uplift of spirits that was almost like hope. She'd taken *steps*. It was going to be okay.

Just as she was turning onto her street, she met two fire trucks, sirens silent, big engines grumbling, making their way back to the barn.

"Wow, look," David cried, popping up in his seat so he could see better. "I bet those are the same ones we saw. That fire must have been right around here someplace. Can we go see it, Mom? Please?"

Summer sighed and said, "Oh, David…"

She guided the Olds around the gentle curve that marked

the beginning of their residential neighborhood, a long row of mobile homes and modest houses, unfenced and widely spaced, separated by grass-pocked gravel driveways and marked by tipsy roadside mailboxes. Up ahead she could see another fire truck parked in the road, its lights still flashing.

"Mom, look." David's voice faded. Silence filled the car.

Summer drove slowly forward, only dimly aware that her heart had begun to pound. She saw people coming toward her now, people she didn't know—her neighbors, walking alone with their arms folded, shaking their heads, or in twos and threes, talking among themselves, walking down the road, turning into driveways, cutting across lawns. Children on bicycles, pumping hard, racing their dogs home. The excitement, whatever it had been, was obviously over now.

Summer pulled the Olds onto the grassy shoulder and parked. A fireman in protective gear glanced at her, then went on with what he was doing, gathering up, tidying up, putting things away. She turned off the motor, opened the door and got out.

"Mom, that's our—"

She turned, arms braced on the door frame, to face her children—Helen standing with her arms on the back of the seat in front of her, staring over it with round, avid eyes; David's face, pale as the moon, his mouth a thin, frightened line. "Stay here," she grated through clenched jaws. "You…stay…in…this…car."

She slammed the car door and walked up the street toward the fire truck. Her legs felt strange, as if her knees had been hinged with rubber bands.

Someone approached her—a police officer. She hadn't noticed the two radio patrol cars parked beyond the fire truck. "Ma'am, I'm gonna have to ask you to stay back outta the way—"

Summer shook her head. "That's my house," she said. "I live here."

Chapter 4

The policeman put his hand on her elbow, at the same time gesturing with the other to someone she couldn't see. "Uh-huh. Okay, ma'am. You want to tell me your name, please?"

"Yes. I'm Mrs. Robey. Summer. And this is my house."

It was hardly true; the ugly little trailer would never be anyone's house, ever again. Where it had stood was a blackened skeleton, a sodden, stinking, smoking gash in the landscape surrounded by yellow police ribbon. The stench of destruction was overpowering; she wanted to gag.

"May I please... I need to sit down."

And then she was in the back of a patrol car, and someone—a policeman—was offering her something in a small paper cup. Water. She took it and drank without tasting, then murmured, "Thank you."

A soft voice, thick and Southern, said, "Ma'am, I'm gonna need to ask you some questions, okay? You feel up to it, or you wanna take another minute?"

She shook her head. "No, that's okay, I'm fine." She focused her eyes on the policeman's face, observing that he was young, black, and didn't look like he was enjoying himself much.

The reason for that became clear a moment later when he cleared his throat, shifted his feet and said, "Ma'am—can you tell me if there was anybody that might've been…uh, in the building?" He coughed and made it simpler. "Was…anybody home?"

Summer stared at him. Bile rose in her throat. She swallowed and said hurriedly, "No. No, there's only me and my children—they're over there, in the car. I just picked them up from day camp." She stopped, then added as if it might be of importance, "We stopped for tacos."

The young policeman drew himself up, looking considerably happier at that news. "Yes, ma'am, well, that's good. I'm sure glad to hear it." He coughed, then frowned again. "Your, uh, neighbors said they thought you folks had some pets?"

"Yes." Funny, how she seemed not to be feeling this. As though she were in a plastic bubble, and the policeman's words just bounced off without touching her. "They were at a friend's house. I was away over the weekend."

There was the soft hiss of an exhalation. "Well, ma'am, sounds like you were real lucky." Summer looked at the officer, who gazed back at her with shadows in his eyes, the shadows, maybe, of memories of other disasters and people who hadn't been as lucky. "Sorry for your loss," he said in a more formal tone.

"Thank you," said Summer. She looked down at the paper cup, which she had crumpled in her hand. "Is there anything else you need right now? I'd like to get back to my children."

"Oh—sure." He stood back away from the open door to make room for her, then reconsidered. "Uh…listen, do you have someplace to go? Somebody you can call? Any kinfolk in the area?" Summer shook her head. "What about friends?"

Friends. She thought about it. She'd been here almost a year, and who did she know? Well enough to ask for a favor of this magnitude? The answer was, with the possible exception of the Motts: *nobody.*

The Motts. Summer's mind filled with the image of Debbie Mott's plump, self-satisfied face, and her stomach recoiled. Never, she thought, in a million years. "We'll be okay," she said softly. "I guess we'll probably go to a motel." Her mouth formed the words, but her brain didn't comprehend their meaning. Not their real meaning. She was safely encased in that nice little plastic bubble of shock.

The policeman nodded and took something out of his uniform pocket—a card. He handed it to her and said kindly, "Okay, then, I'll let you get on back to your kids. Ma'am, this here's the address and phone number of the local Red Cross. You go on down there and show them the police report—we'll see you have a copy—and they'll fix you up with whatever you need, okay?"

Summer nodded. *The Red Cross.* Reality tried to push its way into her bubble along with that name. *It's true. I'm a victim.* She pushed the thought ruthlessly, angrily away.

"Just one more thing." The policeman ducked down so that his head and shoulders filled the car door's opening. "You got any reason you can think of why somebody might want to do this?"

"Do this?" Summer stared at him. In her cocooned state, understanding came slowly. "Do you mean…it wasn't…the fire didn't…just happen?" Trailers burned all the time—she heard about them often on the news.

The policeman's face was impassive. "We won't know that for sure, ma'am, not until the investigators finish their job. But right now I have to say, it does look suspicious."

She desperately needed a breath, but something cold and heavy was occupying the space where her lungs should have been. She shook her head and choked out the word "No."

Apparently taking that as her answer to his original question, the officer straightened once more, at the same time reaching in his breast pocket again, this time for his notebook. "Well, okay, then. We're just gonna need for you to leave us a number, someplace where we can get ahold of you. Work number'd be fine."

"Uh, sure. I work for Dr. Jerry Mott—you know, the mobile vet? I guess you can reach me there. If not, he'll know how to get in touch with me." She gave him the number and watched him jot it carefully down in his notebook before returning it to his pocket. She cleared her throat. "Can I go now?"

"Sure." He stepped back, offering her his hand. She ignored it, instead levering herself out of the patrol car under her own power. Except that she felt it wasn't really her own power, but something outside herself, some unseen puppet master manipulating the nerves, tendons and muscles that operated her body, made it stand erect and begin walking down the sloping, grass-furred driveway. Told it to step carefully around the bare patches where the water from the fire hoses had turned the red clay to sticky, slippery muck. Surely it must have been some other guidance system—automatic pilot?— that told her to stop at the bottom of the driveway and open the mailbox and look inside, just as she did every day when she came home from work. Her own consciousness was still encased in its soft, safe place.

She walked back up the road to where she'd parked the green Oldsmobile, her feet finding their way on the uneven verge while she shuffled through the day's mail: mostly junk, maybe a couple of bills, a plain envelope with Mrs. Robey printed on it, several catalogs…her mind registered none of it. Just ahead on the opposite side of the road, her children's faces hung in the car windows like two pale, not-quite-full moons. And there was another car parked behind the Olds now, a tan sedan that for some reason seemed vaguely familiar. A tan sedan…

"You got any reason you can think of why somebody might want to do this?"

Something clicked on in her brain, shattering her bubble and restoring full power and function. She looked down at the pile of mail in her hands, then shuffled rapidly through it until she came to the plain envelope with her name printed on it. Something about it felt wrong. It just felt *wrong*. She slid trembling fingers under the flap and lifted it, drew out the single sheet of paper, folded in thirds. She stared at it, her mind registering the sound of a car door slamming as the stack of mail slipped from her nerveless hands and hit the ground with a soft, slithery *thud*. Catalogs and envelopes fanned out unnoticed across her feet. She unfolded the paper and stared at the words printed there in block letters, hand-printed letters that matched her name on the envelope.

SORRY WE MISSED YOU. NEXT TIME WE'LL BE SURE AND STOP BY WHEN YOU AND THE KIDDIES ARE HOME.

She felt cold. She wanted to throw up.

"Mrs. Robey?"

Her head came up slowly and she gazed into the melancholy brown eyes of the man from the FBI. She remembered his name: Special Agent Jake Redfield.

"May I?" He reached toward her cautiously, as if he feared either she or the objects she held in her hands might explode if mishandled. She surrendered them, both the note and the envelope it had come in, and watched with silent revulsion as, touching them gingerly only on their edges, he first read them, then tucked them away in an inside pocket of his suit jacket. Taking her elbow in a firm grip, he said tersely, "Get your kids. I think it's a good idea if all three of you come with us."

Summer made a small, sucking sound; her mouth and throat felt sticky, as if from long disuse. "My car—I can't just—"

"Agent Poole here'll bring it." Redfield made a gesture toward the car, in response to which a stocky, middle-aged man with what was left of his gray hair cut in a 1950s-style buzz emerged from the passenger side and slammed the door behind him. He came toward them with a purposeful stride, at the same time sweeping his surroundings with narrow-eyed glances the way Summer had seen make-believe cops do on TV shows. Redfield, too, kept looking around him and making small, fidgety adjustments to his clothing, as if he was preparing for the possibility of some sort of action. And in the process, revealing the presence of a holster nestled in the small of his back. The sight of that gun cleared the fog from Summer's mind like windshield wipers in a drizzle.

"I don't want my children frightened," she said in a low, growling voice she hardly recognized as her own. "They're going to be upset enough as it is."

"Gotcha." Redfield shrugged, and his jacket settled once more into lean and innocent lines.

He released her elbow and reached around her to pull open the Oldsmobile's rear door. The two children shrank away from the opening like wild creatures retreating into their burrows. Before Summer could move to intervene, the FBI man was squatting down to peer into the car and saying in a voice he probably imagined to be cajoling, "Hey, kids, how'd you like to come for a ride with me?"

"Oh, great," Summer muttered as two pairs of blue eyes widened in alarm. She knew exactly what was going to happen next. *Now, children, what do you say if a stranger asks you to go for a ride with him? You just…say…*

"No!" shrieked Helen, shaking her head wildly. "No, no, no, *no!*"

Agent Redfield threw Summer a beseeching look over his shoulder. Arms folded, she glared back at him. His brows drew together, and he turned back to the children with what he probably imagined was a reassuring smile. It made Summer think of Snidely Whiplash. "Look, kids, it's okay—your mom's coming, too."

"Mom?" David said on a rising note of alarm, his eyes zooming in on Summer's. Her little champion.

"You sure do have a way with children," she said under her breath as she elbowed the FBI man aside and gathered her daughter into her arms just in time to head off a full-blown case of hysterics. Behind her she could hear Agent Poole snickering, and Agent Redfield's muttered response, "Hey, just because *you've* got kids…"

"Honey," Summer crooned, "it's okay. Helen, David, this is Mr. Redfield. He's uh…" The FBI? Why did that sound so sinister, so unexplainable? She couldn't say it. "He's a policeman. He needs us to go with him so he can ask me some questions, okay?"

"What kinda questions?" Helen demanded to know, still sullen and suspicious.

"Well, honey, it's about our…house. I'm afraid…"

"Is our house burned up?" David asked, scrambling after her as she backed out of the stuffy car with Helen's arms in a stranglehold around her neck.

"Yes," said Summer on a long exhalation. "I'm afraid so."

"Is everything burned? Everything?" Her son's eyes searched hers, liquid with hopelessness.

"Yes, honey. I'm sorry." She put her arm around his shoulders and pulled him against her side. Her throat felt parched…charred. *Honey, I'm so sorry…Mr. Bunny, after nine years only tattered blue remnants, but I know how much that blanket meant to you. And all your books, your games… Gone.*

"It's a good thing Beatle and Cleo and Peggy Sue are at Jason's house, huh, Mom?" said Helen. "Or they'd be burned up, too."

Summer gulped a breath as if it were a drink of water. "Yes, sweetheart, it's a very good thing." She was conscious of the two men, one on either side of her, hemming her in. Protecting her, she realized. But she felt crowded, suffocated. Suddenly she wanted, more than anything in the world, to be alone. Just to be alone. So she could think about this. So she could realize this. So she could go ahead and be frightened. So she could cry, if she wanted to.

"Mom? Where will we sleep?"

Summer gave David's shoulders a squeeze. "You let me worry about that, okay?"

"Mrs. Robey,…" Agent Redfield was watching her with his dark, sorrowful eyes, the set of his shoulders telegraphing urgency. He jerked his head toward the tan sedan.

"Yes." Summer set Helen's feet on the ground and gave

both children a gentle push. "Go on, now—go get into Mr. Redfield's car."

"How come we aren't going in our car?" David asked.

Our car? Funny how the old car didn't seem so ugly and decrepit now that it was the only thing they had left in the world. She turned to look at it, and even smiled a little at the expression on Agent Poole's perspiring face as he squeezed himself in behind the wheel.

"Why aren't we going in our car? Well, because…" Inspiration struck. "Because, Mr. Redfield's car has air-conditioning!" She gave the FBI man a look of triumph.

He acknowledged it with a shrug but no smile—she wondered if he was even capable of it—and went walking back to the sedan, leaving Summer to collect her purse and the children's backpacks from the Olds and follow.

As she was settling into the passenger seat of the tan sedan, the last remaining fire truck pulled away and went roaring off down the street, leaving them with an unobstructed view of what had once been their home. Silence filled the car. Even Helen was speechless. It was as if a curtain had risen, Summer thought, on a stage set for a play called *Devastation.* Who could have done such a pointless, heartless thing? And *why?*

Agent Redfield started the car and made a U-turn in the middle of the street. "Mrs. Robey…"

But Summer had twisted around in her seat to stare back at the blackened ruin, the singed trees and sodden grass, the sagging yellow tape. *What does this have to do with Hal? What do they want from me?* Her stomach constricted with a hopeless, helpless rage.

"Mrs. Robey," Jake Redfield repeated, speaking in an undertone as he glanced sideways at her, "I'm sorry about this, I truly am. But I hope you understand now what I meant when I said these people mean business."

No, Summer thought suddenly, *not* helpless. Not anymore.

"Maybe you might want to rethink—"

"Re…think…" she murmured, absently frowning. Because

a name had just come into her mind, lighting it up like neon. *Riley Grogan.*

"—*how* you feel about cooperating with us...."

She turned to him, her breath catching, stopping him there. "Excuse me, Special Agent Redfield," she continued in a cold, quiet voice, a confident voice, without a trace of a tremor in it. "May I use your cellular phone, please? I would like to call my lawyer."

The page had come at an opportune time for Riley. He'd been attending a black-tie reception at one of Charleston's best and ritziest art galleries, the occasion the opening of a show by an artist who had recently begun making a name for himself with his abstract representations of social injustice rendered on bits and pieces gleaned from old sharecropper's cabins. As Charlestonians had a way of turning such minor commercial enterprises into major events in both the world of art and in Low Country society, the show had attracted media attention from as far away as Boston and New York City.

Normally, Riley preferred to skip openings, unless he happened to actually like the artist, but in this case the gallery owner was a client of his, and it would have been awkward to refuse. So, since Riley made it a practice never to put himself in awkward situations, he'd resigned himself to the evening and had taken the necessary steps to increase the probability that he might even enjoy it.

But the truth was, he'd found the artist's work disturbing in ways he didn't care to examine too closely. And the strident and overblown praise for the artist issuing in a constant stream from his date, who happened to be the art critic for *Southern Styles Magazine* as well as a former Miss Louisiana, irritated him. He thought it vaguely inappropriate, just off the mark, somehow. In fact, as the evening wore on he'd been finding it more and more difficult to appreciate Miss Louisiana's auburn hair, sparkling green eyes and brilliant smile, which, he'd once thought, along with certain other physical attributes, gave her a startling resemblance to the young Maureen O'Hara. As a consequence, the vibrations from the beeper he wore inside the waistband of his trousers—so as not to spoil the lines of his dinner jacket—had not been an entirely unwelcome interruption.

Summertime had come early to the Low Country, and although darkness had fallen by the time Riley left the gallery in Charleston, the temperature had not. The night smelled of flowers and dust, car exhaust and imminent rain, with a fitful breeze that now and then coughed up, like reminders of a bad meal, odors of the sea and the marshes—the tang of sawgrass and saltwater, with touches of mud and decaying shellfish. It was the kind of evening that even under normal circumstances could stir in Riley a vague and restless disquiet; tonight, coupled with the evocative mood of the show he'd just left, it seemed to have awakened memories that winked on and off in his consciousness like fireflies in the dusk. He drove to Augusta through air as thick and soft as cream, watching lightning flicker across the mountains far to the northwest and listening to Bach on his stereo to keep the memories at bay.

He did allow his mind to dwell some on Summer Robey, though not on what it was about her and her problems that had him making what promised to be at least a four-hour round-trip drive on a muggy Monday evening when he could have been enjoying a candlelit postreception supper—at the very least—with the voluptuous former Miss Louisiana. Generally, he did not believe in wasting mental energy on fruitless speculation, and his client had given him very little information. She had told him only that she was once again in the custody of the FBI and therefore, in keeping with his instructions, was contacting him immediately and saying nothing to anyone.

"*Protective* custody, Mrs. Robey," he'd heard an exasperated-sounding male voice say in the background. "This is for your own safety...."

When Riley had inquired as to what had happened that she was in need of the FBI's protection, her voice had gone quiet, hard as glass and just as fragile. "They burned my house, Mr.

Grogan. My *house.*'' Needless to say, he had understood that she didn't mean the FBI.

"Stay where you are, I'm on my way," Riley had told her, and rung off with the soft burr of her barely audible *"Thank you"* in his ears. It was that sound he thought about. Along with the image of her mouth forming the words, it kept returning to his mind in spite of all his efforts to quell it, like a phrase of music, a tiresome bit of song.

The government building that housed the FBI's small Augusta field office was closed up tight at that hour. At the front entrance Riley identified himself and stated his business through an intercom, and after a short wait he was buzzed into a cubicle where he confronted a directory mounted on one side wall. Momentarily derailed, he was about to select someone at random when the elevator doors to his right suddenly slid open. He muttered a sardonic "Thank you" as he stepped on.

The doors whisked shut and, after a brief ride to an indeterminable floor, opened again on a large, well-lit room crowded with desks, windowed cubicles and computer terminals. It appeared to be empty of people, except for a tall man with dark hair, a shadowed jaw and the patient, sorrowful look of martyrs and bloodhounds. He gave Riley's tux a silent and cynical once-over, shook his hand and said, "Mr. Grogan? Special Agent Redfield. Come with me, please?"

He led Riley through the maze of desks and down a short hallway, tiptoeing, for some reason, past a couple of rest rooms, and paused before a door at the far end, one hand on the doorknob and a finger to his lips. Riley quelled a flare of impatience and nodded. The FBI agent turned the knob and pushed the door partway open. Riley stepped silently past him and into the room.

It was a typical off-duty room, perhaps a bit more generously outfitted than some, crowded with refrigerator and microwave, sink and coffeemaker, a table cluttered with newspapers and crossword puzzle pads, several chairs. There was a large sofa along one wall, and a TV set perched on a bookcase with shelves occupied by a VCR and an assortment of reading material that ranged from a Bible to *National Geographic.*

On one end of the sofa, Summer Robey sat slumped awkwardly sideways with her head pillowed on one arm. The other arm was draped protectively over the body of a small child—a girl, Riley guessed—who lay with her head in her mother's lap. Both were asleep, jaws slack, mouths slightly open, snoring softly. At the other end of the sofa, a boy lay in a tight fetal curl, his cheek uncomfortably pillowed on a backpack. His mouth was open, too, and there was a small, round wet spot on the fabric of the backpack beneath its corner. Even asleep, Riley noticed, the child's forehead was creased in a worried frown.

He backed soundlessly out of the room and pulled the door closed before turning to Agent Redfield and remarking in an acid tone, "You couldn't have taken them to a hotel?" He felt indefinably shaken; somehow he'd forgotten about the children. Lord, of course there were children; she'd mentioned them several times. It wasn't like him to forget a detail like that.

Redfield said dolefully, "Yeah, well…it seems there's just one…slight…complication."

Riley frowned. "Complication?"

A grimace gave Agent Redfield's lips an upward tilt, almost like a smile; he rubbed at the back of his neck. "Seems she has some…other baggage."

"Baggage?"

"Pets."

"Pets." Riley said the word as if it were a foreign language.

"Yeah. Lucky for them, they were at a friend's house—I guess they'd been out of town over the weekend, some family thing—so they weren't involved in the fire. Anyway, she—well, the kids, actually—they insisted we had to go and get them before we did anything else."

"They *insisted?*" Riley repeated in an incredulous tone.

"You have no idea," Redfield said dryly, "how persuasive

they can be. Believe me. It was a whole lot easier to go than not." He looked, Riley thought, like a man who'd recently survived an unnerving experience.

"Humph," he said without sympathy. "These...friends couldn't have kept the, uh, pets for another few days? What kind of pets are we talking about? Cat? Dog? Goldfish?"

Redfield straightened with a laconic gesture for Riley to follow him. "I guess the best way is to show you.... Oh, I think they would have, if they'd been asked," he said, answering Riley's first question as they walked. "I kinda got the feeling they weren't on very good terms—some sort of altercation among the kids, apparently. Anyway, she—Mrs. Robey—she didn't feel like she could impose."

No, thought Riley, she wouldn't. That damned pride. He couldn't decide whether he admired it or not, at least not in a client, but he did understand it. He understood it very well.

"Anyway," Redfield continued, "I figure no hotel in the world's gonna want to take this bunch. Here—see for yourself." He halted in front of one of the rest room doors but didn't open it—took a step backward, in fact, as if he expected a bomb might go off any minute.

Riley gave him a look of annoyance and the door a push.

"Get out!" a woman's voice shrieked as a dog began to bark ferociously. "Get out, get out, *get out!*"

What the hell? At the first words, Riley had jumped back as if he'd bounced off a rubber wall. He threw the FBI man a cold and murderous glance. "Your idea of a joke?"

Redfield wasn't smiling. He shrugged. "No joke. Go ahead—just go on in."

Riley gave him a long, considering stare; he was not in the habit of being made the fool. Beyond the door all seemed quiet now, almost eerily so—no human voices or barking dog, no hurried flushing sounds or running water. He pushed on the door...then pushed it wider.

A woman's voice—a different one, he'd have sworn—muttered evilly, "Go to hell." That was followed by a jubilant

"No wa-a-ay!" as the high-pitched barking began with renewed frenzy.

"Oh, good Lord," Riley said under his breath.

In the middle of the tile floor sat three pet carrying cases, the kind made of plastic with a steel-mesh door at one end. In one, the ugliest cat Riley had ever seen in his life sat and stared at the world with pure, unadulterated malevolence; from another, a very tiny Chihuahua with huge, bulging eyes was voicing a strong desire to tear anything that came within range of its minute jaws limb from limb—or at least, toe from foot. The third carrier was covered with a blue cloth, and apparently it was from here that the voices had issued. Because one was at that very moment muttering, "Stupid...dog," employing an adjective Riley would never have used, at least not around children.

He backed out of the room, bringing the door gently to a close, then stood and stared at it for a moment. "Well," he said. And after a moment, "You people don't have a safe house of some kind?"

Redfield shook his head. "Nothing appropriate for the...you know." His head jerked toward the room they'd just left.

Riley said nothing. Turning on his heel, he strode down the hallway to the big room with all the desks in it. He chose one that wasn't buried in computers and paperwork, leaned his backside against it, folded his arms and waited for the FBI man, who was right behind him.

"Agent Redfield," he said in a soft, even tone, "before I let my client know I'm here, I do have one or two questions for you, if you don't mind."

"I'll do my best to answer 'em for you," Jake Redfield said in a voice just as calm, just as quiet, as he leaned his rear against the desk across the aisle from Riley and folded his arms on his chest in an exact duplicate of his posture.

And then for a few moments there was silence while the two men took each other's measure, like a couple of dogs meeting in an alley, Riley thought, figuring out which one was going to be top dog.

Funny thing was, he had an idea they weren't really all that much different, he and this man from the FBI. Sure, the guy was obviously at the end of a long day that promised to get longer yet, and looked it—baggy-eyed and unshaven and as if he'd slept in his clothes—while Riley appeared calm, cool and immaculate in a dinner jacket and black tie. *Appeared* being the key word—and he just hoped the facade was going to be thick enough to stand up to the fact that at the moment he felt as off balance and ill-equipped as a man trying to tiptoe through a cow pasture in patent-leather shoes. But under their two very different skins, he'd be willing to bet, there lay the same junkyard-dog toughness, a few of the same ideals and principles, and maybe even something else, something Riley would never put a name to or let anybody see. He was pretty sure Jake Redfield didn't, either.

"You mind telling me," Riley said, "just exactly what is the FBI's interest in my client?"

"We consider her an important witness in an ongoing investigation," Redfield answered promptly. "I thought we made that clear to her." His eyebrows lifted. "You mind telling me what it was that would make her feel like she had to call in her lawyer?"

Riley let his lip curl with just a touch of sarcasm. "Maybe you scared her? Maybe your methods were a touch heavy-handed, considering who you were dealing with? That is a nice lady in there. Seems to me, if you want cooperation from nice people, it generally works best to ask nicely."

Redfield snorted. He rubbed at the back of his neck and muttered, "We're not who she needs to be scared of."

"Ah, yes. My client mentioned you think this involves a gambling syndicate?"

"Gambling, among other things—yes. One of the biggest left in the country. I've—*we've* been trying to nail the lid shut on these people for a long time." The FBI agent's face had a dark and tense look, as if his jaw were clenched and his blood pressure rising. After a moment Riley saw him take a deep breath and give his head a quick shake, as if it were a self-control regimen he practiced frequently. "Never quite been able to manage it. Can't quite get anything—or anybody— that'll stick through the whole system of due process, if you know what I mean." He threw Riley a resentful look. Plainly, the agent thought that lawyers should have been required to wear a special security pass stamped Enemy.

"I can certainly sympathize," said Riley evenly, not bothering to point out that he wasn't a criminal defense attorney and therefore had little if not nothing to do with the government's failure in their quest to stamp out organized crime. "But what does this have to do with my client?"

"We want her husband," Redfield said softly, his eyes like long, dark thoughts. "Hal Robey. We think she can help us."

Riley made a disgusted noise. "My client has no idea where her ex-husband is. When he disappeared he left her and the kids flat broke, did you know that? If she knew where he was, don't you suppose she'd be after him herself?"

Redfield shrugged. "Maybe…maybe not. All I know is, the syndicate we're interested in wants Hal Robey, and they have come after his wife in a very serious way. To me, that says they must have some good reason to think she can give them what they want. Since we also want Hal Robey, and would very much like to find him before the bad guys do, we have to pay attention to that. You follow me? We have no choice but to look very hard at Mrs. Robey. The difference between us and them is that we don't burn down people's houses and threaten to hurt their children to get what we want."

There was a hard, unhappy silence. Then Riley straightened and said quietly, "I believe I will see my client now."

There had been a year in Summer's childhood when the winter rains came early and stayed on into May in the California deserts and mountain foothills. They hadn't known about El Niño then; old-timers called it the year of the Hundred-Year Flood. For a while, California was in its glory. The desert bloomed with carpets of wildflowers, some that appeared only once or twice in a lifetime, and poppies and brush grew thick and lush on the slopes. And then in June the rains ceased and the Santa Ana winds blew down the canyons, and the vegetation became tinder. And the fire season began.

As the hills and forests and subdivisions of Southern California burned and firefighters and equipment poured in from all over the country to help wage the unwinnable war, base camps sprang up near those communities in the most desperate states of seige. That year, one such tent city had been located in Summer's hometown, because of its proximity both to an airfield large enough to accommodate the water bombers, and a reservoir that would be their source of water.

At the height of the holocaust, Summer's daddy, Pop Waskowitz, the town's chief of police, had taken his children to visit the camp. While Evie had run around taking pictures and home movies for a school social studies project, and Mirabella had fussed and fumed over what she considered to be rampant inefficiency and disorganized chaos, Summer had stared in silent sorrow at the firefighters coming in from the line. Too exhausted to eat, they would fall asleep where they hit the ground, sometimes with their heads pillowed on knapsacks, hard hats or bare ground. Their smoke-blackened faces and red-rimmed eyes had haunted Summer's nightmares for weeks afterward.

She was dreaming of those faces again. Of young faces crusty with soot and eyes aged and hollow from staring into hell itself. But…for some reason the faces were David's—all of them. No, some of the faces were Helen's, too. And when she tried to touch them, the blackened faces—her children's faces—crumpled and disintegrated and turned to ashes, each and every one. Crying, she kept trying to reach out to them, trying to touch them, one after the other, until there were none left. Yet…she could still hear their voices! She could hear them calling her.…

"Mommy! Wake up! Mom, a *man's* here. Wake…up."

Summer opened her eyes and immediately thought she must still be dreaming. How else could she account for this surreal dissolve from the nightmare horror of her children's burned and blackened faces to the vision of masculine beauty that stood before her now? An angel, perhaps? But…in *evening dress?*

But of course it was not a dream. And if Cinderella, down on her knees in the fireplace, dressed in her tatters and rags and up to her elbows in ashes and soot, were to suddenly look up and find the Prince standing there in all his royal splendor, she could not have been more dazzled than Summer was when that fact became apparent to her. Or more humiliated.

"Oh, gosh—I must have dozed off," she mumbled, struggling to shift Helen off her lap with one hand so she could sit up, wiping at her cheeks with the other. Had she been crying? Snoring? Her mouth and throat were dry. She cleared her throat and at the same time tried desperately to stifle a yawn. "Mr. Grogan—thank you so much for coming. I—"

"Why are you wearing that?" Helen asked from her battle station at Summer's side, up on her knees with her arms folded and her chin jutting out, and the expression on her porcelain face one more of suspicion than awe.

"Helen—"

Riley Grogan said, with none of the adjustments to tone and manner adults usually employ when addressing small children, "I was at a party. I didn't have time to go home and change." He regarded his inquisitor through half-closed eyes while she considered that, her head tilted at a judicial angle.

"I'm sorry," Summer said in a low voice.

"Don't be." Somehow his voice managed to be both crisp and comforting. He glanced toward the far end of the couch, where David was frowning and twitching, clinging to his troubled sleep. "If you'd like to get your things together, I'll get you out of here now."

Hope and gladness carried Summer to her feet before she remembered. Her shoulders slumped as she turned one to Riley Grogan, averting her face so he wouldn't see the defeat and worry she knew must be written there. "That's nice of you to offer, but I don't know where we'd go. I'm told the Red Cross will provide us with shelter—I'll check into it tomorrow—but I don't know if they'll take the animals. The hotels—''

"You just let me worry about that." He leaned down to give David's shoulder a shake. "Come on, young man—rise and shine. Time to go." Not yet fully awake, David rolled himself into a sitting position, still clutching the backpack to his chest and blinking slowly, like a fledgling owl.

"Time to go *where?*" Helen demanded as she hopped off the couch.

"I'd be interested in the answer to that question, myself," Jake Redfield said quietly from the doorway. "We still have some questions we need to ask Mrs. Robey."

"My client won't be answering any more questions tonight," Riley Grogan said, taking Summer's elbow in a firm grip and ushering her toward the door. As Helen wedged herself between Riley and her mother, and David slid bonelessly off the couch to shuffle along in their wake, Summer's eyes anxiously followed the FBI man, wondering how he would respond to her lawyer's implacable declaration.

For one moment it did look as if Agent Redfield might try and stop them. "I'm gonna need to know where you're taking my witness," he said in a belligerent tone, but his face said he already knew it was a lost cause.

As they met in the doorway, Riley paused, and Summer saw the two men exchange a long, measuring stare. And she knew with a sudden primitive awareness that the silent struggle had much less to do with her and her current predicament than their words might suggest. More, perhaps, to do with the thunder of hoofbeats and the clang of antlers echoing on a cold autumn morning. That awareness stirred along her skin and her pulse quickened.

"Is my client under arrest?" her lawyer softly asked, and the FBI man made a sibilant noise of disgust. "In that case, where my client goes is none of the government's business."

Redfield stood his ground a moment longer, then turned his head away. "At least let me know where I can get ahold of her."

"You can reach her through me." Riley drew a card from his jacket pocket and offered it to the other man in a motion both controlled and graceful. "Right now I'm taking Mrs. Robey and her children someplace where they will be safe and can rest undisturbed. Give it a couple of days and then call my office. If I think Mrs. Robey is up to it, she'll be available to answer your questions at that time. Now—Mrs. Robey? Shall we go?"

Still caught up in the primal spell of it herself, Summer allowed herself to be towed along for several steps before the realization kicked in that she was being treated exactly as if she were the spoils of that recent masculine power struggle. She halted, more like a balky child than a reluctant bride, and pulled her arm free of Riley Grogan's grasp. She was obscurely pleased when he stopped and looked back at her in utter astonishment, as if an inanimate object had suddenly acquired legs and voice.

"Excuse me," she said, "but *I* would like to know. Where, exactly, are you taking us?"

Riley stepped back and leaned down so that his face was close to hers. "Can we talk about this later? Like…outside?"

It was very quiet in the hallway. On the edges of her vision Summer was intensely aware of her children's wide-eyed, listening stares, and beyond them, Jake Redfield, alert and interested, his face looking as if it might even smile. She inhaled through her nose, struggling to take in air that had suddenly become thick and warm as fur. "No," she said, through lips that barely moved, "now…please."

The silence held for perhaps three suspenseful seconds more. Then Summer felt the breeze of a silent exhalation, and once more the pressure of Riley's fingers on her elbow. He said to the three interested spectators, with mocking courtesy, "Would y'all please excuse us?" as he drew her with him into the empty rest room and closed the door.

She felt light-headed; her ears were ringing. Afraid to give herself time to think about why that should be so, Summer launched into what she knew was a pointless protest, delivered in harsh whispers. "I'm not about to let you just haul us off without knowing where it is you're taking us." *I will still have some control over my life. I must.*

For a long, tense moment he gazed at her, his eyes dark and thoughtful. Then, as if he understood, he suddenly nodded. That astonished her so much that she felt as if the bands that were holding her together inside had just snapped, leaving everything loose and trembly.

"Mrs. Robey, you know the situation better than I do. Not only do you have children and animals with particular needs, but there's the security aspect to be considered. Someone has tried to do you harm. They may do so again."

"Yes," Summer whispered, and swallowed. "That's why I can't go to my family. Please understand, I can't take this—my trouble—home to them."

Again he nodded as if he truly understood. "Which is why I believe I have the only solution. I'm taking you home with me."

"Home—with *you?* No." Instinctive reaction forced the word from Summer's lips. She repeated it in a whisper, her breath gone. "No. Absolutely not. I can't—*won't* let you do this."

Pride. Riley's temper flickered and flared like heat lightning, and he had to turn his back on his client for a moment to let the breezes of reason cool it down. He understood the woman, but that didn't make dealing with her any easier. In some ways, it may even have made it harder.

He turned to her again, his eyes sliding downward past her face, the dangerous shoals of terrified eyes and a too-vulnerable mouth, as he reached for her hands. No-nonsense hands. A doctor's hands. A mother's hands. He held them for a moment, feeling their strength, their gentleness, their competence. Then he let them go and slipped his hands to her wrists. A woman's wrists. He felt their fragility.

"Tell me something," he said softly. "If you were to break these, what would you do?" She made a small, surprised sound. "No, really—if you were to break both of your arms, say, in a fall, what would you do? Would you hire someone to feed you, dress you, brush your teeth for you? Would you ask a friend?'' She shook her head in silent denial and tried to pull her hands away. He held them tighter. ''No—better yet, what if you had an illness, a life-threatening illness? Would you consult a doctor?'' He knew she was staring at him now, angry but unresisting. Bracing himself, he met the pride and fury and challenge in her eyes with all the strength of his own will. Knowing they were two of a kind. *But I'm the stronger, Summer Robey. You may not want to accept it, but it's true. I'm stronger because I've already been through my crucible. And yours is just beginning.*

''Say you consulted a doctor. What if he told you you needed rest, treatment, tests—would you take his advice? Would you do what your doctor said? Or would you say, 'Oh, no, thank you, but I can't let you do that'?'' He'd quoted the last in a feminine falsetto, and almost…almost thought he caught the glimmer of a smile.

If so, she banished it with an in-drawn breath and said flatly, ''It's not the same thing.''

Riley shook his head and lifted her captured wrists so that their eyes waged silent war between them. ''Oh, no, Mrs. Robey, it is the same thing. You have a life-threatening situation here, and I'm the doctor who's going to get you through it. Sooner or later, you're going to have to relinquish control and put yourself in the doctor's hands.''

''But…should I do that?'' Her wrists jerked in his grasp. ''What if he's wrong? Doctors don't have all the answers.''

''No, they don't.'' Without realizing it, he'd pulled her hands close to his chest. Now he found himself stroking the quivering tendons in her wrists with the tips of his fingers. His voice emerged unexpectedly thickened. ''No, they don't. But there comes a time when you have to decide whether you trust your doctor or not. If you don't, and you want to live, then you'd better find one you *can* trust. You follow me? So this is the time. Make up your mind now, Summer Robey. *Do you trust me?*''

Chapter 5

Do you trust me?

Such a simple question. One she could not possibly answer. Because the only answer she could have given him at that moment was "No! No, I don't trust you."

She didn't trust anyone, and probably never would again.

That realization came to her like a knife thrust straight to her heart. She gasped at the pain of it, then murmured, "It's not that simple."

She stared at her hands, doubled now into fists, and right below them Riley Grogan's fingers wrapped like manacles around her wrists. He had strong fingers, she noticed, big hands to match his frame, hands that were rather more rugged than she'd have expected, but which fit the image she'd carried of him in her mind. The *other* image. *The street fighter.* They did seem out of place, though, emerging from those pearly white cuffs with their gold-and-onyx cuff links, and the soft black fabric of the jacket sleeve. And they were immaculately clean, so scrubbed the skin had a buffed look, like fine leather, with perfectly manicured nails and the gleam of gold and onyx on the right ring finger. Her own hands looked grubby as a child's by comparison.

For some reason that made Summer think again of Cinderella, whose hands must have been rough and chapped from the soap and water, with nails broken and black from the ashes and soot of the hearth. What must *that* poor girl have felt as she watched the Prince take her hand in his royally pampered one and gracefully raise it to his royal lips? Why, Summer thought, didn't any of the books, movies or plays ever tell you what was going through *her* mind? At the very least she had to have been dying of embarrassment.

Summer fixed her eyes on Prince Ch…uh, Riley Grogan's pristine shirtfront, unstuck her tongue from the roof of her mouth and said firmly, "It's impossible. I have my job. The children have—"

"Your kids aren't going anywhere, I'm afraid. And neither are you." His voice was as implacable as when he'd put the FBI man in his place. "Think about it. As long as you three are targets—"

Summer stared at the tiny mirrors that were Riley's black onyx studs, feeling dazed, as if she'd been hypnotized by them. Suddenly the whole thing seemed like a nightmare to her. "This is crazy," she muttered. "I'm a veterinarian, for God's sake. A mom with two kids. This sort of thing just doesn't happen to people like me."

"Hard as it is for you to believe and accept," Riley drawled in that calm, patient and suddenly very Southern voice, relaxing his hold on her wrists so that it became at the same time gentler and more compelling, "somebody *is* out to do you harm. All you need do to remind you of that fact is to think about what happened to your house trailer."

Summer closed her eyes. Oh, God, she thought, swaying a little. It isn't a nightmare. It's true. It really has happened. They had nothing—except, thank God, they still had one another, and the animals. The clothes on their backs. Whatever had been in the children's backpacks. And, of course, that wretched car…

"This is no time for misplaced pride, Mrs. Robey." Riley's quiet voice had taken on a slightly harder edge.

Summer thought, *Pride?* What pride? How could she possibly have any pride left? She couldn't even work. She couldn't go to her family, not even to leave the children. Oh, God, she thought, what if they came after us there? How would she ever live with herself if she brought this mess to Bella's family? To Mom and Pop? To Evie?

"Our first priority," said Riley, "is gonna have to be your safety—yours and the kids'. That's what you need to be thinking about right now."

"Yes." *My children.* The thought was strangely calming. Conscious, suddenly, of warmth and pulse beats, Summer opened her eyes to find that her wrists—in fact, her forearms—were cuddled up against the stiff white shirtfront she'd been staring at so intently only moments ago, and that the pulse beats were her own, tapping joyfully against the smooth pads of Riley's fingertips. Letting her gaze travel upward, she found what seemed to be the same pulse—no, not a pulse, but a muscle, a tiny knot of tension—beating in the side of Riley's jaw.

A strange hollowness filled her, a dizzy, light-headed feeling she hoped was only exhaustion. Carefully removing her hands from their gentle restraints, she said, "Yes, of course you're right," and took a breath. "Right now, I have to think of the children."

Was it like this for you, Cinderella? she wondered as she turned her back on the totally incongruous vision of the Prince standing there in the flesh before her. She went to the sink, turned on the water and plunged her wrists into the stream in a determined effort to drown those tap-dancing pulses. Was this what prompted you to throw caution and good sense to the winds and go riding off with a man you hardly knew? Was it just that you knew you couldn't possibly stay where you were a moment longer? Did you feel you had no choice? Maybe, she thought, it wasn't true love after all, just simple expediency.

It occurred to her then, that trapped between the devil and the deep blue sea, if a person were scared enough of water, the devil might not look all that bad.

Not that she suspected Riley Grogan of being the devil in disguise, or anything even close to it. In fact...

"It's you I'm concerned about, Mr. Grogan," she informed him quietly as she reached for a paper towel and then turned to the rest room door, an ironic little smile on her lips. "I don't think you have any idea what you're getting yourself into."

"Oh, Lord, what have I gotten myself into?" Riley muttered the words aloud sometime later that evening—or more accurately, early the next morning—as he sat in his study nursing a large brandy and a bandaged finger. If anybody had asked him, he would readily have admitted it was no accident that the words were arranged in the form of a prayer.

Except for the fitful and distant grumble of thunder, his house was quiet. Blessedly quiet. He relaxed in it, slouched down on his spine in his favorite chair with his feet stretched out on the matching ottoman, the snifter cradled on his chest. His eyes were closed as he savored, along with the old-woodsy aftertaste of the brandy, both the quiet and the thunder—the latter because it echoed his mood at the moment, the former because he had an idea it might prove to be the last of such moments for a while.

He had a headache, and his finger throbbed to the dirgelike pace of his heartbeat. And it was becoming increasingly clear to him that he had lost his mind.

There were few things in life Riley Grogan valued more than his privacy. He considered his home his personal refuge, a haven that in the past he'd guarded as jealously as a wolf would guard his lair. Yet, inconceivable as it seemed, there were at this very moment asleep in one of the several extra bedrooms he called "guest rooms"—though he seldom if ever had any—not one stranger, but three: an exhausted woman, who happened to be his newest client, and her two minor children. Oh, and had he mentioned her cat and her dog? And—he stared balefully at his bandaged finger—one apparently demented parrot.

What *had* he been thinking of?

As if his mind had been waiting for that question, had already rewound his memory tapes to the proper place and had just been waiting for the order to push Play, he found himself watching a replay of that scene in the rest room at FBI headquarters in Augusta, those last few moments before she—Summer Robey—had pulled her hands from his and turned to wash them and her face in the sink. He'd never forget the way she'd looked at him then. Doomed but not defeated, like a magnificent wild creature caught in a trap. He'd never forget the way he'd felt, either, as if something had struck him hard in the chest and momentarily interrupted the normal rhythm of his heart.

He hadn't known whether to be relieved or sorry when she'd left him immediately after that, focusing instead on her kids. While she'd been doing whatever one did to get children ready for a trip, Riley had gone to get his car. Following Agent Jake Redfield's instructions, he'd driven around to the back of the building and up to what had appeared to him to be a blank wall, which had opened, James Bond-like, to admit him to an underground garage. In that stuffy, dimly lit cavern, he and Redfield had transferred various pet accessories from an anonymous FBI sedan to the trunk of Riley's Mercedes—food and water dishes, assorted bags of dog, cat and parrot chow, cat litter and the appropriate container for same, something covered with carpeting that Jake had told him was called a cat cave, and what appeared to be a miniature-size jungle gym. Enough equipment, it had seemed to him, to outfit a small invasion force. At least, he'd thought, it didn't look as if he was going to have to stop at an all-night pet shop on the way home.

The children, however, did require a stop at some vending machines for crackers and chocolate milk, which Riley made damn sure were eaten and all traces disposed of before they were allowed anywhere near the Mercedes. He and Redfield had then escorted everyone downstairs to the garage via a special express elevator.

It was while he was helping to find places for three pet carriers and two kids in the back seat—his suggestion that the carriers might ride better in the trunk had been loudly over-ruled—that Riley had managed, though he still couldn't figure out how, to get his finger within range of that damn parrot's beak. That had brought about a short but chaotic delay in their departure while Jake went in search of a first aid kit and Summer tried her best to calm hysterical children and livestock while simultaneously assessing the damage to Riley's person.

"It's not broken—hardly even bleeding. You're lucky," she had pronounced when order had been restored, more or less. Riley, experiencing sensations similar to those caused by slamming a finger in a car door, had seen no reason to answer that. "A parrot's beak can easily snap small branches—and bones," Summer had explained in a tone half instructive, half scolding, as if Riley were a not-very-bright child. "You should never, ever put your fingers in a parrot's cage—especially one who doesn't know and trust you."

But to tell the truth, he'd hardly been aware of his injury just then. He'd been watching Summer, watching her capable hands as they gently examined his finger, watching a frown of concentration etch a deep crease between her brows, watching a stray strand of her hair float in the breeze of her breath.

He'd discovered he liked seeing her in this mode—relaxed, confident, less tense than she had been up to now. He wondered if it had even occurred to her that she was holding his arm, tuxedo sleeve and all, imprisoned between her arm and body, and that when she shifted to find a better hold, or better light, she'd turned herself neatly into the circle of *his* arm, with her back turned to him and her head bowed low over his wounded hand so that her nape was unselfconsciously bared to him. He could have counted the hairs that had escaped from her haphazard ponytail, he thought, if there'd been more light. If there'd been less, he would only have had to lower his head a little, shift his arms a few degrees...and his mouth could have savored the taste and texture of the velvety skin drawn taut over the vulnerable bumps of her spine....

Absurd notion. She was his client, a mother, and absolutely off-limits. But it had been a very long day and an unexpectedly unsettling evening, and he supposed he must have somehow been reminded of Miss Louisiana and her uncanny resemblance to Maureen O'Hara. Thinking of what might have been.

Agent Redfield had returned about then with a first aid kit, and Summer had made short work of bandaging up Riley's finger, all the while tweaking his masculine ego with remarks about the insignificant nature of the injury. He'd consoled himself with the thought that naturally she'd say that—it was her bird that had inflicted it, after all. Technically, she was liable for the damage. Not that he'd have said so. Just a minor legal point.

They'd left the FBI garage in a convoy—Redfield first, with a mannequin sitting beside him in the passenger seat of the tan sedan as decoy for anyone who might have observed the departure with interest—and no one present questioned the need for such a precaution. After five tense minutes, Riley's Mercedes rolled silently out of the garage, with its passengers crouched low and hidden from the view of any of those watchers who might have remained behind. It was then, as he'd guided the big car down an alley that seemed as dense and dark as a tropical jungle, through streets where humidity drifted in the car lights like dust and hung overhead in a gauzy yellow shroud, that he'd realized that all thought of his wounded finger, incipient headache and the sensuous Miss Louisiana had faded from his mind. The night was like a sauna, but the sweat that trickled down his spine was cold. *Evil* was out there, somewhere. He could feel it. Unlikely as it seemed, evil had touched this woman and her children. And because he had committed himself to keeping them safe, it had touched him, too.

That was when it had first come to him, the question she'd

suggested to him, the question he'd been asking himself ever since: What in the world *was* he getting himself into?

Riley knew evil very well. He knew what it was to be stalked by it, to lie hidden and chilled while evil hunted him through the long, dark night. But it had been a long time since he'd made a solemn vow to himself that he would never live in that kind of fear, or in the proximity of evil, ever again— thirty years, as a matter of fact. Ironically, thirty years almost exactly. He'd conducted his life ever since with that vow as his guiding light, had chosen to go into civil instead of criminal law because of it. Because he had no desire to rub shoulders with the criminals and predators of this world; he'd seen enough of those. Not that civil law didn't provide him with ample opportunity to witness more than his share of wrong-doing and shady dealings and other shabby aspects of human nature. But in his practice, those generally had more to do with avarice and greed than with pure, out-and-out evil. And as it happened, other people's greed had provided Riley with the means to insulate himself against evil. He'd done a damn good job of it. Until now.

What had he done? And *why?*

There in his study, in the blessed silence of the wee hours of morning, Riley sipped his brandy and thought about it. But the only answer he could come up with hung in his mind like a pale oval moon. Summer Robey's face. Summer Robey's eyes…

For the first time in many years, Riley awoke with his skin prickly and clammy, breath thick in his throat, heart pounding. *Danger!* Something was there—*right there,* surrounding him. He could hear it rustling…feel its warm, moist breath.

Already charged with adrenaline, he opened his eyes. His fingers digging deep into the arms of the chair were all that kept him from exploding out of it. There before him, inches away, a face hung like a small, oval moon.

Voices whispered hoarsely. "See? I told you he was awake."

"Well, he is now." A second moon appeared beside the first, this one a little farther away. "You woke him up, that's what you did."

"Did not."

"Did too."

"Uh-uh—Beatle did. See?"

At that point Riley realized that something was prodding him—very lightly—in the groin. Then on his abdomen…belly…ribs…chest. A third face appeared, a goblin face—dark, almost black, with huge, round buggy eyes. It was much smaller than the first two but so close to his own it eclipsed them both. Something cool and wet—a tongue!—slapped across Riley's lips…then his nose. *Aagh—into his nostrils!*

He swiped at it, a maneuver that only seemed to excite the tongue's owner, who apparently viewed the slap as some sort of game. Tiny feet danced an eager tattoo on his belly and chest as Riley threw up his hands in a futile attempt to defend himself. But he was simply no match for that tongue, which feinted this way and darted that way and managed to hit its targets with unerring accuracy.

Finally, somehow, he managed to sputter, "Umph—get…it…*off*…of…me!" And just like that, the onslaught ceased.

Then, for a few moments, Riley simply sat—or more accurately, *lay*—half in and half out of his favorite chair with his legs sprawled across the ottoman, the bathrobe he'd wrapped himself in just before settling down with his brandy so few hours ago hitched up around his neck and gaping open on his chest. He lay there, breathing hard and glaring at the three small faces, which had prudently moved back a step out of range.

"We're sorry we woke you up." The voice came from the largest of the faces as it attempted to hide behind the perked-up ears of the smallest. It sounded apprehensive, and matched the worry crease that had dug itself in between the sky-blue eyes and childish brows. Riley realized that he'd seen eyes like those, and an almost identical pleat, before.

He cleared his throat and managed to scoot into a more-or-less erect position, just as the third face thrust itself brashly forward. Nothing scared about those eyes—uh-uh, no, sir. No sign of a worry crease there.

"Beatle has to go outside," the second voice announced. *Helen*—that was the child's name. And why did that immediately make Riley think of *hellion?* "Mom said we have to ask you first, in case there might be a burglar."

"Burglar *alarm.*" That was the other one, the boy David.

"That's what I *meant,*" said Helen, scowling at her brother before turning her inquisitive gaze back to Riley. "*Is* there?"

"Yeah, as a matter of fact." Riley pushed himself upward and out of the chair and walked over to a small box on the wall beside French doors that opened onto a trellis-shaded patio, rebelting his robe as he went and silently blessing the foresight that had made him put on pajama bottoms under it. Both children shuffled their way into close formation right behind him, David still clutching the dog, who was apparently named after an insect, though in Riley's opinion it bore a closer resemblance to a praying mantis than a beetle.

"Is it real loud?" Helen inquired as Riley punched in the appropriate code and deactivated his security system.

"Sure is."

"Can I hear it sometime?"

Riley glanced down at the small, upturned face wreathed in pinkish-blond curls, pretty as an angel's—and at the most unangelic gleam in those china-blue eyes. "In all probability," he muttered as he pushed open the French doors and stepped out onto the patio. Children and dog tumbled after him, hard on his heels.

The morning heat and humidity slapped him in the face and he inhaled a lungful of air that was like slightly cooled bathwater, perfumed with honeysuckle and roses. For some reason that image brought the thought of Summer to his mind. Summer Robey, that is. He wondered if she was still asleep, up there in his ''guest room''; wondered even more at the small but unmistakable disappointment he'd felt when it had been the children rather than their mother who'd awakened him.

Then, remembering the indignity of that awakening, he decided he was just as glad after all that there hadn't been a beautiful woman there to witness it.

''Where's your mother?'' He asked the question casually, checking the watch he hadn't bothered to take off the night before. It was early yet—almost obscenely early. There was still plenty of time to go over some things—such as the ground rules for this arrangement, before he had to leave for work. ''Still asleep?''

He got no answer from Helen, who was already off exploring, stalking across the lawn with her hands firmly planted on her hips, like a new landlord surveying her most recent acquisition.

Meanwhile, David had put the dog down on the patio. Riley winced as the mutt ventured onto his pristine turf, promptly squatted, then moved on, one tiptoeing step at a time, ears alert, every muscle quivering.

David glanced up at Riley, still wearing that worried frown. ''She said she'd be down as soon as she finds something to put on.''

Oh, Lord. The fact that his houseguests literally had nothing but the clothes on their backs had completely slipped Riley's mind.

''Oh,'' he said, when he realized he'd been scowling at the poor kid for several seconds without saying anything, thereby causing the worried look to intensify to one approaching alarm. ''Well—''

But just then Helen came skipping back around the corner, making her way toward them and looking like the cat that had stumbled on a whole nest of canaries. She gave Riley a sideways look, then sidled up to her brother and tugged on his shirttail.

David squirmed away from her, then reluctantly bent a little to allow his sister to whisper in his ear. And went absolutely still. He gave a small gasp, the lines between his eyebrows vanishing as his eyes opened wide. "Really?" The word was an airless squeak. "Oh, boy..." His head snapped toward Riley as if operated by levers and springs instead of muscle and sinew. His ears were pink and his eyes glowing. Breathlessly, worshipfully, he said, "You have a pool...."

"Yeah," Riley allowed, "I do."

"Ask him, ask him," Helen hissed, hopping up and down at her brother's elbow.

The boy tried, but the words seemed to have formed a log-jam in his throat. The effort it cost him to sort them out and get them moving again made him go even pinker, but in the end he managed to whisper, "Can we...*please,* Mr....um..."

"Riley."

"Please, Mr. Riley, can we go swimming? We'll be careful, I promise. We're real good swimmers—I'm even on a team. And we won't run on the deck, and we won't splash...much. Can we? Please?"

"Yeah," Helen echoed, "can we?"

Riley stared down at the two upturned faces, one flushed with hope, the other squinched up with what he could only have described as glee. Oh, Lord, he thought. These two blue-eyed urchins squealing and splashing in his beautiful pool, which he'd had designed, situated and landscaped to create the most harmonious and tranquil environment possible? He hadn't planned for such a circumstance—hadn't considered it would ever come up. Couldn't even imagine it.

And how could he possibly say no?

Fully aware that he was stalling for time, he folded his arms on his chest and said sternly, "Well. It appears you've already answered most all of my objections—except for one big one. Don't you think you should ask your mother?"

"She'd just tell us we have to ask you," David said quickly, as Helen's head bobbed in rare agreement.

"Hmm..." Riley rubbed his chin. "Okay, what about suits?" He was rather pleased to have thought of that; of course all their clothing would have been burned in the fire.

Naturally, buying replacements, including bathing suits, was one of the first items on his list of priorities, but right now what he needed most was to buy himself some time. Time to get used to this…invasion. Time…

"We have suits," said David eagerly. For an exclamation point, Helen added a jubilant little hop. "They're in our backpacks. We were gonna go swimming at Jason's, but then *stupid-head* here, had to go and squirt him with *grape juice*—"

"Am not a stupid-head! You are!"

"—and then our house burned down." For once even Helen had no punctuation to contribute. Both children gazed at Riley in round-eyed silence.

Seconds ticked by while Riley gazed back at them. Dammit, he didn't know what to say. He couldn't account for the fact that his chest suddenly felt as if it had been filled with gravel. Finally he cleared his throat. "Well, okay, then. Go put your suits on. You can swim after breakfast. But only if someone's with you. *And if your mother says it's okay…*"

But the children were already beyond earshot as they rocketed through the French doors and into the house, their gleeful shouts flung back at him like pebbles from under a spinning tire. "Mom! Mom! Mr. Riley said we can go swimming! He said we can go in his pool! Where's my bathing suit? Mom—where's my backpack? Mom—"

All the noise and excitement, of course, brought the dog at a dead run. She came in at warp speed, carrying a golf ball in her mouth, and skidded to a stop on the flagstones. Finding herself left behind and apparently forgotten, she stared intently for a moment or two at the closed French doors. She looked over her shoulder at Riley. Then, on paws so tiny and delicate they hardly seemed to touch the ground, she trotted over to him and dropped her trophy at his feet.

Even Riley had to admit that was pretty cute. "Well, okay, thank you very much," he said magnanimously, and was bending down to retrieve the golf ball when, to his annoyance, the little mutt snatched it up in her jaws and pranced away with it, stopping just beyond his reach.

He swore under his breath. The dog looked at him, then opened her mouth and once more let the ball drop. It made a small "pock...pock...pock" as it bounced on the patio flagstones. The dog—Beatle—watched it until it had stopped rolling, then cocked her head and looked up at Riley. Her eyes were huge and round, and every muscle in her body seemed on hair-trigger alert, as if she were about to speak.

Riley, however, was not about to be suckered a second time. He folded his arms on his chest and growled, "Okay, what do you want, a medal?"

"A simple 'good girl!' would absolutely make her day," Summer said with a soft laugh as she stepped out onto the patio.

Riley turned, a whole string of stock "good morning!" phrases in his mind. But the words seemed to hang somewhere between there and his lips, run aground on the shoals of feelings he hadn't known were there, lurking just beneath the smooth-flowing surface of his conscious thoughts.

She did look like summer personified, all right, standing there in his old blue bathrobe—a former favorite of his, coincidentally, which had become so threadbare and worn he'd banished it some time past to one of the guest room closets. Now he wondered why. It didn't look like a ragbag candidate, not on her. It matched her eyes. It draped softly over her body. She looked like blue sky and sunshine, fresh breezes and flowers. And her eyes had a misty look.

She said softly, "I hope you know you just made their day."

Riley cleared his throat. "Oh, yeah?"

She nodded. "I don't know if I mentioned it, but David was on a swim team in California. It was so good for him— he's not a naturally active child, you know, like Helen is. It was good for his self-esteem, too. I know he's been worried about keeping it up...keeping fit...." Her voice trailed off, and she gave herself a little shake. "Anyway, thank you."

"You're welcome," Riley said absently. He was watching her as she bent down to scoop up Beatle, who had gone into raptures at her appearance, dancing on her hind legs and frantically jabbing the air with tiny front paws. He frowned as Summer endured, with eyes and lips firmly closed, the same treatment he'd gotten earlier from that lightning-quick tongue, then gave the dog's ears a scratch and set her back on the flagstones. He frowned because, for what may have been the first time in his adult life, he felt ill at ease with a woman.

The problem was, he couldn't *place* her, not here, not in this setting. Something like running into your dentist's receptionist in the grocery store—he couldn't quite figure out who she was. Summer Robey in court had been one thing to him— the adversary. In his office yesterday morning she'd been something else—the prospective client. He was well-experienced in dealing with those. A little less experience with last night's incarnation, the traumatized client, perhaps, but still a role he was reasonably comfortable in. But who in the hell was she now, standing here barefoot and sun-kissed in his old bathrobe, on a morning that smelled of honeysuckle and roses? His houseguest? Well...yes. And still his client, too—he couldn't let himself forget that. But somehow, it seemed to him, more than either of those. As hard as it was to admit it to himself, he didn't have the faintest idea how to treat her.

Talk about the children, he decided. That was usually safe. He cleared his throat and remarked, "Seems to me that boy worries a lot."

The words hadn't been meant as a criticism, Summer knew, but they pricked her heart just the same. Instead of answering, she scooped up the golf ball and tossed it onto the lawn, then watched with Riley as Beatle bounded after it, keeping her smile firmly in place. When she glanced at Riley, she saw that he hadn't bothered to make even that effort.

"I hope you don't mind," she said, hunching her shoulders and plunging her hands deep into the pockets of the blue flannel robe—movements that felt stiff and unnatural to her as a puppet's. "I found this in the room next to mine. I thought, since—"

"No, of course I don't mind—you're welcome to it." His

tone was polite but aloof, and his gaze slid only briefly toward her before returning to Beatle, who, having run down his "quarry," was now growling and shaking it violently to insure a quick "kill." "I'm sorry—I should have thought to find something for you last night."

"No, no—that's all right. We were all tired."

Once more silence fell between them and was instantly filled with the hum of morning...and miniature canine snarls. Summer listened to it all for a few moments, then forced an unsteady laugh. "You have no idea," she said in a low voice, "how awkward this feels."

His eyes flicked back to her, and this time, before he could veil them with his usual grace and faultless courtesy, she caught a look of surprise—surprise, and a glimpse of something darker, something that told her how wrong her statement had been. Not only was Riley Grogan feeling the same awkwardness she was, but it was a state he abhorred. Naturally, she thought, remembering the way he'd faced her in a courtroom and in his office, with the quiet confidence that had made her think of jungle cats. The way he'd faced down the FBI man on his own turf and promptly taken charge. Riley Grogan was not a man who would ever be accustomed to feeling at a loss.

She smiled, making it a hopeful invitation to him to do the same. "Just yesterday I hired you as my attorney. And today..."

Today, she was standing barefoot on his patio in the soft, sweet-smelling morning, dressed only in one of his old bathrobes. And the man she'd envisioned last night as Cinderella's Prince was facing her not ten feet away, not armored in elegant evening clothes, but rather endearingly rumpled and unshaven in a navy blue robe that she knew must be silk, with his hair falling over one patrician eyebrow in the sort of disarray she thought novelists must be describing when they employed the word *rakish*.

Poor Cinderella, she thought as she swallowed, dry-mouthed. What a shock it must have been for you, waking up that first morning in the Prince's palace, to see your polished and graceful royal suitor for the first time as…a man. Did your heart pound like this? Did your mouth suddenly taste like dust?

She took a deep breath and just managed to hold on to the smile. "This seems…really, really strange."

Yes, and what was this sudden preoccupation with Cinderella, anyway? It never had been one of her favorite stories—oh, well, except for when she was a little girl and had identified so strongly with the way she'd taken care of the animals, and those adorable little mice…. But now that she was grown up—well, actually, she *did* have a cat who looked an awful lot like old Lucifer….

"Strange…" Riley's voice rumbled, bringing her back to the here and now with a start. He gave a snort of irony and looked away, scrubbed a hand over his face, then shook his head. She was more than relieved when he finally faced her again, this time wearing his version of her own smile—a bit wry, more than a little bemused. "Yeah, I guess it is, at that. Well, I don't imagine either one of us planned on this happening. Since it has…as I said last night, I don't see we had any other choice. For right now, anyway. You'll be safe here until we can come up with a more comfortable arrangement for you. Meanwhile—"

He was interrupted by a bloodcurdling scream.

Chapter 6

Bloodcurdling. Earsplitting. And hair-raising. Riley could actually feel the goose bumps rising up on his arms and the back of his neck.

He exclaimed "Good God!" just as Summer was murmuring in heartfelt dismay, "Oh, no…" She heaved a sigh and closed her eyes. Riley said acidly, "I take it that's…" and held up his bandaged finger.

She nodded, then winced as two more screams shattered the morning's peace, issuing from almost directly overhead. "I'm so sorry—the children must have uncovered her carrier. She's just feeling left out. Parrots need a lot of attention. And they tend to vocalize when they're unhappy. As soon as I find a nice central location for her, I'm sure she'll settle down."

A nice…central…location. A dark cloud seemed to drift across Riley's sun. Which one would that be? he wondered gloomily running several possibilities through his mind. The morning room, just off the kitchen, full of light and flowering plants, where he so enjoyed taking his morning cup of coffee? Or maybe the informal living room that opened onto the pool and waterfall with its shade plants and cool green ferns, and the soothing sounds of water, so relaxing after a tense day in court. Not the kitchen! God help him if Mrs. Abernathy should arrive to find a bird in her immaculate domain!

"Ah," he said, and left it at that, then raised his voice several notches. "Perhaps if we go inside…?" And he nearly tripped over Beatle, who was trying her best to crawl inside his pajama legs. "What the hell?"

The pink in Summer's cheeks darkened as if he'd slapped her. "Oh, gosh—I'm sorry. Here—let me." She dropped to her heels at his feet. He felt her hair brush his knees as she rose again, cradling the trembling dog in her arms, breathlessly trying to explain. "I'm so sorry—she's terrified of Cleo."

Riley's estimation of the dog's intelligence rose considerably, but he made no comment as he took Summer's elbow and steered her through the French doors, which he shut firmly behind them. The screams, muffled by the walls of the house, seemed to diminish slightly in volume, if not frequency. He drew a breath, then exhaled it as he said, "Coffee. I could sure use a cup—how about you?"

She threw him a grateful look. "Oh, that would be great. I'll make it, if you'll just show me where everything is."

"Should already be made. It's on a timer. My housekeeper generally sets it up before she leaves in the evening." He paused, frowning. "Reminds me," he said after a moment, taking care to keep it to a businesslike drawl that carried no trace of the regret he was feeling. "I guess I'd better call Mrs. Abernathy and tell her the good news." Summer glanced at him, her eyes asking the question. He answered it with a wry smile; Lord, but he was going to miss Soon-Li Abernathy's cooking, an eccentric combination of Deep Southern and classic Chinese that he realized he'd never fully appreciated until now. "That she's about to get a vacation of unspecified duration," he explained. "With pay, of course."

Summer's expressive mouth formed an O of dismay. He stopped the anticipated apology with a shake of his head and a touch on her elbow, which he then used to guide her through the swinging door and into the kitchen.

"Can't be helped—the fewer people know you're here, the better," he said briskly, as the aroma of fine Colombian bade him a reassuring welcome. Riley liked his coffee as most things, simple, straightforward and rich.

He opened a cupboard while Summer set Beatle down on the floor. He gave the dog a sideways look, then decided he'd best just ignore it. "Here you go—cups are in here." He indicated the one that had been set out ready for him as he took another from the cupboard. "Why don't you go ahead and help yourself. What can I get you? Take anything in it?"

"Thanks—just some nonfat milk, if you have it. And artificial sweetener."

That threw him. Already halfway to the refrigerator, he halted and lifted a shoulder in apology. "Uh…I don't believe I have either one of those."

"That's okay—just some sugar'll be fine." He got out the sugar bowl while she poured coffee for them both. Then he picked his up and sipped it while he watched her spoon sugar and stir. After a moment, without raising her head, she said, "I can make the coffee from now on, if you like—and anything else I can do to fill in for your housekeeper…if you'll just…I don't know, give me a list—"

Riley snapped his fingers. "Speaking of which—you need to make me a list of everything you can think of that you're going to be needing—you and the kids. That's including food—you already mentioned sweetener and skim milk. I don't know what the kids like." He thought fleetingly, and with longing, of the Cantonese delicacies Mrs. Abernathy was in the habit of preparing and leaving for him to reheat for his evening meal, on those rare occasions he ate at home. Ah, well… It's temporary, he reminded himself. A few days at the most. "And," he added, "anything else you need—clothing, of course."

"I thought…the Red Cross…"

He let a snort tell her what he thought of that idea. "You

just write down the sizes for me and I'll have my secretary pick up what you need.'' Danell had a couple of kids and would no doubt know where to go. He seemed to recall having heard her mention some sort of *mart* or other.

Summer didn't reply, but held her cup with both hands while she blew, then sipped. Above the line of the cup he watched the familiar lines of worry form between her eyes. *Like her son's...*

He knew what she was thinking, and that her pride was wrestling with her need...and losing. Compassion crowded his chest, bumping aside the confusion about where she belonged and how he was supposed to treat her. All he knew was that he wanted to spare her even one more moment's humiliation. That he wanted her smiling and confident again. He was trying to think of a way to make it all right for her, to tell her he'd add the expenses to the bill she was going to work off for him, if that's what she wanted. But just then, as if allowing that one thought about the child into his head had caused them to materialize, suddenly here they came. Following a brief but noisy overture that included the clatter and thump of footsteps and childish exclamations and giggles, both children burst through the swinging door and into the kitchen.

''*There* you are,'' said David, breathless with impatience. He had on swim trunks—the loudest Riley had ever seen— and a towel draped over one shoulder. Riley couldn't help but notice that the boy seemed to have put on some self-confidence, too, along with the outfit.

Helen, meanwhile, was chanting ''Break-fast, break-fast'' as she made her way across the kitchen in a series of bunny hops. She was wearing a bathing suit as well, a black tank suit with a white polka-dot ruffle around the hips that bounced up and down as she hopped. On her feet she wore pink plastic flip-flops decorated with daisies. They made loud slapping sounds on the floor tiles. ''I want *Luck...y Charms!*'' she announced as her final hop carried her into her mother's arms for a good-morning hug. ''Can I have Lucky Charms, Mom? Can I?''

Over her daughter's bouncing curls, Summer's eyes met

Riley's, eyebrows lifted in question. "Sorry," he said with an apologetic shrug, "guess you'd better add that to your list."

Suddenly he felt like an interloper in his own kitchen. As he turned, sipping coffee, to gaze out the window, behind him he heard the refrigerator door open and Summer's voice saying, "No cereal this morning. This morning I think we'll have…raisin toast! And…orange juice…and bananas! How's that?" A chorus of mixed cheers and complaints answered her.

Riley headed for the morning room, badly in need of some peace and solitude. But damned if there wasn't that silly beetle-dog, clickety-clicking along right at his heels. He halted and looked down. The mutt stared back at him, head cocked, huge round eyes glowing expectantly.

"Okay," Riley growled under his breath, "you can come. But no talking—you got that?" He'd have sworn the damn dog grinned.

But when Riley got to the morning room's step-down threshold the Chihuahua came to a dead halt and refused to accompany him any farther. As the dog went scampering back to the kitchen as fast as she could go, skittering and sliding on the slippery tile, Riley shrugged and turned to the wicker-and-glass-topped table where he was accustomed to sit and savor the morning sunshine along with his first cup of coffee. Then he, too, halted, much as Beatle had before him. No doubt for the same reason.

There on the tabletop, squarely in the middle of the hand-woven Peruvian place mat that marked Riley's customary place, was something that resembled a hairy, dirty and some-what moth-eaten pillow. It was a mottled black and gray in color, with patches of bilious yellow scattered here and there, and had a plumed appendage that it flicked every few seconds in an offhand, unmistakably contemptuous manner. On the opposite end from that twitching plume Riley could just make out a face with a protruding pink tongue and a pair of mar-blelike yellow eyes with narrowly slitted pupils.

"Oh, good Lord," Riley said, sighing, "what next?" He waved his arm. "Go on, cat—*get!*" The cat's tail twitched.

"Look, cat, if you think I'm going to pick you up, you're crazy. You're in my place. Now, get the hell out." He and the cat regarded each other. The cat blinked at him with the lazy insolence of a large reptile.

In the kitchen, David was carefully picking all the raisins out of his raisin toast. "Mom, can we go swimming right after we eat?" he asked as he added one to the growing pile on the edge of his plate. "Mr. Riley said we could if you say it's okay."

Summer sighed inwardly but didn't say anything about the raisins; he would eat them eventually, she knew—David had always been funny about mixing foods. "Mr. Riley is a very kind and generous man. I hope you remembered to thank him," she added as she reached across the counter to confiscate Helen's toast, into which the child had bitten holes where eyes, nose and mouth should be and was now wearing as a mask. "And of course, it goes without saying—"

She stopped, as the man himself suddenly appeared at her elbow. She straightened hurriedly and wiped her hands on the flannel robe. Helen seized the opportunity to retrieve her toast-mask, which she proudly displayed for her host's benefit, sticking her tongue through the mouth hole and wiggling it horribly.

Riley cleared his throat and murmured politely, "Can I see you for a moment, please?" He beckoned silently, his expression unreadable.

Mystified, Summer followed him across the kitchen and stepped down into what she decided must be one of the loveliest rooms she'd ever seen. Semicircular, with multipaned windows all around, it seemed to shimmer with light. There were blooming plants on every sill, white wicker chairs with comfortable cushions, a glass-topped table with—

Oh, God. "Oh, *Lucifer*—I mean, Peggy Sue!" she gasped. She couldn't bring herself to look at Riley, who had halted in the doorway and was stoically sipping coffee. She rushed to scoop the cat off the tabletop. "I'm so sorry. I don't know how—I didn't dare leave her in the room with Cleo. They don't—''

''Let me guess,'' said Riley, wiggling his bandaged index finger above the handle of his coffee cup. ''Cat and bird don't get along?'' Summer nodded. ''Let's see,'' Riley drawled, ''cat and dog don't get along. Dog and bird don't get along.'' He made a sharp little sound of irony with the side of his mouth. ''Mrs. Robey, I must say, you have an interesting household.''

Summer cleared her throat miserably. ''Well…''

''I seem to recall reading somewhere that cats can shed at will,'' Riley interrupted. ''Does this—'' he picked up the place mat, holding it gingerly with thumb and forefinger ''—mean it's true, or is your cat suffering from some sort of molt?'' His tone was pleasant, but Summer couldn't meet his eyes. Images of the Prince in his formal clothes shimmered in her mind— his immaculate white shirtfront and elegant black dinner jacket now covered with cat hair.

She cleared her throat and mumbled, ''I'm so sorry. Please let me have that—I'll see that it's cleaned. If you'll show me where your washer and dryer are—I'm going to need to wash mine and the children's clothes, anyway—so if you have anything…'' Her voice trailed off, finally bogging down in the swamp of this latest humiliation.

''Summer.''

The gentleness in his voice was a surprise. Her chin jerked upward and she sucked in a breath that burned like arctic cold as she forced herself to face him—this man she couldn't seem to stop thinking of as the Prince; the powerful and distinguished lawyer she'd all but begged on hands and knees to take her as a client; the impossibly elegant Southern aristocrat whose peace she and her family had so completely annihilated.

He took a step toward her as if he meant to touch her, but his eyes flicked at the cat in her arms and he evidently thought better of it. He paused and brought his gaze back to hers, and she braced herself for the impact.

Once more it wasn't what she expected. She was prepared

for disapproval, anger. Censure. Contempt. Maybe even…pity, which would be worst of all. She was not prepared for the steady blue gaze that seemed to enfold her in a cloak of calm and safety. There was something invincible about those eyes, so that she instantly felt comforted, like a child in a nightmare soothed by a mother's touch, but at the same time, frighteningly, dangerously vulnerable.

"Listen, there are bound to be some things we're going to have to work out." He spoke in a lowered voice so the children, who were being suspiciously quiet in the next room, would at least have to strain to overhear. "That's to be expected."

Summer hid her panicky swallows in Peggy Sue's billowing fur and managed to nod. The old cat's snarling purr drilled its way through her sternum, melted into her chest and from there through her whole body, like a slow-motion electrical charge. Her vision misted and blurred…and when it cleared, Riley Grogan was her lawyer again. Unmistakably, in spite of the silk robe, bandaged finger and beard stubble, the man she'd confronted last winter in a Charleston courtroom and pleaded with just yesterday across a desk of polished mahogany. The man in whom she'd placed her absolute confidence, and to whom she'd entrusted her children's lives.

He glanced at his watch and frowned. "I'm gonna have to get going. You'll run up that list for me while I'm in the shower?" He held out his coffee cup for her to take and waited, brows arched, for her affirmative. "Good—now, what else was it you wanted to know? Oh—the laundry room's upstairs, down at the end of the main hall, door on your right. Okay? Anything else?"

Temporarily dazed, Summer shook her head. Then, as he was walking away, she followed him into the hallway and gulped out, "Oh—the phone. Is it okay if I…?" Halfway to the stairs he paused and looked back at her, the frown on his face more quizzical than annoyed. "I really should let someone in my family know what's happened. I know my sister— if she can't get ahold of me, she's apt to call out the marines."

Riley glanced toward the kitchen doorway. Summer was sure the children were too busy pelting each other with raisins at the moment to eavesdrop, but he stepped closer to her and lowered his voice before he spoke.

"By all means, call your sister. Tell her what you have to, to make sure she doesn't worry, but don't let her know where you are, understand? You, me and the feds are the only ones who know you're here, and that's the way they—and we—want to keep it. That means you don't answer the phone if it rings. There's a lock on the front gate, and an intercom, but nobody's expected—except for Mrs. Abernathy, and I'll call her—so if anybody buzzes the house, don't answer. We're pretty secluded here, but I want you and the kids to stay away from the front gate, anywhere you might be seen from the road, okay? Just as a precaution," he added when he saw the deepening consternation on her face. Once again he made that movement with his hand as if he meant to touch her, then glanced at the cat in her arms and changed his mind.

"You're safe here," he said softly. "Okay?" He waited for her nod, then answered it with his own. He started to turn away, then for some reason, hesitated. Inexplicably, Summer's heart quickened. Her body felt warm—too warm. Then, with a look of alarm, he all but bolted for the stairs.

"Mom! Mom!" Summer braced herself as her children surged around her like an incoming tidal wave. "We're all done eating—can we go swimming now? Please? Can we, can we?"

"Clean up your mess first. And—oops—" she made a lunging grab for the Chihuahua as she raced by hard on Riley's trail, but missed "—quick, David, grab Beatle. You both know the rules about swimming alone. You're not to go near that pool until I'm out there, you hear me?"

David's reply was unintelligible, muffled by Beatle's happy tongue, and Helen was too busy exploring the gymnastics possibilities of the stairs and banister rail to answer at all. Summer allowed her shoulders to slump with her silent exhalation as she watched her esteemed attorney and reluctant host make his way up the long, curving staircase and disappear from sight.

How he must hate this, she thought. He was being polite— very nice, really—but she knew she and the children were driving him right up the walls.

She reminded herself that it was only temporary. That Riley or the FBI would find them a more suitable place soon. There *must* be someplace else they could go. *Some place safe.*

Or, they would find the people who were responsible for the phone calls. For the threats. For destroying her house. Maybe they'd even find Hal, now that the FBI was involved. *Surely it's going to be okay.*

''You're late,'' Danell sang out by way of a greeting when Riley sailed into his office sometime later that morning. ''Client's waitin' on you.'' She extended her arm over her head, holding up a handful of pink slips for him to grab on his way past her desk. ''Your messages, in order of priority. Hey, what happened to your finger?''

''Thanks…I caught it in a door.'' He took the messages and shuffled through them, noted that the one on top was from his investigator, Tom Denby, then tucked them into his jacket pocket and said, ''Dan-*nell*…''

She turned her eyes to him. ''Yes, boss?''

''I wonder if you'd do me a favor.''

''Now, you know I'd do anything in this world for you when you bat yo' eyelashes at me like that, sugah,'' she purred in a syrupy drawl. The phone sounded its discreet electronic tone. ''First, though, I'm gonna take this call,'' she added in her normal voice, which was Southern enough to begin with. ''Would you excuse me, please? Good morning, law offices.'' She listened alertly, glanced at Riley, then murmured, ''Yes, sir, just one moment, please,'' and punched a button. ''You might wanna take this one,'' she said, offering him the receiver. ''The man says to tell you it's Jake, and it's urgent. You want it in your office? I already put the client in there.''

Riley set his briefcase down and got the receiver tucked in

between his shoulder and jaw, and Danell punched the button for him. "Jake," he boomed out in a "Hey, old buddy!" kind of way. "What can I do for you?"

The FBI man's cop-monotone was a low rumble in his ear. "Uh…yes, Mr. Grogan, I'm calling to update you on our…situation." There was a cough, and in a slightly more animated tone, he asked, "How're Mrs. Robey and the kids? Everybody settled in okay?"

"Oh, fine, fine, couldn't be better," said Riley jovially, showing his teeth to Danell, who just rolled her eyes.

"Uh-huh. And all the, uh, animals?"

"Oh, great."

"So, I take it you didn't have any unwanted company on the trip? Nobody followed you?"

"No problem—not a thing," Riley drawled.

"Okay, good…good." There was the sound of a throat carefully cleared, some papers shuffled. Then he said, "Thought you'd want to know. Just got the report from the Augusta police. The fire was arson. No attempt to disguise the fact. And something else. The place had been tossed before it was torched—a thorough job of it, too. No leads, either. Nothing. Nada." A pause, and an exhalation. "A professional job. Pretty obvious warning."

Riley felt a chill between his shoulder blades. He held on to the smile for his secretary's benefit, but it was starting to feel twitchy. "Yeah? Who for, I wonder?"

The only reply to that was a snort. And then, softly, he said, "I hope I don't have to tell you, Grogan." Another pause. "It'd be best if nobody knows about your, uh, houseguests—and I do mean *nobody*—you follow me?"

"Sure do," said Riley.

"I don't suppose she's feeling up to talking to us this morning?"

"Don't think so."

"Uh-huh. So, what am I supposed to do, wait for you to get around to us?" Jake sounded sarcastic.

"That's right," said Riley, with a big grin for Danell. Ignoring the FBI man's swearing, he handed the receiver back to his secretary, who cradled it and gave him a sideways, borderline put-out look.

"Didn't sound all that 'urgent' to me," she said with a sniff. When it came to guarding his precious time, the woman was a regular rottweiler.

"Ah, don't mind Jake. He's an old acquaintance," Riley lied with a placating smile and an easy shrug. "From law school. Only gonna be in town for a short while and wanted to know if we could get together for a drink. So I guess you could call it urgent, in a way." He picked up his briefcase.

"You wanted me to do you a favor," Danell reminded him, only partly mollified.

"Oh." He paused, frowning. *It'd be best if nobody knows....* He turned back to her. "Uh, yeah—would you see if you can clear the afternoon for me? I have some personal business I need to take care of." He took a couple of steps toward his office, then pivoted once more, took a message slip out of his pocket and slapped it on his secretary's desk. "And while you're at it, get Tom Denby on the phone."

With the exception of a few particularly stressful times in his life, Jimmy Joe Starr had never been much of a worrier. That didn't mean he wasn't now and then *concerned.* The way he saw it, there was a big difference between worrying about things he didn't have any control over, and being concerned about the happiness and well-being of the people he loved. And that about described where he was at the moment. He was concerned, because lately it seemed to him that the person he loved most in this world hadn't been either well *or* happy.

Now, Mirabella did have her moods; she'd warned him of that fact way back when she'd been tryin' her best to talk herself out of marrying him, and he'd had occasion since then to exercise the patience and understanding he'd promised her then. Moods he was used to. Moods he could handle. But what he wasn't used to and didn't have the first idea how to deal with was this feeling he had that his Marybell was keeping something from him. Not that he expected her to tell him everything—he didn't. Jimmy Joe, like his six brothers and sisters, had been raised to respect a person's right to privacy, and he didn't consider that right any less sacred just because the person in question happened to be his wife. But there did come a time when a person's right to privacy got to be outweighed by a loved one's concern. There were times, he truly believed, when a man's beloved's personal business became *his* business. Jimmy Joe was sort of thinking this might be one of those times.

He was loitering over his third cup of coffee and thinking about that when Mirabella came downstairs with Amy Jo on her hip and a worried look on her face. Marybell *was* a worrier, he knew that. But this was the same look she'd been wearing for a while now, the one that had Jimmy Joe so concerned.

"Problems?" he asked quietly, girding himself for battle.

She drew a quick breath, then frowned. "Where's J.J.?"

"He rode his bike over to Mama's. He and Sammi June wanted to get in some work on that hideout they're buildin' before it gets too hot." Jimmy Joe pushed back his chair and held out his arms. "Here, let me take her—you go on and get your coffee. Come on, sweetie pie, give your ol' Daddy some sugar."

Amy Jo lunged for him and happily babbled, "Daddy-Daddy-Daddy," as she wrapped her arms around his neck and about half strangled him. He got her strapped into her high chair and poured some Cheerios onto the tray to keep her occupied. He waited until Mirabella had poured herself some coffee and settled into the chair across the table from him before he tried again. "Hon, something botherin' you?"

She heaved a testy sigh. "Oh, I can't get ahold of Summer, that's all. Something seems to be wrong with her phone."

"That what's been keepin' you awake nights?" Jimmy Joe reached across the table and gently touched the bluish smudge under one of Mirabella's eyes. She swiped angrily at his hand, which he drew back and held up in mock surrender, and she threw him what he'd come to call her "F & F" look—furious and frustrated.

"I'm sorry," she said, sighing. "I don't know why I'm so...I'm just a little bit tired, I guess."

Keeping it real casual, Jimmy Joe sipped coffee and said, "Think maybe you ought to see a doctor?"

"No!"

The denial came so quickly and so vehemently, Jimmy Joe's heart about stopped. He felt himself turn cold. He opened his mouth to ask...Lord only knew what—and damned if the phone didn't pick that moment to go and ring. So then he had to sit there and wait, with his heart booming inside his chest, while Mirabella—since she was closer and quicker—got up and went into the office just off the kitchen to answer it.

She was gone quite a while; Amy Jo had run out of Cheerios and he was up getting her some more when she finally came back. She had a funny look on her face—it seemed to Jimmy Joe she was less worried now and more stirred up, if that made sense.

"That was Summer. I knew something was wrong. I *knew* it," she said, breathlessly exultant; there wasn't anything Mirabella loved more than being right. And Jimmy Joe knew his part well; he waited in expectant silence while his beloved drew breath for the dramatic denouement: "They had a fire at their place!"

"Oh, Lord." He set down the Cheerios box and prepared for the worst. "How bad?"

A frown made a little watermark in Mirabella's forehead. "I guess the damage was pretty bad. She says they're staying with friends. But everybody's okay—the kids and the animals—that's the important thing." But she sounded distracted.

"You need to go?" Jimmy Joe asked quietly. She gave him a startled look and quickly shook her head. "Well, then," he said, "she and the kids need a place to stay? Maybe what she ought to do is come on over here. We've got plenty of room."

Mirabella was still shaking her head. "I asked her, but she

says no, the kids have day camp, and of course she's got her job. She says they're fine and not to worry...."

"But you're goin' to, anyway, aren't you?" He went up behind her and put his arms around her and pulled her back against him, resting his chin on her silky red hair as he drew a long breath, just inhaling the sweet Mirabella smell of her.

She seemed to want to go along with it for a moment, but then shook her head and muttered in kind of a thick, husky voice, "I *knew* something was wrong. You know, I've been dreaming about her. Evie, too. I just wish I'd hear from *her*. Dammit, why doesn't she ever call?"

It came to Jimmy Joe suddenly that his beloved was dangerously close to crying. And because that didn't happen often, and because like most men he tended to panic whenever he thought it might, he tried to hold it off with some snuggling and sweet talk.

"You missing your sisters, is that it?" he murmured against her ear, gently rocking her. "Feelin' a little broody?" His hand skimmed downward over her breast, on down to her belly. It was when he did that, and the woman he adored suddenly froze up on him—just went rigid as a post—that somewhere way in the back of his mind a light came on.

"Marybell?" he said in a wondering tone as his fingers fanned slowly over her barely rounded stomach. "You're not...*are you?*"

So it was that when Jimmy Joe's beloved abruptly burst into tears on that particular occasion, it wasn't consternation he felt but a tremendous wave of joy.

Chapter 7

Riley's home was his castle. There had been a time, just after he'd bought the place, when he'd gotten an almost baronial satisfaction out of driving up to his front gates, punching in his security code, delivering the password and watching the gates—the drawbridge—swing back to admit him to his castle keep. There'd been a purely visceral kickback then—call it pride, call it power—from all he'd achieved against so many odds. Power to insulate himself from the world's dangers, pride in the zone of beauty he'd built around himself as a buffer against its ugliness. It had been a long time, though, since he'd felt that kick or, with the exception of April when the azaleas were in bloom, paid much attention to the beauty.

He was bemused, therefore, to discern a quickening of his heartbeat as he stopped the Mercedes beside the security box that evening, after a long—and curiously entertaining—afternoon spent in a suburban Charleston Wal-Mart. He wasn't quite sure what was responsible for the phenomenon—apprehension, perhaps, but a touch of excitement, too, and even anticipation. He felt much like an explorer setting foot on an uncharted island possibly inhabited by headhunters.

But the most bemusing aspect of it was that he didn't really mind—not the way he normally would have such an anomaly—such a huge glitch in his carefully orchestrated life. He didn't care to ask himself why that was so, or what it was exactly that was responsible for his unanticipated lightness of heart. Or why, as he proceeded along the brick-paved drive shaded by old magnolias and live oaks festooned with Spanish moss, he was whistling under his breath, not Mozart or Bach but some popular ditty he didn't know the name of that he'd heard over the loudspeaker at Wal-Mart.

What he *did* mind was being barked at by someone else's dog when he attempted to enter his own house.

"I *live* here, you canine dimwit," he growled, only to be answered in much the same tone, albeit nonverbally.

Choosing prudence over dominion, Riley halted and glared over his armload of shopping bags at the minuscule sentry standing stiff-legged and resolute in the kitchen doorway, bared white fangs and raised hackles steadfastly denying him entry. "Hey," he growled back, "I've got shoes bigger than you. So back off." About then the absurdity of the situation struck him, though he didn't let the amusement he felt creep into his voice. "What do you think you are, a damned *rott-weiler?*"

"I'm afraid she probably does," Summer said with a sigh, coming from the kitchen to scoop the Chihuahua into her arms. "Yes…yes…what a good *girl* you are…my *brave* champion…" She paused to wipe her face. "I really believe dogs lack a sense of size. Oh, my goodness." She broke off to stare openmouthed at the packages in Riley's arms. "What is all that?"

For the first time, possibly because the kitchen light was behind her and as a consequence that distracting mouth of hers was hidden in shadow, it occurred to Riley that she had a very nice speaking voice—a California voice, devoid of any accent, but rather low-pitched and with a musical quality he found pleasant. The kind of voice that was probably calming to small children and animals—a useful asset for a vet.

She was laughing as she stepped aside to let him through the doorway. "No wonder Beatle didn't recognize you."

"There's more," he said as he deposited his load on the island countertop. "If you want to, you can give me a hand."

"Oh—yes, sure."

He paused, then, to watch her set the dog on the floor, noting that she was wearing the same clothes she'd had on when she'd come to see him at his office the day before—tan slacks and a pale green sleeveless shell—but that they looked clean and freshly pressed. As she bent over he noted, too, the slender lines of her back and arms, the way the fabric pulled taut over her buttocks and thighs. Things he didn't normally allow himself to observe in a client.

She straightened, dusting her hands, forcing him to shift his gaze quickly. He cleared his throat and said, "Where are the, uh...?" and held his hand out, palm down, waist high.

"The children? They were upstairs watching television, but I have an idea they must've fallen asleep." Her mobile mouth gave him the briefest of smiles. "Otherwise, I'm sure they'd be here to welcome you. They didn't get much sleep last night. And they spent a good part of the day in the pool. They were pretty worn-out."

"Ah." With a twinge of shame at the relief that news brought, he held up his index finger, adorned now with only a discreet flesh-toned bandage, and arched his eyebrows in question. "And the, uh...?"

The worry-crease sharpened between her brows. "Oh, I hope it's okay—I put her in the living room. You know, the room that overlooks the pool? I put a sheet down on the floor to protect it—I'm sorry, there will be some mess. With birds it goes with the territory, you know." Her smile flickered again, on and off, as if it had a faulty connection. "I'm sorry. I know this has got to be a terrible nuisance for you. But it was closest to where we all were for most of the day, and she needs the reassurance of being around people she knows and trusts.''

"Really." Riley kept his voice neutral as he held the door for her and they went together into the warm, muggy evening. He glanced at her and she nodded.

"There's been so much upheaval in her life."

In the waning light he caught the sheen of humidity on her face, the tops of her shoulders and along her collarbones. The air around him seemed to thicken.

"Moving, you mean," he said, and cleared his throat. "Yeah, I'd think a parrot would be somewhat difficult to travel with." He glanced at her and frowned. "You mind if I ask why you didn't just leave her behind in California? Seems to me it would have been easier on everybody."

She was silent for a moment, watching her feet on the uneven brick paving. Then she leveled a look at him. "There are some things I've had to do in the past couple of years where I felt like I had no choice in the matter. My decision to keep the animals wasn't one. Sure, I could have left them— all of them. And yes, things would be a little easier for me now. And for you."

She looked away, leaving him feeling diminished, somehow. A little ashamed. After a moment her voice came back to him, along with a laugh as soft and forgiving as a breath of the evening air.

"Peggy Sue—my cat?—I got her as a gift for my sixteenth birthday. I named her after an old fifties song—it was the seventies, but there was a big fifties revival at the time: 'Pretty, pret-ty, pret-ty, Peh-he-gy Sue'—remember it?" Her voice grew husky. "She's twenty years old now—do you have any idea how old that is for a cat? No wonder she's ugly and cranky, huh? So, for that should I have put her down, or left her behind to finish her days with strangers?"

Again she paused, this time to kick absently at an uneven brick in the pathway. "And Cleo—parrots are very intelligent, you know? It's like having a preschool child." Riley saw her shoulders lift, then a moment later heard the sigh of an exhaled breath. "Her owner brought her to me after her mate had been killed accidentally. She was grieving, and they thought she'd die, too. She wouldn't accept another mate, but she was beginning to bond with us—the children and me—when…all this happened. If I'd given her away she likely *would* have died." She glanced at him, then as quickly looked away. "And poor little Beatle—we got her because one of my clients, a breeder, wanted me to put her to sleep. You know why? Because her ears are damaged and won't stand up, so she's no good to show. That little dog would give her life for any one of us.…" She broke off suddenly. They'd reached the car. She stood and stared intently at it, her back rigid, arms folded across her waist.

Riley felt an urge to put his hand on the back of her neck and massage it until her shoulders relaxed and her body eased back and melded with his like a hand in a glove. Instead, he reached past her, opened the door and popped the trunk, then said gruffly, "Guess we should take the food in first."

They each made two fully laden trips, mostly in silence, before the car was empty of all the shopping bags and various-size boxes and plastic-covered clothes hangers.

After the last trip, Summer stood with her arms full of shoe boxes and garment bags and surveyed the already overflowing countertops. She gave a feeble-sounding laugh. "Do you do this for all your clients?" So many packages…the thought of what he must have spent gave her a horrified, panicky feeling.

"Only those I'm keeping locked up in protective custody," Riley drawled, but with an edge to his voice.

She had no trouble taking the hint; obviously he didn't want to talk about it. He probably wasn't any more comfortable with the subject than she was. Okay, so as difficult as it might be, it looked as if she was going to have to accept Riley Grogan's generosity and swallow her pride—again. One more lump to add to the ones she felt sometimes would choke her. She wished she could feel grateful; instead she felt inadequate and ashamed.

Riley turned from the open refrigerator, frowning as he

weighed a bag of peaches in one hand, a plastic package labeled Caesar Salad in the other. He held them both out to her, eyebrows arched in that querying way of his.

She took a breath, swallowed the lump and said, "Lettuce, yes, peaches, no—they should be left out to ripen. Here—just let me put these…" She gave up looking for a place to set down her armload and ducked into the hallway, where she dumped everything in a pile at the foot of the stairs. She returned to find Riley staring at a note she'd fastened with cellophane tape to the refrigerator door.

"What's this?" He focused on the note and read, "Crayons—"

She felt herself blush scarlet. What must he think of her? And after he'd just spent a small fortune! Her chest constricted with shame. "After you left this morning I thought of a few things to add to the list—but there's absolutely no hurry. I just thought it might help to keep the children occupied—you know, since they can't go…" She stepped closer and raised her hand to snatch the note away.

But he eluded her by shifting slightly and bracing his arm against the door. "Lint roller?" He turned his head to give her a look along his shoulder, his expression, except for the elevated brows, impassive.

She coughed, her face on fire. "You know—for the cat hair."

He went on looking at her, so close to her she could see the pores in his skin, the dark stubble of a day's growth of beard. He'd looked at her much the same way that day in court, she remembered, with a distance of several yards, a lawyers' table and a witness box between them. And if he'd made her feel trapped and impaled then, at close range like this he was even more intimidating. She couldn't think. Could barely breathe. Because all at once she knew that she had gravely misjudged Riley Grogan.

Oh, she'd recognized him as a fighter that day, in spite of his elegance and polish, but now she knew that the image she'd carried away with her that day had been more make-believe than real. She'd seen him as an actor playing the part of action hero in a movie with herself as the director. She'd thought of him as a tool she could control—and dispense with, when her need of him was over, as easily as a director yells "Cut!"

Only now, facing him over salad makings in his brightly lit kitchen, did she realize how foolish she'd been. Riley Grogan was no movie actor or make-believe hero—he was the real thing, a flesh-and-blood man, a strong man made of muscle and bone and sinew. She could feel the heat from his body, smell his sweat and aftershave, hear the rasp of his breathing. And she suddenly knew that, if there *was* violence and passion in Riley Grogan, hidden away beneath the elegant facade he presented to the world, it would not be hers to command.

Wrenching herself away from such close proximity and unnerving thoughts, she turned to the pile of shopping bags on the island counter and began to paw through them, pulling in a breath that seemed to clot in her lungs like heavy cream. "All I can say," she said huskily, "is that your secretary must have gone a little nuts. This is…" Her fingers, exploring the contents of one of the bags, came upon the silky coolness of nylon…the raspy luxury of lace. *Too much. It's just too much.*

"I'm afraid you can't blame her," said Riley absently, still frowning at the contents of the refrigerator. "I didn't ask her, after all."

Summer's fingers froze. Then, like someone peeking through her fingers at a scene in a horror movie, she lifted one edge of the bag. Her worst fears confirmed, she closed her eyes. "So," she said faintly, after pausing to clear her throat, "you did all this yourself?" *Lingerie. He did—he bought me underwear.*

Even with his back to her, Riley could hear the dismay in her voice…the precarious quality of blown glass and soap bubbles. It occurred to him to wonder if she even knew how fragile she was.

To give her time, he reached into the refrigerator and got his fingers around the necks of two bottles of his favorite brand of imported beer. He carried them to the counter, opened a drawer, took out a bottle opener and popped the caps, then turned and held one out to her. She looked startled but took it, studied the label for a moment, then lifted it to her lips.

"Would you like a glass?" he asked politely.

She shook her head. "This is fine." She took a sip and murmured, "Thank you."

Riley leaned against the counter and indulged himself in a long swallow of his beer, then said in a quiet, matter-of-fact tone, "I didn't ask my secretary to do the shopping, because it seemed best that the fewer people who know you're here, the better." He paused for another swallow and to give that sentence a moment to sink in, then grinned. "And frankly, I couldn't think of a plausible explanation to give her for why I was needing women's and children's clothing all of a sudden. After all—" he frowned in mock seriousness "—I do have a certain image to protect."

He was mystified by how pleased he felt when she smiled.

She took a hefty swig of beer that left her lips glazed, then frowned and tilted the neck of the bottle toward him to indicate a return to serious discussion. "Listen—I know you have an...active social life." He heard what was unmistakably a small burp. "You mustn't let us interfere with it."

She looked startled when he chuckled. "You know that, do you? How come you know so much about me, Mrs. Robey?"

She shifted slightly, leaning one hip against the counter, and Riley felt his gaze being drawn slowly and inexorably downward by the movement and the subtly relaxing lines of her body. He couldn't help himself.

She gave her head a toss, and he jerked his eyes back to her face almost guiltily to find that her lips were pursed and shiny with moisture, her eyes the fierce, burning blue of glaciers. "You don't think I'd come to you without checking on you first, do you? With my children's lives at stake?"

"Well..." For the first time in his memory his tongue seemed to have stuck to the roof of his mouth. He drank some more beer to loosen it. When, he wondered, had it gotten so warm in his kitchen? So heavy and humid? He hoped the air-conditioning wasn't going out again. Oxygen-deprived, he suppressed a yawn and mumbled, "Well, the only excitement I have planned for this evening is an early bedtime. Your kids aren't the only ones needin' to catch up on sleep."

He couldn't keep his breathing even as he watched her walk toward him...until it occurred to him that her only purpose in doing that was to dispose of her beer bottle. Feeling vaguely foolish, he moved to one side to give her access to the sink, then watched her rinse out her bottle and extend a hand to ask silently for his.

He surrendered it, and again availed himself of the unforeseen pleasure of watching her hands as she held the bottles under the faucet's stream...the seconds seeming to slow and elongate so that the flowing water became oil and each movement of her hands a slow and sensual caress. What was it about her hands, he wondered—her hands, the water, the fresh-soap smell of her. He couldn't for the life of him think why those things suddenly seemed so erotic to him. This simple domesticity, the casual intimacy of it, wasn't at all his style. He'd always preferred the more stylized courtship rituals—flowers and candlelight, elegant dinners, weekends in the Bahamas....

"Do you recycle?"

He straightened and jerked his head toward the kitchen's outer door. "I think Mrs. Abernathy has a bin...."

While she was disposing of the bottles, to give himself at least the illusion of useful occupation, he picked up the first thing at hand—a plastic-wrapped package of meat—and scowled at it. Returning, she reached around him to take it from him and in doing so brushed against his arm. He felt a charge go through his chest, a vibrating rhythm like the subsonic boom of bass speakers that he realized with a small sense of shock must be his heartbeat.

"Filet mignon." She shook her head as she pulled open the freezer door. "I hope you didn't buy this for us. The children and I are just as happy with mac 'n' cheese." She paused

then, and he saw her shoulders slump. She looked at him over
her shoulder, eyes dark with contrition. "I didn't even think—
of course you must be hungry. Can I make you something?"

Riley was not often at a loss for words—another of his gifts,
and one reason he was such a success at his chosen profession.
But at that moment his mind was a blank, his speech-
processing centers totally nonfunctional. And he knew why.
Because, yes, he definitely was feeling pangs of hunger, but
they weren't located in his stomach. And because, yes, he'd
have liked very much for her to make him something, but it
wasn't filet mignon. And because he knew very well that what
he was feeling was absolutely unpardonable—the woman was
a client, a recent crime victim, a protected government witness
and an unwilling guest in his home. And because in spite of
all that he knew, if she came one inch closer to him, he was
probably going to kiss her.

The silence had already lasted too long. Long enough to
become vibrant with unspoken suggestions and innuendo, long
enough for the heat to gather in Summer's cheeks and the
questions in her eyes, long enough for the sweat to bead on
Riley's forehead and upper lip. Way too long for graceful
exits, plausible explanations or any chance of redemption.

Still, what could he do but try? He gave his head a slight
shake, cleared his throat and said, "I'm sorry—" all of which
he knew only made it worse "—what did you say?"

She touched her lips with the back of her hand, cleared *her*
throat and murmured, "I said, you must be hungry. I can cook
one of those steaks for you, if you—"

"Mom?"

Never had a child's voice sounded sweeter to Riley. He
turned to see the boy David standing in the doorway, blinking
in the harsh kitchen light. He was wearing briefs and a dark
T-shirt with the words The Truth Is Out There printed on it.
For some reason, he thought, the child's knees seemed knob-
bier than they had in the oversize swim trunks, his legs spin-
dlier, his shoulders narrower and more vulnerable.

He felt Summer brush past him, so closely he felt the tickle of her hair on his face, saying breathlessly, "Oh, honey—what's the matter, can't sleep?"

David nodded, at the same time throwing Riley a look that held a strange kind of appeal, but more, he thought, of mute embarrassment. The boy's mother put an arm around his shoulders, forming a barrier of privacy with her body, but Riley could hear her voice murmuring words of comfort, David's voice answering. He heard the words "bad dream."

"Would you like Beatle to sleep with you?"

Again David threw Riley that unfathomable look, half wistful, half ashamed, then nodded. His mother walked him into the hallway, still talking to him in her low, soothing voice, her strong hands gentle on his shoulders and the back of his neck, ruffling and then smoothing his hair. *Mother's hands...*

"Git up outta that bed, you little piece a...! What'd you do with it this time, huh? You got it hid, you better tell me where. Better not a'poured it out, or I swear I'm gonna beat the tar outta you. Don't you dare run from me! Hey, boy—you come on, now, you git back here! Go on, then—sleep with the snakes, ya little weasel! Hey—yer gonna hafta come back some time—y'hear? I'll be waitin' fer ya. I'll be waitin'...."

"He had a nightmare," Summer said, coming back into the kitchen. She was wearing her worry lines again, and a flushed, defensive look that made Riley realize he must be frowning. He nodded and muttered something, he didn't know what. He felt chilled, and there was a heaviness in his chest he couldn't dislodge.

She brushed past him and began to take groceries out of plastic bags and arrange them on the countertop with rapid, almost angry movements. "Look—he probably wouldn't want me to tell you this—it embarrasses him, okay? He had a...a bunny blanket. It was destroyed in the fire. He's trying to be grown-up about it. He's trying so hard to be grown-up...about

a lot of things. And I wish—'' She ducked her head and he
saw her make a surreptitious swipe at her cheek with one hand.
Then she lifted her chin and threw him a defensive look. ''I
know you must think he's way too old to sleep with a security
blanket. He probably is. But dammit—'' she stopped to take
a deep breath, and when he said nothing, continued in a de-
liberately calmer tone ''—he's a very sensitive little boy who's
had a lot to deal with, and if a lousy blanket could make him
feel safer and more secure, I was *damned* if I was going to
take that away from him. And now that those…thugs…have
robbed him of that, I'm going to do whatever I can to make
him feel safe without it, okay? I'm sorry if you think I'm
babying him, or spoiling him—''

''Mrs. Robey,'' Riley said stiffly, ''I'm afraid you've mis-
understood me.'' Unbelievably shaken, he turned and stalked
out of the kitchen.

Riley looked forward to spending his weekends quietly at
home catching up on his reading, Saturdays and Sundays being
the only days he had time to do justice to a newspaper. He
saw no reason why this weekend should be any different just
because he happened to have three extra people sharing his
living quarters. His plan was to walk down the drive to the
gate while it was still relatively cool, then barricade himself
in his den with the papers and a large cup of coffee while
Summer and the children were occupying the kitchen. Once
the diminishing decibel levels informed him that they had ad-
journed to the pool, he would emerge from his lair just long
enough to fix himself a hearty brunch—a nice omelet, perhaps—Mexican-style with plenty of salsa. Or, if his sweet
tooth was in charge, French toast made with that cinnamon-
raisin bread he liked so much.

There was a reason Riley could feel optimistic about his
plans for the weekend, in spite of the recent catastrophic
changes in his household's population and routine. The truth
was, ever since the incident in the kitchen on Tuesday evening,
it had been apparent that Summer was doing her best to avoid

him. And doing a pretty good job of keeping the children and animals and their associated debris out of his way as well, with the help of the crayons and the lint roller, and a few other things she'd since added to the list—such as powdered pet deodorizer, and something in a spray bottle that seemed to work magic on the revolting puddles Peggy Sue habitually threw up on the carpets, almost always where Riley would be sure to step in them in his stocking feet. In fact, except for the samples of their artwork that now decorated the refrigerator and most of the windows in the kitchen and garden room, he saw little of the children. In the mornings, Summer contrived to keep them busy upstairs in their suite of rooms—showering, coloring or watching cartoons on television—until Riley had left for work. He had no idea how they spent their days, and truthfully, hadn't given the matter a lot of thought. In the pool, he imagined. He did have a vague idea they might be constructing themselves some sort of hideaway out in the backyard. Summer had asked him about it, and since it seemed to him a relatively harmless way for the children to occupy themselves, as long as nothing already in existence was altered or destroyed in the process, he'd given his okay. But he'd seen no signs of such a project, and had heard nothing more about it since.

In any event, by the time he arrived home, which was customarily around eight o'clock in the summertime, Summer would already have fed her brood and hustled them off upstairs once more, leaving a place set for Riley at the table in the morning room, and his dinner on the counter, neatly covered with aluminum foil. He told himself he was pleased with this arrangement. The forced cohabitation was working out very well. And if it suddenly seemed unusually lonely to be dining, as he'd always done, with only Mozart for company, he told himself it was just as well, and much better for the health of the attorney-client relationship.

The first part of Saturday went according to plan. Riley retrieved his newspaper, stopped in the kitchen long enough to pour himself a cup of coffee and retired with both to his study minutes before he heard the first thump on the stairs. He had worked his way through the national and local news and was well into the business section when he heard a timid knock on his door. Lowering the paper to his desktop, he let the glasses he'd recently begun to wear for long, uninterrupted bouts of reading slide onto the tip of his nose, frowned over their tops and said, "Yes? Come in...."

The door opened silently, and the boy, David, stuck his head tentatively around it. "Hi," he said, his eyes shifting to one side.

"Hey," said Riley, and waited.

The boy's eyes slid to the other side of the room. "Mom said to ask you if want some breakfast. She's makin' blueberry waffles."

"Waffles, huh?" In spite of himself, Riley's mouth began to water. "Uh...sure. Tell your mother yes, thank you. That sounds good."

The boy's head disappeared, and a split second later came a bellowed "Mom, he said yes!". Riley picked up his newspaper.

Alerted by subtle changes in air currents, or a sixth sense, perhaps, he lowered it again to find that, instead of leaving and closing the door behind him, David had entered the room and was wandering silently, gazing around him in apparent awe. Riley watched him over the tops of his glasses, saying nothing.

Presently David sighed, craning his neck to take in the bookcases that filled the entire wall behind Riley's desk from floor to ceiling, and said, "You sure have a lot of books."

"Mmm-hmm," said Riley.

"Did you read all these books?"

"Most of them, yes."

David's head swiveled and his jaw dropped. Then, lifting one shoulder in a belated attempt to look unimpressed, he sniffed and said, "I like to read books." His gaze slid wistfully back to the shelves. "Maybe...you could let me read some of yours sometime."

Riley coughed and harrumphed. "Oh, well, I don't know about that. These are probably too grown-up for you. I don't think they'd be very interesting...." Then, to his astonishment, he heard himself say, "Now...I might have some books upstairs you'd like." He rubbed at his unshaven chin and regarded the boy's solemn but hopeful face. Damn, the kid did look like his mother.... He cleared his throat. "How old are you?"

"I'm nine—almost ten."

"Think you're old enough for *Tom Sawyer?*"

Instead of answering, David heaved another sigh. "Mom reads us stories. She read us *James and the Giant Peach,* and she was reading *Black Stallion*—that's about this horse that gets washed overboard in a shipwreck, you know, and this boy tames him? But anyway, I guess she can't now because it got burned up in the fire."

Once again, Riley found himself with nothing to say. After a moment David shrugged and went on with his artfully aimless exploration, head tilted to one side like a potential buyer in a not-very-interesting art gallery. When he'd made a complete circuit of the room, he put a hand on one hip, gave Riley a sideways look and inquired with a poor attempt at nonchalance, "Don't you have a computer?"

"I do," Riley responded with a nod. "I keep it at my office."

"Oh." David's eyes shifted as he tried hard to hide his disappointment. "How come?"

"I keep it there because my secretary is mostly the one who uses it."

"Oh." The boy's shoulders sagged, then hitched upward in another of those brave little shrugs. "I used to have a computer when we lived in California. My dad used to play with me all the time." He turned suddenly, his face alight with an enthusiasm overpowering enough to carry him right to the edge of Riley's desk. "You can do really cool things on a computer, did you know that? There's all kinds of stuff, especially if you have a CD-ROM drive. Like, I had this encyclopedia, you

know? And—oh, yeah, there's Puzzle Wizard—I really like
that one, there's all kind of neat puzzles you can solve. And
there's games, too. My dad gave me a whole bunch of games
one Christmas—Battle Beast, Mech Warriors—only Mom
wouldn't let me play with most of 'em. She said they were
violent and gross, and she made my dad take 'em back. She
was pretty mad at him.''

"Hmm," said Riley, who was only half paying attention.
He was watching, out of the corner of his eye, the evil-looking
creature that had just slunk around the edge of the door—
which David, naturally, had neglected to close. The boy's
monologue faded to a background hum; the focus of Riley's
attention had narrowed to the cat's silent progress toward him
across the Persian rug. The last thing he saw before it disappeared behind his desk was the moth-eaten tail held aloft like
a plume waving over the head of a rather seedy potentate.

Riley felt himself tensing up. Where in the hell was the
beast now? More important, what was it doing? A moment
later, he had his answer. There came a horrid scratching sound
and what felt like about a dozen needles pricking him in the
legs. Something heavy landed squarely in the middle of his
lap. Riley gripped the arms of his chair and pressed himself
backward as the cat, her expression disdainful, casually sniffed
his chest and then turned herself around, managing to trod
heavily on some sensitive parts of his anatomy in the process.
A loud wheezing, grinding noise began to emanate from her
as she slowly stretched herself out and placed her front paws
on the desktop. After carefully sniffing out the area, she swiped
Riley several times in the face with her tail, then hauled her
hind half stiffly up and onto his newspaper. There she
crouched, staring intently at the door.

Riley had heard David's mother calling but was holding his
breath to avoid inhaling cat hair and couldn't answer. While
he sat frozen, not breathing, her advance guard, the dog Beatle,
came dashing headlong through the narrow gap in the door,
caught sight of the cat on top of the desk and skittered to a
halt. The cat lazily arched her back. The dog gave a yelp and

scampered back the way she'd come, while the cat placidly arranged herself like a mildewed stole across Riley's newspaper.

An instant later, Summer stuck her head through the door. The smile on her lips vanished like the sunlight when a cloud gets in the way, and she closed her eyes and softly breathed, "Oh, Peggy Sue..." She pushed the door wide and started forward.

Riley let his breath out and held up a hand like a traffic cop, stopping her there. He rose, one eye on the drift of cat hair that scuttled across his desk, blown by the breeze she'd made, and said briskly, "Never mind—I was done with it, anyway. David mentioned waffles?"

She stepped quickly back, giving him a lot more room than he needed. Oh, yeah, she was avoiding him, all right—why was that beginning to annoy him?

Her smile returned, though, as she gestured toward the kitchen. "I left some for you. But I was coming to ask you— where do you keep your lawn mower?"

"Lawn mower?" He had to stop and think for a moment. "Lord, I don't know. In the gardener's shed, I imagine—that's the door down at the far end of the garage—but I couldn't tell you what kind of shape it's in. My gardener generally uses his own, I believe. Why on earth do you want to know?"

"Because," she began in the same patient tone he'd heard her use with her children, "I noticed your lawn needs mowing. And since I figured your gardener was probably on paid vacation, too, I thought I'd mow it for you. If that's okay." And all the while she was saying that, a rosy flush was creeping across her cheekbones.

Chapter 8

Riley halted opposite her in his study doorway. Undiagnosed tensions crowded his chest. "You don't need to do that."

She raked a hand back through her hair, which, since most of it was caught up in her haphazard ponytail, left the short parts around her face wildly—and rather endearingly—askew. She was wearing a new pair of shorts, he noticed. But with it she wore one of his cast-off shirts with the sleeves rolled above her elbows and the tails knotted around her waist and the top buttons open to show a deep slash of cream-colored throat. For some reason, she seemed to prefer his old clothes to the new ones he'd bought for her.

"Yes, I *do*," she said in a low voice, while her eyes begged him to understand.

Well, he did understand. Maybe he understood pride too well. Because he had *his* pride, too, dammit. He wondered if she knew what it cost him to swallow it now and grudgingly say, "Well, I guess we can see what kind of shape it's in."

He stalked past her, down the hall and through the kitchen, through the mudroom and out the back door, mired so deeply in the mystery of his wounded thoughts that he was halfway across the yard before it occurred to him to wonder if he was going to need a key to get into the gardener's room; it had been that long since he'd had occasion to go there himself. Riley was not in any way, shape or form a do-it-yourselfer; he was accustomed to having his castle run like a well-oiled machine, and he paid people generously to see that it did, and to insure that he personally would never have to concern himself with the details. Somewhere in the back of his mind he supposed he must have realized that eliminating the services of his housekeeper, gardener and pool man was probably going to have some effect on the workings of the machine, not to mention his own participation in its maintenance. Of course he had. He just hadn't prepared himself for the possibility that a woman—any woman, much less a client and a guest in his house—would be mowing his lawn for him. It didn't make him proud to discover that he felt that way, either—Lord, he was all for equal opportunity, or sure had thought he was.

To Summer's relief, the gardener's room wasn't locked. She was right behind Riley as he pushed the door open, waved aside a few spiderwebs and stepped over the threshold. She spotted the mower, a green one that looked almost new, pushed over in the far corner but accessible enough. And she was encouraged to see that it was encrusted with a spattering of dried grass, as though it might have seen fairly recent use after all.

"Looks okay," she said as she dropped to one knee beside the mower. She unscrewed a cap, stuck a finger into the opening, sniffed it and nodded. "Seems to have plenty of gas." She straightened and took hold of the handle.

But when Riley said gruffly, "Here, I'll do that," she let go of the handle and moved aside as quickly as she could.

It had been another near miss. Once again they'd come close to touching…his masculine scent filled her nostrils; his body heat wafted like a breath across her skin. Heart pounding against the arms she'd folded humbly across her waist, she stood and watched him wrestle the mower through the doorway. Her own breath seemed to stick in her throat. *Oh, dear,* she thought, but beyond that her mind simply refused to go.

How was it, she mused, that the man could look so elegant even in tan Dockers and a white polo shirt? And she realized, as she found herself staring at them, that it was the first time she'd ever seen his bare arms. How was it that a lawyer, who presumably spent all his time in offices and courtrooms, could have arms so well-muscled and deeply tanned? Did he play tennis or golf? Enjoy a daily workout at a gym? The idea of Riley Grogan sweating and grunting under a set of barbells was simply mind-boggling.

At the moment, though, he was squatting beside the mower looking like any other perplexed suburban weekend gardener—though surely about a hundred times more handsome than most. And it suddenly occurred to Summer to wonder if he'd ever in his life used a lawnmower before. Did he even know how to start it? What should she do if he didn't? She could hardly shove the man aside and take over, not when it was his lawn and his mower. Not without risking grave damage to his masculine ego—which, she was beginning to realize, to her utter bemusement, was every bit as fragile, for all his strength and confidence, as that of any other man's.

And yet, how long could she stand here and let him suffer?

As Summer pondered her dilemma, a delicious, quivery feeling came over her. It had been such a long time since she'd felt it, it took her a while to recognize it for what it was: *amusement.* She suddenly felt an almost overpowering urge to laugh. *At Riley Grogan!* The only thing keeping her from it, in fact, was the hand she'd had the foresight to clamp tightly over her mouth.

Oh, Lord—she couldn't go on like this—she really couldn't. In another second she was going to explode with laughter. Male ego be damned—she had just made up her mind that she was going to have to speak up before she giggled and made things worse, and had peeled her fingers away from her face and cleared her throat in preparation for doing so, when salvation arrived from an unexpected source.

David, whose presence Summer had all but forgotten, pointed and said, "You have to pull on this thing right here."

Tossing her a look that could only be described as smug, Riley rose to his feet, so abruptly that Summer, who was already leaning forward to point out the necessary steps to achieve ignition, had to spring back to avoid a collision. Meanwhile, Riley took his place at the helm, grasped the ring David had shown him and gave it a mighty tug.

The mower gave a derisive snort and then was silent. Riley pulled the cord again. Same thing. And again. And...yet... *again.* Finally, with sweat pouring down his face and fire in his eyes, he turned to Summer.

Who once more peeled her fingers away from the bottom part of her face, cleared her throat and stepped forward. "Maybe," she said carefully, "it would help if you primed it."

She then reached down, pumped the primer bulb a few times, straightened, adjusted the choke, set the throttle, grasped the ring and pulled. The mower snorted...snarled...and died. Unperturbed, she made a minor adjustment to the choke and tried again. This time the snorts and snarls settled nicely into a roar, which, by easing up on the throttle, Summer soon tuned to a businesslike growl. Without further ado, without even daring a backward glance, she steered the mower onto the lush and overgrown lawn.

And, oh, didn't it feel good!

She was flushed with success, the June sun was hot on her back, sweat was pouring into her eyes, and she could feel the vibrations of the powerful machine running up her arms and into her chest and belly. She could even feel them in the fillings in her teeth. The muscles in her calves and thighs, arms and back protested...and then rejoiced in the exercise. The grass smelled so sweet she could almost taste it. The air was heavy with humidity, but she felt light. She felt confident and capable. Exhilarated and strong.

And not once today had she thought of herself as poor Cinderella. Or, thank heaven, of Riley Grogan as the Prince.

Back on the path, Riley and David stood side by side in identical poses, hands on hips, watching Summer cut a widening swath through the grass. Presently Riley looked down at David, who returned his gaze with mute sympathy, then after a moment just sort of wandered off, as if he found the whole episode vaguely embarrassing.

Riley knew how he felt. But while his masculine pride had definitely taken a body blow, he was discovering that there was something intensely erotic about the sight of that particular woman pushing a powerful machine around his backyard. She'd only been at it a few minutes, but she was already drenched with sweat, her face flushed and shiny with it, loose strands of her hair lying on her neck and cheeks in wet corkscrew curls, the soft material of his old shirt sticking to her body in dark patches. Her body moved with the unstudied grace of the naturally strong and healthy, the muscles in her legs bunching and relaxing as she pushed and pulled and maneuvered the heavy machine through tight spots, the sunlight turning the fine hair on her thighs to golden down....

Riley's stomach growled, reminding him he hadn't gotten around to eating the breakfast Summer had left for him. But it wasn't blueberry waffles he was hungry for, not then.

Scowling, he turned and stalked back into the gardener's shed. There was no point in trying to go back to his study, not with the cat having usurped his newspaper, and with Summer putt-putting around out here he'd never be able to stay inside and concentrate, anyway. And, if he remembered right, he'd seen—yes, there they were—a pair of hedge clippers. Old-fashioned hand clippers, nothing power-driven, thank you—his ego had taken about all the beating it could stand for one day. He took them down from their hook and gave them a few practice snips to make sure they were in working order, then carried them outside.

Way off down in the back beyond the wooded slope, he seemed to recall having seen some bushes that had looked as if they could use a trim. Hell, he thought, might as well have a go at them, since the morning was otherwise shot. Lord knew he could use the exercise—not to mention a way to work off some of this unanticipated sexual tension—and there was the additional perk that, since there were so many trees down in that part of the property, he'd be working in the shade.

The bushes—he had no idea what kind they were, but they did have some rather nice flowers in the spring—were as rampant as he remembered. Obviously the gardeners hadn't been in this part of the grounds in a while, which made him feel the more valiant and enterprising, precisely what his bruised male ego needed. Riley surveyed the clump and mapped out his plan of attack. He'd start at the sunny end, he decided, then work his way toward the trees and into the shade. Whistling tunelessly, he set to work.

He'd been at it maybe fifteen minutes or so, long enough to work up a good sweat, and was maneuvering underneath a good-size magnolia, whacking away and feeling good about the progress he was making, when all of a sudden the bush he was chopping on emitted an earsplitting shriek. That startled him so he let go of the clippers, which landed, points down, on his instep at the precise moment a voice a few inches from his ear yelled, "Hey, you're cutting down my fort!"

Pain stabbed through his foot. He straightened violently, unfortunately right underneath a sizable branch of the magnolia tree. Riley's head met the branch with a considerable amount of force, and then for a short while his world became mostly bright lights and dark blotches.

When his senses returned to normal function, he found that he was lying on his back in some prickly leaves, gazing up at the face of a small, blond angel, who kept poking his cheek with her finger and saying solemnly, "Are you dead? Huh? Are you dead?"

Before Riley could put together an intelligent response to that, the face abruptly vanished. He heard the crunch of footsteps and the crashing of underbrush, and a voice of diminishing volume yelling, "Mom! Mom! Mr. Riley's *bleeding!*"

Was he? Riley sat up slowly, swearing as he fought off a wave of nausea. Yes, dammit, he was; he could feel the trickles working their way through his hair in several directions—toward his forehead, his ears, even down the back of his neck. *Damn.* In another minute he was going to look like an ambulance case. There were already spots of blood on his shirt. He groaned, as much in mortification as in pain, as he pulled the shirt off, wadded it up and pressed it against his head.

As if that weren't enough, his foot hurt like bloody hell. He was wearing an old pair of canvas boat shoes with no socks, which was what he always put on for his Saturday of reading and relaxation. He knew he should have changed into heavier work shoes before tackling those bushes. But he hadn't. And as a result, it appeared he'd stabbed himself in the foot with the damned hedge clippers. He couldn't even bring himself to look at the result.

Summer was plowing methodically up and down the lawn when she caught the flash of movement out of the corner of her eye. She cut off power to the mower, wiped sweat from her eyes with her shirtsleeve and said sternly, "Hey—what's the rule about lawn mowers, kiddo? We *wait*—". Then she lowered her arm and got her first good look at her daughter's flushed and sweaty face. Alarm narrowed her focus instantly. Bending closer, she said, "Honey, what is it? What's the matter?"

Helen was shaking her head and gasping like a netted fish. "I didn't mean to, I didn't mean to, Mommy. You have to come quick, Mr. Riley's hurt because I yelled and he got scared and poked himself with the scissors and then he hit his head and now he's just lying there on the ground bleeding and I don't know if he's dead, but 'cept his eyes are open—''

"Wait," said Summer. "Slow down. Take a breath. What are you talking about? You said Riley's *bleeding? Where?*"

Helen turned and pointed. "Down there."

"No, I mean—oh, gosh, never mind—"

David arrived on the scene just in time to inquire in a superior tone, "Oh, boy, what'd she do now?"

"I didn't *mean* to," Helen wailed, scarlet-faced. "He was gonna cut down my fort! So I just screamed, and then he said a bad word and dropped the scissors on his foot and then he *jumped,* and bumped his head on the tree *real hard!* But I didn't mean to hurt him, Mommy, I didn't, I didn't!" With that she turned and ran for the house as fast as she could go.

"Hey—" David yelped. "What'd you do to Mr. Riley? You better not've hurt him—darn you—hey!" And he took off after his sister.

For a second or two as her eyes followed her offspring, Summer hesitated. Her mother's radar definitely sensed trouble. But obviously, "lying on the ground bleeding" had precedence over a possible sibling tiff. "Down there," Helen had said. Summer sighed and started across the grass. After the first few steps, she broke into a run.

Riley was sitting up when she found him, to her extreme relief; okay, Helen did have a tendency to exaggerate, but still... He had his back propped against the trunk of a magnolia tree, one leg drawn up, the other straight, and Lord help her, he'd taken off his shirt. He'd wadded it up and was holding it pressed to the top of his head. And yes, she could definitely see bloodstains on it.

Summer slowed her steps, asking her heartbeat to take its cue from them and do the same. But for some reason it only seemed to accelerate as she drew closer to the injured man. For God's sake, what was the matter with her? Had it been so long since she'd seen a grown man's naked torso up close and personal like this? Or was it just that it was *this* man's body?

This, after all, was Riley Grogan, her lawyer; the oh, so elegant man-about-town Riley Grogan, whose unclothed body she would never in a million years have expected to see.

Oh, God, especially not like this. Alone with him in hot, damp, shady woods that smelled like the dawn of time…his smooth, tawny skin—not suntanned so much as naturally olive-toned—shiny with sweat and speckled with blood, flecks of decayed leaves and bits of grass clinging to the dark hair that patterned his chest and torso, the muscles of his shoulders and belly taut and quivering….

"Well," Summer said in a voice she had to struggle to keep steady, "you're alive." Riley opened one eye and regarded her morosely as she ducked under a limb of the magnolia. "Helen's sure she killed you."

He gave a short gust of laughter. "It's a wonder she didn't—damn near gave me a heart attack. Scared the…you-know-what outta me when she screamed like that. Thought for sure I'd got her with the damned clippers."

"How bad is it?"

He hissed and said "Ouch!" when she lifted up an edge of the bloody shirt, then continued in an airless mutter as she bent over him and began to explore his scalp, combing through the soft, dark thicket of his hair. "Well, it rang my bell, that's for sure. Must've opened a cut, because it's bleeding quite a bit, but I think it probably looks worse than it is—sure did put the fear a'God into your daughter, anyway… Hey—" he drew back, laughing silently "—how come your hands are shaking? What kind of doctor are you, anyway?"

"An animal doctor," she reminded him. "Hold still, please, I'm not used to working on humans." His body was so hot she felt on fire…his scent burned like brandy in her throat.

"So, why don't you just pretend I'm an animal?"

"Good idea—hold still, *Rex*…" And when he turned, his breath caressed her sweat-damp breasts like a cooling breeze….

"*Rex?* Ouch!"

"I told you to hold still. There now," she said in a thickened purr as she restored the folded shirt to its original position and gave it a pat, "that's a good boy...." She sat back on her heels, trembling inside. "That's going to need stitches."

Riley swore. "The hell it is—" He tried to rise, then sank back with a hiss of pain and swore some more. "Don't know about my foot, though," he said in a constricted, self-pitying voice. "Hurts like bloody hell."

"Let me see." Summer crawled along his side on her hands and knees, then scooted around to face him and lifted his injured foot into her lap. Carefully, she drew off the shoe and set it aside. Funny, she thought dazedly, how vulnerable feet are. Bare feet especially. *Men's* feet...

She looked up at Riley, who had leaned forward to stare at the bluish-white, pigeon-egg-size lump on his instep. His eyes lifted to hers and held on. She couldn't seem to look away from them, even while her fingers delicately manipulated the bones in his foot. His eyes were so close to hers she could see her tiny reflection in the black depths of the pupils.

"Well?" he asked in a cracking voice.

She licked her lips, then murmured, "The skin's not broken—that's good. Can you wiggle your toes?" He did so. She moved her hands over his arch—God, how hard it was not to make it a caress—and pressed. "Does this hurt?" He shook his head, and she could feel the faint stirring of air on her hot cheeks. She eased his foot carefully away from her lap and cleared her throat, not once but twice. "Okay, I don't think anything's broken. But you should probably have it X-rayed to make sure."

"The hell with that," Riley growled. "Help me up. A little ice...some Advil...I'll be fine."

She got quickly to her feet. "Can you stand on it?" He gave her a look, and a moment later, with her help, he did. "Do you want your shoe?" He nodded, and then held his breath against the pain while she knelt down and eased it onto his foot. And when she rose up again, making it seem like

such a natural thing Riley couldn't think of a way to avoid it,
she'd somehow eased herself in under his arm and had taken
some of his weight on her own shoulders.

She's comfortable like this, he thought unhappily as they
made slow progress up the wooded slope, through the shrub-
bery and across the lawn. This was her natural place—helping...doing for...taking care of...others. Always others.

He found himself thinking about the other night in the FBI
garage, how he'd enjoyed watching her work on his injured
finger, and the way she'd seemed to forget herself and her
worries for that brief time. And how intensely attracted to her
he'd been. Now here he was, under very similar circumstances,
and while he was finding her no less attractive—if anything,
more so—he couldn't seem to derive the same enjoyment from
the situation.

To distract himself from the pain he was in, he let his an-
alytical mind have a go at solving the puzzle, but couldn't
come up with any answers. Except to conclude that, while he
had no problem with Summer Robey in the role of ministering
angel, sometime between last Monday night and this Saturday
morning he'd decided he did not like being the one she was
ministering to. And what in the hell was *that* all about? God
help him, he didn't know. But *something* had changed.

It was obvious to Summer, when David intercepted them
on the flagstone patio just outside Riley's study, that he'd been
looking for them. He looked upset, and uncharacteristically
angry. And she thought, *Uh-oh, now what?*

Whatever he'd been angry about, he forgot it instantly when
he saw Riley. His mouth dropped open in dismay and his
brows drew inward, and he didn't even seem to hear when
Summer asked him about Helen. His eyes were huge and violet with anxiety as they clung to Riley, and his voice was
hoarse as he asked, "Is he hurt bad, Mom? Is he gonna be
okay?"

"I'm fine," Riley growled, drawing himself staunchly erect.
Shunning Summer's help, he hobbled to the French doors.

"Just a bruised foot and a little cut on my head—don't know what your mother's making such a fuss about."

The worry didn't leave David's eyes, but he eagerly nodded. "Yeah, I know, sometimes she does that." He lurched in front of Riley, clumsy as a puppy in his efforts to get to the French door first. "But...are you *sure* you're okay?" he asked as he held it open for them. "Honestly? You look terrible. You got blood all over—"

"Looks worse than it is," Riley cut in. "Trust me—I'll live."

Men, Summer thought. "Hey—" she said in a low voice as she clamped a hand on her son's shoulder just in time to prevent him from dogging Riley's heels right on into his study, "I want to know where your sister is—right now."

"I don't know!" David wiggled his shoulder impatiently out of her grasp. He threw an anxious look after Riley's retreating back, then turned on Summer, the anger once again hot in his eyes as he hissed, "Mom, what if she really did hurt him, *bad*—huh? What if he gets mad at us? *Then* what?"

"David—"

"What if he tells us we can't stay here anymore, Mom?" His voice was quivering, tears unbearably close. "It's all Helen's fault—it *is*. She just goes and *does* stuff, you know? What if—"

"That's not going to happen." Summer kept her tone brisk because she understood her son's worry too well, and knew how dangerous gentleness would be just then—for both of them. She put her arm around her son's thin shoulders and pulled him in for a quick encouraging hug as they walked together into the house. "Okay? Now—you know what you can do for Mr. Riley? Go and get a tray of ice out of the freezer—use the oven mitt so it doesn't stick to your fingers!" The last was a shout, as David was already halfway to the kitchen.

Summer went into the hallway and found it empty.

"Up here," said Riley quietly.

She lifted her gaze to the stair landing. He looked back at her, his hands braced on the railing. After a long, silent moment, she took a deep breath and exhaled it in a sigh. "I suppose you heard that."

He nodded and said gruffly, "That boy worries too much," then he turned to continue his slow progress up the stairs.

Summer caught up with him near the top. "He's trying to grow up too fast," she said, slightly out of breath. But the ache in her chest had nothing to do with exertion. "Since his father left…"

Riley didn't say anything, but she sensed a flinching withdrawal in him, as if he were an animal she'd touched in a sensitive spot, and too well-trained to bite.

Knowing that in those circumstances it was best to move as quickly as possible past the sore place, she said cheerfully, "David's getting some ice. Cold compresses should help that foot. But I still think you ought to have that cut looked at. How long has it been since you had a tetanus shot?"

He threw her an irritable look. "I don't need a damn tetanus shot. Look—" as if regretting his retort, he held up a hand and took a calming breath "—if you think I'm going to spend my Saturday afternoon sitting in a hospital emergency room, you're crazy." And then, almost as a double-take, he added, "You're a vet—why can't you sew me up?"

Summer's response was a close imitation of his, without the irritation. "I could, if I had the proper supplies. Look, if you think I'm going to put stitches in your head with a sewing needle and thread—and you a lawyer?—*you're* crazy."

He gave a short bark of laughter, then his face darkened again. "Well, I'm not going to the hospital."

Summer almost smiled; he sounded so much like a balky little boy. Like David in a snit. Instead, she gave a put-upon sigh. "Lord above, you're a stubborn man. All right, I guess I'll have to see what I can do. Please tell me you at least have a first aid kit?"

He did, in the mudroom. David came clumping up the stairs

just then, out of breath, eyes sparkling with his eagerness to help, so Summer took the ice tray and oven mitt from him and sent him back down for the first aid kit. Then she turned to Riley. "Okay, where do you want me to do this?"

"I don't know—I guess the bathroom's the best place." He turned and marched down the hallway and through a doorway.

Hurrying after him, Summer found herself a moment later in another of those circumstances she would never in a million years have ever expected to be—in Riley Grogan's bedroom. She had time only for brief impressions: the warmth of honey-toned wood; soft green walls and furnishings in deep, mysterious blues, colors that were repeated in the Persian rugs and in the framed art—mostly watercolors—that hung on the walls. Somehow she knew they weren't prints, not even the signed, limited-edition kind. It's so like him, she thought. This room, like everything about him, was handsome and graceful, classy and elegant, well-ordered and…not impersonal, exactly, but…intensely private. *Like everything about him. Except us. The children, the animals and me. We don't belong here. We don't fit.*

Riley hobbled across the room without stopping. Summer followed him through a pair of open double doors at the far end, through a dressing room larger than most bedrooms, with walls lined with built-in shelves, drawers and closets in the same golden wood—no wonder he always looks so nice, she thought, trying not to stare—and into what was simply the biggest and most luxurious bathroom she had ever seen.

"My word," she breathed, staring in frank awe at an enormous tile-enclosed whirlpool tub in a sky-lighted alcove filled with blooming orchids, "does it come with dancing hand-maidens, too?"

"Of course," said Riley, without missing a beat. "But I thought it best to give them all a vacation of unspecified duration—"

"—with pay, of course," Summer chimed in with a nod and a wry smile. She looked around, hands on her hips. She thought, it's like being inside his skin.... His scent, the unique and indefinable man-smell along with touches of soap and aftershave, mingled with the residual dampness of his morning shower, seemed to hang in the air like fog. It was inescapable; it permeated her being with every breath she took.

"Okay, well...here, I guess—" she indicated the commode, lowered the seat and lid "—it may be tried and true, but it's still the best place." She looked Riley in the eye, gave the lid a pat and said firmly, "Rex—sit."

He gave her a look and a snort of surprised laughter, but obeyed. "You're enjoying this, aren't you?" he remarked as he surrendered his shirt to her outstretched hand.

"Oh, yeah," she said dryly. Okay then—this seemed to be the way to handle the situation—keep it light. Silliness and banter. Jokes. She could do this. With a shallow breath of relief, she dropped the shirt onto the floor and bent over him. "Okay, let's have a look...."

Oh, how wrong she'd been. Light banter and silly jokes were no match for the wave of sensation that washed over her the moment she touched him. She'd doctored angry pythons and terrified pit bulls with steady hands and nerves of steel, dealt with traumatized horses and fighting, clawing cats without a qualm. So why, as she felt the damp silkiness of this man's hair on her fingertips, was her heart in her throat and her belly filled with knots?

She had to ask him to bend down, but found that she could only whisper it. Why, when every inch of her seemed soaked in sweat, did her mouth feel dry as dust?

And instead of doing as she'd asked, Riley simply looked at her. Time stopped. Suddenly, for Summer, the world consisted of the busiest, noisiest silence she'd ever heard, empty of words but filled with booming pulses and humming nerves, crowded with unspoken messages, discoveries, declarations...denials. *This can't be happening!*

But the thought was there in her mind, plain as day and delicious as sin, the same one she could see in the eyes that held hers in thrall with their hot, smoky look, intoxicating as whiskey. *He wanted to kiss her. And she wanted him to kiss her.* Oh, yes, she could see it in his eyes, in the pulse that throbbed at the base of his throat, in the sudden, reflexive tightening of his hands on his thighs; hear it in his quickened breathing; feel it in the heat that rose from him in almost palpable waves to envelop her like a wet towel. She could *taste* it—taste *him*—smooth skin over firm muscle, sweat-slick on her lips, salt on her tongue…the sweet, salty taste of a man's sweat…. Oh, God, it had been so long.

Her stomach knotted and coiled. Almost on a level with his ears! Would he hear it? She was trembling inside. If she touched him now, he would have to know!

"Mom! Mom, where are you guys?" Summer closed her eyes as sneakers squeaked on tile. "Oh, there you are. Is this it? I looked where you told me to and it wasn't there, so I just looked around and…I found it."

She turned to take the large metal box from her son's proudly outstretched hands. "Yes, honey, thanks—that looks like just what we need." Behind her she could hear Riley take a quick, deep breath and let it out, long and slow. Her own heart was racing like a panic-stricken rabbit's, but her voice was calm, and her hands, she was pleased to note as she placed the first aid kit on the countertop and popped the latch, did not shake.

"Can I watch?"

"*No,* you may not. What you *are* going to do, young man, is go and look for your sister. *Now.* You got that? And don't come back until you've found her."

David addressed an unhappy "Yes, ma'am" to his shoes.

Riley watched as Summer took the boy's face in her hands and tilted it up for a quick kiss, then turned him around and gave him a firm but gentle push toward the door. And he felt a familiar ache forming like sickness in his chest.

He heard her take a quick breath as she turned back to the

counter and the box of first aid supplies. "Well, now, let's see what we've got."

She kept her eyes averted, he noticed, carefully avoiding looking at him, or at her own image in the mirrors that stretched the whole length of the counter. There were mirrors behind her, too, and Riley watched her without her knowledge as she sorted through the kit, taking out what she needed and setting it carefully aside on the tile. He studied her angular, almost patrician profile, noticing the way her hair grew in a cowlick on one side of her forehead and gave her face a quirky, slightly asymmetrical look; noticing that when she wore it pulled up in a ponytail like that, it showed darker, almost doe-brown underneath, with streaks of sun-yellow above; noticing the soft tendrils of drying hair that wafted around her temples and along her neck. Oh, she did have a lovely neck....

Once she raised her head, tilted it slightly but without looking directly at him and murmured, "Cotton swabs?" Distracted, he indicated the drawer he thought the most likely, and she nodded and went to look, giving a nod and a satisfied "Ah" when she found them.

She turned to the sink then, and Riley went back to studying her while she turned on the water and let it run hot, pumped liquid soap and worked it into a lather, which she slathered all the way up above her elbows. She had long, firmly toned arms...strong, broad shoulders...supple back...slender waist.

Thank God, he thought, she wasn't ever going to know how close he'd been to putting his hands on that waist, spanning that firm and supple back and, if she was willing, pulling her down astride him right there where he sat. And if he was lucky, she was never going to know how much he still wanted to do that very thing, or guess that even now he could feel the weight of her smooth-muscled thighs pressing on his, feel the moist heat of her body soaking through his old shirt...imagine himself opening it, and the slick-slippery meeting of her breasts with his chest...the slap of her belly against his...the taste of her mouth, the feel of those supple, mobile lips moving under his...the ripe-peaches smell of her hair...and her hands, those strong, no-nonsense hands making imprints in the muscles of his back....

"Ready?" Was it his imagination, or did she sound as breathless as he felt, standing there looking at him with her eyes alight, drying her hands on a towel. She handed him the towel almost absentmindedly; he took it and gave his face and neck, shoulders and torso a cursory wipe with it before laying it across his lap—a seemingly casual act, but oh, how grateful he was for that towel just then.

"I could sure use a shower," he muttered. *A cold one.*

"You can shower when I'm finished...I'll lend you one of my shower caps, if you like." She was frowning at his scalp. "Am I to assume you'd rather I didn't shave off *too* much of your hair? Just kidding."

Riley snorted. "You're a regular riot, Doc."

"Gee...my other patients don't seem to mind. Okay, hold the towel up to your face while I pour some of this hydrogen peroxide into the cut...little bit more...okay, that's good. Now some antiseptic..."

"Ouch!"

"Don't be a baby...the sting just means—"

"It's doing its job, I know. Hurry it up, will you?"

"Almost done. Now—I'd like to put a couple of these little butterfly bandages across the cut to close it, but I'll have to snip off just a lit-tle teeny bit of hair. Is that going to be okay? You won't even see it, I promise."

Lord, how vain did she think he was? "Do it," he muttered. "Get it over with." He closed his eyes and held his breath; it wasn't pain he was trying his best to shut out, but her scent, her nearness. His stomach growled; he was helpless to stop it.

"Hmm," she said softly, her voice just a breath away from his ear, "that's right, I guess you never did get to eat your waffles, did you? They're still there, you know, in the kitchen.

When we're done here, I can warm them up for you, if you like. They'll crisp up nicely in the toaster.''

There it was again—that mystifying little irritation. She sounded like somebody's mother. Which definitely wasn't what he wanted from her, not then. Not ever. ''Gee, Doc,'' he said sarcastically, ''do you normally offer your patients blueberry waffles after surgery?''

''No...I usually give them doggy treats...okay—that's it. Done.'' She stood back, her eyes innocent. ''Beatle probably wouldn't mind sharing some of hers, if you'd prefer.''

He didn't know whether to laugh or growl; what he wanted to do was pull her into his arms and kiss her until she couldn't breathe. He might have done it that time, and the hell with the consequences, if at that moment David had not come bursting through the doorway at that pace all children seem to prefer, somewhere just below a dead run. Right behind him was the beetle-dog, her toenails clickety-clicking on the tile.

''Mom—'' naturally he was out of breath ''—I looked and looked, and I can't find her *anywhere*. I called, and even Beatle helped search. Helen's gone, Mom, I swear. She just *vanished*.''

Chapter 9

"Take a deep breath," Summer ordered. "Calm down. Now—she can't just vanish, can she? So she has to be here somewhere. Unless—" She looked at Riley.

He shook his head. "She couldn't get past the perimeter of the grounds, not without setting off the alarm."

"Okay, then. She has to be here. Tell me where you looked."

David lifted his hands and hitched up his shoulders as far as they would go. "I *told* you—I looked *everywhere*."

Summer straightened and threw Riley a look of apology. "She does this sometimes. When she's angry, or afraid she's in big trouble, she…hides. Right now—" an ironic smile tugged at her mouth "—she's afraid she's in big trouble because she thinks she may have killed you." She drew a deep breath and gave her son's shoulders a squeeze. "All right, I think we should start in the house, don't you? Come on—we'll take it one room—" And she was already turning to hustle the boy ahead of her out of the bathroom. She stopped, though, as Riley struggled to his feet, and shooed him back with a wave of her hand. "No, no—that's okay, stay there. No need for you to bother yourself. Here—" Distracted, she paused at the sink where she'd dumped the tray of ice cubes, pulled up the stopper and turned on the tap, then dropped in a washcloth. "Put this on your foot. I'm sure David and I can find her."

Riley reached over and turned off the water. "If she's hiding because she's afraid she's hurt me," he said reasonably, "then seeing me alive and well ought to reassure her. Maybe she'll come out of her own accord. And if she doesn't—" he bit on his lip as he tested his foot, decided the pain was entirely manageable and then nodded "—then I probably know some hiding places you don't. This house has a few odd nooks and crannies."

For a moment she hesitated, and he could see the struggle in her eyes—a brief one, an automatic rejection of the idea of anyone helping her more than a real objection, he thought. Then she nodded in acceptance and abruptly pivoted, following her son from the room. Riley raised his eyes skyward in a silent appeal for patience and hobbled after her.

As they were passing through his bedroom, he observed what looked like a fat furry pillow squarely in the middle of his bed. Summer saw it, too, and halted dead in her tracks.

"Oh, Lord, I'm sorry. Here—just let me take her—" She threw him a look of pure misery and bent over to pick up the cat, trying her best, it seemed to him, to do so without letting any part of her touch any part of the bed. No small feat, given the size of his bed.

Riley's mind suddenly became crowded with images and associations, all having to do with Summer and her proximity to his bed, thoughts he had no business entertaining, even for a moment. His belly grumbled ominously. "Leave her—let her sleep," he growled, waving Summer out of his bedroom with an impatience bordering on urgency.

They commenced the search at one end of the upstairs hall, taking it one bedroom at a time, opening doors and drawers and cupboards, peering into closets, behind draperies and under beds—any space a five-year-old body could possibly squeeze into as well as a few it couldn't. They'd finished the two empty rooms on the north side of the house and were about to move on to the one Summer was occupying when Riley noticed that the dog Beatle appeared to have taken an interest in one of the doors across the hall. He paused to watch her as she sniffed and snuffled at the bottom of the closed door, then raised her head and gave a soft "Wuf."

Summer looked down at the Chihuahua, then up at Riley. He raised his eyebrows; she shrugged a *who knows?*

Then David, with a faith born of innocence, said, "Hey, Beatle, did you find her? Huh? Find Helen, Beatle—where's Helen? Come on—let's go find Helen." And he turned the knob and opened the door. Beatle scampered into the room. Riley and Summer exchanged a look, then followed.

It was very warm in the room. Riley knew it could get downright hot in those south-facing rooms in the summertime, in spite of air-conditioning and the huge magnolia trees that had been planted on that side of the house long ago to provide shade for the tall casement windows. It was precisely why Riley had given his guests quarters on the north side, though the south rooms were larger and certainly brighter.

While Riley stood frowning in the doorway, thinking about that, Summer walked on into the room, calling, "Helen? Honey, are you in here?" She opened a wardrobe door. David dropped to his hands and knees and peered under the canopy bed.

Meanwhile, the dog Beatle hesitated only long enough to give the rug a sniff, then scampered over to the window, put her paws up on the sill and uttered that same small but decisive "Wuf."

It was then that Riley realized the window was open. "The balcony," he said, and started forward.

Summer, too, was moving toward the window, moving like a sleepwalker. "Helen? Honey…?" She put her hand on the window casing and leaned out.

Riley's house had been built in the sumptuous twenties, in

a Southern Gothic style more typical of Savannah than Charleston. All the upstairs windows had narrow balconies trimmed with wrought iron, meant more for decoration than actual use. Still, he thought, a child might easily hide on one, crouched below the level of the windowsill....

Summer was looking down, up, all around. But it was obvious the balcony was not occupied. She stepped onto it and peered over the railing. She looked down...and Riley could feel his heart trying to bang its way out of his chest. But there was no scream of horror and grief, and moving up behind her, he could feel her body relax slightly.

And then...go absolutely rigid. In a spasmlike reflex her hands clutched the railing, so hard the knuckles went white, and she cried out, *"Oh, my God..."*

Never, in all his life, had Riley heard such terror in a human voice. It had to be the worst sound he had ever heard. He went icy inside as his mind struggled to form the terrible question. But by then Summer had turned blindly into him and was hiding her face against his chest. And without thought he folded his arms around her and held her tightly while his eyes searched for what she'd already seen that had frightened her so.

Leaves. All he could see was those damned leathery, greeny-bronze magnolia leaves. The huge tree filled the window, its branches in some places extending over the balcony railing to scrape against the walls of the house. Oh, hell—and the gardener had just mentioned something to him last spring, he remembered now, about it being time to trim those back. He'd been in the middle of a tricky court case and hadn't wanted to be bothered just then with calling the tree people. And had apparently forgotten about it. *Damn.*

He saw it now—splashes of hot pink and lemon-yellow, colors Mother Nature never put in a magnolia tree. He even remembered the outfit—one of the ones he'd bought—pink shorts with a pattern of tiny cartoon characters, Disney, he thought, and a yellow sun top with a large version of the same characters on the front.

"It's okay, it's okay," he murmured hoarsely, stroking Summer's hair. He could feel her trembling. "She's all right. I can see her. She's all right."

She jerked away from him with a loud sniff. "She's not making any noise," she said in a strained voice as she leaned over the balcony railing, trying to see through the leaves. As if, he thought, she were clenching her teeth together to keep them from chattering. "That's not Helen. You don't know—"

He gave a short, ironic laugh. "I think she's too scared to move. Talk to her—keep her calm. Tell her we're gonna get her down, okay?" But Lord in heaven, how?

Summer called in a high, thin voice, "Helen? Mommy's here, honey…Mommy's here. Are you okay? Answer me, sweetheart." For a moment, it seemed, they all stopped breathing. And then they heard it—a barely audible whimper. Riley saw Summer close her eyes. Her face was bleached bone-white and shiny with sweat, as if she were about one deep breath away from fainting, but her voice sounded calm enough. Only he would hear the knife edge of panic in it as she called, "Okay, that's my girl. You just hang on tight, now, okay? Don't try to move. We're coming.…"

Riley put a hand on her arm, then gripped it tightly. "Not this way, we're not," he said in a tight undertone. "That branch will never take the weight."

"But I can see her—"

"So can I." The kid was stretched out flat on her stomach with her bottom toward the window, her head toward the trunk, arms and legs clamped tightly around the limb. "She's too far out to reach from here. We'll have to get her from below."

"If she falls…" Summer's face was a mask of terror.

"She's not going to fall." And if she did—*Dear God, if she did?*—he was never going to forgive himself. Never. He leaned over the railing and looked down. Lord, it was a long way down. And the kid was so small.… He drew a deep breath. "There's a limb below this one. Big enough to stand on. If I can climb up to it—"

She threw him a wild look, which he imagined was about equal parts surprise and doubt. "Are you sure you... I mean, maybe I should—"

Well, he thought, who could blame her? Climbing trees didn't exactly fit the image he worked so hard to build for himself. Would she even believe him, he wondered, if he told her there'd been times he'd slept in one?

"Hey," he said in a cracking voice, "you may find this hard to believe, but I have climbed a tree or two." His smile felt cramped.

It was the first time she'd ever seen that smile, Summer realized; a dark, off-center smile, with haunted, remembering eyes. Something about it shook her even then, a small earthquake that rocked the underpinnings of her most basic conceptions of the man, and she filed it away for pondering over...later.

"There's a ladder," said David. Summer and Riley both turned to look at him. He nodded, eyes round with eagerness and bright with fear. "I saw it. Over behind the garage. It's a big one, too."

Summer clamped a hand to her mouth, stifling a small whimper. Riley touched her arm and said in a low voice, "Stay here—keep her calm. Young man—" he put his hand on David's shoulder as he passed him "—you come with me. Show me where you saw this ladder."

"Come on!" David was so wired he seemed about to jump out of his socks. He'd be feeling it, too, Summer realized as she watched them go off together, Riley's hand on the back of David's neck seemingly all that held him to the ground. He'd feel the guilt, the sense of responsibility for this. Her heart ached for him. If anything happens to his sister, he's going to blame himself—

Nothing is going to happen. She's going to be all right. *She has to be all right.*

Somewhere way off in the distance, thunder grumbled. A breeze sprang up, making the magnolia's leaves rustle with a dry, crackly sound. Helen whimpered and uttered a thin, terror-filled cry. "Mommy!"

Summer spun back to the railing. "Helen, it's okay—I'm right here. Mr. Riley's gone to get a ladder, okay? We're gonna have you down in just a minute—you just stay right where you are and hold on tight, you hear me? Hey, I know what—let's sing a song. Okay? You sing, too, sweetie. Winnie the Pooh, Winnie the Pooh..."

Though it couldn't have been very many minutes before she saw Riley and David come jogging around the far corner of the house, each holding one end of an aluminum extension ladder, those were, undoubtedly, the longest minutes of Summer's life. Through every one of those minutes she had to fight the compulsion to climb over that balcony railing and onto that limb against all common sense, somehow convinced that, if she could just get her hands on her child, if she could just *touch* her, everything would be all right. Through every one of those minutes the terror, unspeakable, unthinkable, unimaginable terror, held her heart in a grip of ice. Through every one of those minutes, as she spoke her calm words of encouragement and sang her daughter's favorite songs in a quavering voice one good breath away from hysteria, she prayed. *Oh, God please...*

She watched, helplessly leaning over the wrought-iron railing, as far below, Riley placed the ladder against the tree limb, set it firmly and began to climb. He was wearing neither shirt nor shoes, she saw with a small sense of shock; she'd forgotten all about his injuries, and so, it seemed, for the moment at least, had he. Spots of sunlight dappled his naked back and shoulders as he climbed, so that he seemed almost a part of his surroundings, a half-wild creature of the forest primeval, and a far, far cry from the Riley Grogan whose normal habitat was the courtrooms and ballrooms of Charleston. And yet, no less graceful, no less confident. As if he were as much at home in this world as that one.

It all happened rather quickly then. Making it look easy, Riley pulled himself from the ladder onto the limb and unfolded himself until he was standing upright. Then, holding on to and climbing through smaller branches, he moved along it until he was directly below the place where Helen clung to her precarious perch. Summer heard the low, soothing murmur of his voice; leaves rustled and branches thrashed; and then came the cry she had prayed for: "Okay—I've got her!"

She couldn't hold back a gasp, and it was more than half a sob. But it wasn't over yet, she knew that. As if her gaze alone could keep them from falling, she did not take her eyes off Helen's lemon-yellow top and Riley's sweat-glistening shoulders until she saw that they'd made it safely to the top of the ladder. Then she tore herself away from the balcony railing, dove through the window into the bedroom and dashed headlong for the stairs.

He was just stepping off the bottom rung when she got there. She'd been running full-tilt, not even aware of her feet touching the ground; now, a few feet away from her goal, she halted. Afraid if she took one more step the shaking would catch up with her and her legs lose the strength to support her. Afraid if she tried to speak a single word she would burst into sobs. So instead she stood and looked at the two of them—at the man whose face and body were streaked now with dust and sweat; and at the little girl who was clinging to him, her legs clasped around his torso, her arms in a death grip around his neck, face buried against his chest, like a large, brightly colored starfish.

"Wow," David was yelling. "Wow, you *did* it! Boy, was that *cool!*"

Riley spoke in a soft-gruff voice to the top of Helen's head. "Hey—here's your mama. You can let go now."

He was walking toward Summer, and she could see him trying, without success, to peel Helen's arms from around his neck. Summer burst out laughing—and finally into tears.

"Hey, missy," said Riley firmly, "you're on good old terra firma now—you're gonna have to let go of me." But then Summer saw him give up trying to pry his burden loose and suddenly wrap his arms around her and envelop her in a comforting hug, much as he'd enveloped Summer just a short while ago. And after a moment she saw her daughter's small body relax.

Then all at once Helen drew back and looked at Riley's face. Alarm sparked fleetingly in his eyes as she took dead aim, then pounced forward and kissed him—hard—on the nose.

Clearly shaken and teary-eyed from the blow, he croaked, "Uh…well, you're welcome," while Helen turned to grin valiantly over her shoulder, her dusty, tear-streaked face not the least bit vanquished. But she went on clinging to her rescuer's neck until the last possible second, making it plain that it was only with great reluctance she was allowing herself to be transferred to Summer's arms.

To which a hot, sweaty, grubby little body had never felt so welcome, or so sweet. Summer tried to scold. "Helen— honey, what on earth where you *thinking* of?" But then she had to bury her face in her child's hair just once more, breathe in the dusty, salty, little-girl smell—liberally laced with chlorine, naturally. And nothing had ever smelled so wonderful.

At her elbow, David was beside himself, waving his arms and screeching, "What did you do that for? Helen, sometimes you are such an—"

"David," Summer warned in a tremulous voice, "not now. Not another word, do you hear me?"

He threw her a furious look, then frowned at his feet and muttered, "Yes, ma'am."

"Helen, did you say thank-you to Mr. Riley?"

They all turned, but Riley was no longer there.

When they went back into the house, Summer heard the sound of water running upstairs in his bathroom. A little later, while she was shampooing the dust and spiderwebs out of Helen's hair, she heard footsteps on the stairs and the distant sound of a door closing. And from the window in the children's room she watched the Mercedes back out of the garage and roll away down the long, curving drive to finally disappear under the canopy of live oaks and their waving fronds of Spanish moss.

I don't blame him for leaving, she thought. What are we doing to him? What am *I* doing?

She felt such a heaviness inside. And at the same time, wired and edgy, as if her skin had been charged with electricity. *Yes, like that,* she thought as thunder rumbled suddenly outside. *Just like that.*

Though that particular storm passed them by well to the north, the thunderclouds lingered through the afternoon, hanging over them like a threat while the heat and humidity became almost palpable and the sun played a malicious little game of hide-and-seek with poisonous-looking clouds. Summer finished mowing the lawn with one eye on the sky, her skin prickling with that peculiar sensation of awareness, as if every nerve and cell were *listening…*

Afterward, with the thunder still keeping its distance, she gave in to the children's pleadings and let them swim, even joining them in the pool, wearing the streamlined white tank suit Riley had bought for her. It wasn't the first time she'd worn it, but for some reason today everywhere it touched her, with her skin in that strange, sensitized state, it seemed to itch and burn, as if she'd broken out in an all-over rash.

It's the weather, she told herself; all this electricity in the air. Sure, they all felt it—the children were wired and nervous, Cleo was shrieking dire warnings from the living room, and Beatle was upstairs shivering and shaking under David's bed. California-raised, none of them had quite adjusted yet to thunderstorms. Why should she be immune?

By early evening Riley still hadn't returned. The sky had turned the ugly blue-black of bruises. It was as dark as if night were falling, even though Summer knew that at that hour, somewhere up there beyond the clouds, the sun must still be high in the sky. Thunder rolled and rumbled almost continuously; the wind picked up, howling and moaning around the house like some wild creature denied entry, lashing out at the trees in its disappointment and rage. Summer covered Cleo's cage with a cloth to calm her and while the children watched with round, worried eyes, made popcorn in the microwave. And all the time, her skin prickled, the back of her neck tensed, and her ears seemed to hum with...*listening.*

When the popcorn had finished popping, she poured it into a big wooden bowl and carried it upstairs. Then they all—including Beatle—climbed onto Summer's bed, pulled the edges of the comforter around them and settled down to watch Walt Disney's *The Jungle Book,* Helen's favorite video, on the VCR. David and Helen had already watched it several times—Summer had asked Riley to rent it for them a few days ago and he'd purchased a copy instead, so she'd made up her mind not to ask him for another one. And now, seeing it herself for the first time in years, she began to get an inkling of what might have inspired Helen to crawl out onto that tree limb!

Meanwhile, the storm hit like an artillery barrage. The thunder no longer rolled and rumbled; it cracked and boomed and shook the house. Rain rattled against the windows and the wind screamed like a creature in agony. Beatle crawled under the covers and the children huddled closer against Summer's side—but she noticed they never once stopped the methodical relay of popcorn from the bowl to their mouths, or took their eyes from the television screen.

Through all that terrible din, Summer bumped up the volume with the remote control and sat tense and still, trying her best to concentrate on the movie. But every nerve ending in her body vibrated...*listening.*

Right in the middle of the climactic battle between Shere Khan and Mowgli, there was a *crr-aack!* that rattled the windows, and the lights went out. Both children yelped—partly in fear, Summer was sure, but also in outrage that their movie had been so cruelly interrupted. Though it wasn't late enough for the darkness to be total, she sent David next door to his room to fetch the flashlight she'd given him to keep under his pillow—a bit of extra security to take the place of his bunny blanket. After all, who knew how long the electricity would be off? Then, to pass the time and help allay the children's disappointment, they sang all the songs they could remember from the movie, and Summer let them pretend to be Kaa, and hypnotize her with the flashlight.

Somewhere in the midst of that, the lights came on, but they were having so much fun, instead of starting the movie going again, they just kept on with their game. So it was, that David was crooning "Come to me-e-e...Mom-cub..." while Summer walked around on top of the bed in stiff-legged circles with her eyes crossed and her arms thrust limp-wristed straight out in front of her, and Helen was rolling around on the comforter shrieking with laughter, when Beatle suddenly gave her soft "Wuf!" of welcome, jumped off the bed and scampered over to the half-open door.

The door opened slowly inward. Summer froze, and for several long seconds before she remembered to uncross her eyes, stared at the twin Rileys that hovered there, framed in the doorway.

David broke off in midsentence and Helen's giggles subsided, and in the stillness they heard the thunder, which they'd all completely forgotten about, go grumbling away in the distance. In that stillness, Summer felt her heart beating hard and fast. Because at that moment she knew at last what it was she'd been listening for.

Riley had been dismayed, to say the least, to arrive home at the height of the storm to find his security system shut down and his front gate locked up tight. He'd immediately called the security company from his car phone, and was told that the automatic lockdown in the event of a power interrupt was a fail-safe feature of the system, to prevent intruders from gaining access by cutting off the power. The gate could, he was assured, be opened manually, with a key. Which, of course, Riley did not happen to have with him. Which meant he had no choice but to sit in the car and wait for the storm to pass and hope the power would be restored soon. If it didn't, as soon as the rain let up, he planned to climb over the damn gate and walk to the house and get the damn key.

He was uneasy about Summer and the kids, though, alone

in the house and without power in the middle of one of the worst storms of the season. At least he had the assurances of the security company that the house alarm system would remain active on its backup batteries for a minimum of two hours. Although what in the hell good that would do anybody was beyond him, when the "armed response" unit wouldn't be able to get through the front gate!

Needless to say he was out of sorts and edgy as hell by the time the perimeter lights flashed bright and the courtesy light came on again above the intercom and keypad. He punched in his code, waited, drumming his fingers on the steering wheel in rhythms that were in no way in sync with the Vivaldi concerto on the CD player and, once the gates were open, gunned through them with an angry little spurt of gravel.

By the time he pulled up in front of the garage, the rain had slackened off to a light mist. When he opened the car door he was greeted with the busy dripping, rustling, rushing sounds of the earth setting itself to rights, and off to the west, a strip of crimson sky showed through between indigo clouds and lavender earth. He popped the trunk, got out and locked up the car. Then, taking with him one of the smaller, if heavier of the boxes from the assortment in the trunk, he went into the house.

All seemed quiet. Although there were lights on and remnants of an appetizing smell, the kitchen was empty. Then he heard sounds—voices, laughter—coming from upstairs. A woman's voice…children's laughter—until recently, alien sounds to him and to this place, and yet, somehow incredibly alluring. Drawn as if by a siren's song, Riley hefted the box and began to climb toward the laughter.

Just outside Summer's room he halted. Through the half-open door he could see them, the children laughing, rolling around on the bed like puppies, Summer—a grown woman!—walking around on top of the bed as if she were in some kind of trance, with her arms out in front of her and her eyes crossed and a goofy smile on her face, that sun-streaked hair out of its ponytail and tousled all over the place. Something shivered inside him.

He couldn't intrude; he knew very well what an outsider he'd be in that room. He was about to do it—just back away and leave them to their game, when that silly little beetle-dog gave him away. Then, of course, he had no choice but to push the door the rest of the way open and announce himself.

They all froze when they saw him. Of course they would. The laughter died, and he heard the soft gasps of breath drawn and held. He had an impression of eyes bright with mischief, of smiles struggling to hide, but it wasn't the children's faces he was looking at. The only face he really saw was crimson with embarrassment; the eyes that met his—once they'd un-crossed—were wide and almost black with dismay. And the mouth…ah, that mouth. She had no way of knowing how beautiful she was to him then, crossed eyes and all. How in-credibly sexy. And thank God, he thought, for that.

Then everyone moved at once, it seemed, like a tableau coming to life. David sang out, "Hey, look—it's Mr. Riley!" as he scrambled off the bed and ran to meet him, at the same time Helen was chanting, "Hi, Riley, Hi, Riley," in time to her frog-hops across the mattress. And as for Summer, well…there is no sedate way for a grown woman to get down off a bed when she's standing upright in the middle of it.

Riley watched her ponder the problem, trying to decide whether to crouch down and scoot, or just do it in one big giant step, and he realized that for the first time all day he actually felt like laughing. He wondered whether, if not for the presence of the children, he might have put the box down and gone over to her, put his hands on her slender waist, perhaps, to help her down. It amazed him, how much he wanted to.

"Whatcha got in the box, Mr. Riley?" The boy was stand-ing in front of him, fidgety, torn between curiosity and good manners. Riley set the box down on the floor and folded back the flaps.

"Books!" David yelled as he sank to his knees on the rug.

"Oh, man—Mom, lookit this! Here's *Stuart Little* and *Charlie and the Chocolate Factory, The Indian in the Cupboard*...and a whole *bunch* of *Black Stallion* books, Mom! Isn't this cool? Now you can finish readin' it to us. Will you read to us tonight? Huh? Please?"

Summer had come slowly, incredulous and silent, to peer over her son's shoulder. Now she straightened to give Riley a dark, desperate look. "I can't let you do this." She muttered the words for him alone.

He shrugged and answered her the same way. "Fine. If you don't want 'em, you can just use 'em while you're here—or not, that's your choice. After you're gone I'll find some children's hospital to give 'em to." And he felt disappointed without knowing why.

He bent down to scoop up a great big picture book about dinosaurs and handed it to Helen, who was watching round-eyed and, for once, silent. "Here, little girl, this one's for you." He left her looking as if he'd just conked her with a mallet and turned to tap her brother on the head. "You—come with me. I've got some things in the car you can help me with." And he walked out of the room.

With his longer legs and a head start, he made it to the stairs before they'd all untangled themselves enough to follow. He could hear them coming behind him on the stairs, like a small elephant stampede, but at the bottom David passed him and got to the car first. Riley heard him shout. 'Oh, *cool!*" while he was still making his way through the kitchen.

"Is this a *computer?* It is, isn't it? Did you buy a computer?"

"Sure did," said Riley, joining him at the Mercedes' open trunk. "You convinced me. Okay, now—"

"Mom! Mr. Riley bought a computer! Isn't this *cool?*"

"Okay, here—you can carry this one. It's the keyboard, I think. And you, kiddo—' he fished a smaller box out of the trunk and thrust it at Helen "—think you can manage this? It's the mouse."

"Mouse." She giggled.

"Okay—you can take those to my study. And don't run!"
They went running off at top speed. And that left Riley alone
and face-to-face with Summer.

She was standing beside the car, one hip leaning against it,
arms folded on her chest, her face, with the light from the
kitchen behind her, in shadow. She'd gathered her hair up and
scraped it back into that damned ponytail again; suddenly he
wanted to take the rubber band, or whatever she'd used to
hold it together, rake it off and throw the damn thing away
somewhere where she'd never find it. And then he wanted to
comb his fingers through her hair, bury his hands in it…let it
fall like cool silk against his skin.

"I can't let you do this," she said again in a gravelly voice.

It was the second time she'd said that. The first time, he'd
felt it like…fingernails across his skin, raising his hackles and
a few goose bumps. This time, it got *under* his skin. He felt
himself go cold and still. Leaning his hands on the edge of
the trunk, he raised his head and looked at her and said softly,
"Mrs. Robey, are you telling me I can't buy myself a computer if I choose to do so?"

She shook her head and gasped, "I didn't…" then turned
and walked into the house. And he felt as if he'd slapped her.

He didn't see her again until later that evening. He was in
his study, surrounded by various pieces of computer hardware,
scowling through his glasses at an instruction manual the size
of a dictionary and counting teeth in a multitoothed plug when
she appeared in his doorway.

He put aside what he was doing at once; he'd never seen
her look quite like this before, and he didn't know whether to
be alarmed or stimulated. Her body seemed tense, as if, he
thought, she'd rather be anywhere than where she was. Her
expression was multilayered and indecipherable.

"Excuse me," she said softly, "I'm sorry to bother you.…"

"You're not. What is it? Something wrong?"

She shook her head. "Everything's fine. I just wanted to
say I'm sorry. And—oh damn." She closed her eyes, took a
breath and started again. "I really hate to ask this of you—"

Riley's heart beat faster. Ask something? Of him? He could hardly wait to hear what it might be.

"Do you suppose—would you mind if..." Another dead end. Another deep breath. And then out it came in a rush. "The children would like you to tuck them in."

Chapter 10

"Tuck...them in?" Riley shook his head, not because he hadn't heard or understood the meaning of the words, but because they made no sense to him.

Summer sagged against the door frame and folded her arms across her waist. "You know, in bed? It means—"

"I know what it means."

And sometime during the second or two it took him to say that, his mind had exploded with images...of corn-silk hair on crisp pillowcases, of rosy-cheeked faces with sweet, smiling mouths and sky-blue eyes full of trust and questions, soft-skinned arms and plump little hands reaching up to him.... And with the images, came a white-hot, blinding flash of *fear*. He'd faced violence and even death, gone up against cutthroat lawyers and hostile judges with millions of dollars on the line, and worse, stared down Southern mamas hell-bent on making him a son-in-law, and he'd never known fear like this. And for what? An act millions of men all over the world performed every night of their lives—were probably performing right now, in fact, at this very minute?

Millions of fathers. But he was not a father. Had never been one. And for his entire life had reconciled himself to the vow he'd made never to become one. How in the world had he come to this?

"I know it's a lot to ask...." Her lips formed an unstable smile. "They can be very insistent." She turned to leave. "I'll tell them you're in the middle of something. They'll understand."

The hell they would. "Not at all," Riley said in his Trusted Family Solicitor's voice—Southern, confidence-inspiring, just a little unctuous. "Don't mind a bit. Be right there." He couldn't have felt more fraudulent if he'd been about to step onto center stage at Carnegie Hall and attempt to perform the *Brandenburg Concertos.*

"You don't have to do this," Summer said in a low voice when he joined her. "Really." She faced him bravely in the narrow confines of the doorway, eyes clinging to his, liquid and impenetrable as ponds.

He gazed into them for a long time before he murmured, with a thickening tongue, "Look, I don't mind sayin' goodnight. It's not a major deal, is it?"

She shook her head and her lashes fell across her eyes. "No, of course not."

"Well, then." But all his senses vibrated with awareness of the lie, and from the tension he felt in her, even across the inches that separated them, he knew that she recognized it, too. It *was* a big deal, he just didn't know exactly what kind of deal it was. Some sort of mileage post, perhaps, on a journey for which he had no road map nor known destination. He only knew that once he passed this post—or had he already done so?—in either case, there could be no going back now to the safe, secure place he'd started from. That place was lost to him forever.

The children were sitting up in their side-by-side twin beds, waiting for him. And holding their breaths, it seemed, from the way they released them when they saw him, in gusts of excited giggles. Beatle leaped down from David's bed and came to meet him, dancing on her hind legs and shadow-boxing in delighted greeting.

Riley said "Hey—" in the gruff, Southern way, and bent down to give the little Chihuahua a tickle as he moved between the beds. "So—" his stomach was jumping with nerves "—you want me to tuck you in, I hear?" Both children nodded eagerly. He frowned sternly at them. "Well, now, I can't very well do that unless you lie down, can I?"

There were hushed gasps as the two children instantly flopped down onto their pillows, breaths once again held, giggles stifled. David, though, popped right up again and propped himself on one elbow to ask eagerly, "Did you get the computer put together yet?"

"Not yet," said Riley, "but I'm workin' on it."

"I'm pretty good with computers. I could probably help you—you know…if you needed any help—setting it up and stuff."

"Oh, I'm definitely going to need help. Not tonight, though, okay?" He reached down to touch the boy's hair, noticing as he did that the dog had jumped up on the bed and, after a few swipes at the kid's chin with her tongue, was making a nest for herself against the curve of his thin body. Riley remembered then what Summer had told him about David having lost his security blanket in the fire. Did the dog know somehow, he wondered, who was in greatest need of her comfort?

"You'll tell me when, right?"

"You bet. That's a promise." He turned then to the other bed, where the little girl lay rigid in feigned sleep, eyes squinched shut, nubs of baby teeth bared in an irrepressible grin. "And you, missy—" he began, but his voice ran aground on a shoal of gravel. The image of cherub curls and rose-pink cheeks against the pillow blurred and wavered…began to change subtly. Riley's heart gave a lurch; fighting panic, he forced the child's face ruthlessly back into focus, cleared his throat and was able to say gruffly, "What's that you've got there?"

Her eyes popped open and she held up the small plastic lizard she'd been clutching to her chest. "Godzilla!"

"Godzilla, huh?" He examined the toy warily. "Looks pretty mean to me. I bet he keeps all the bad guys away." Helen nodded her enthusiasm. Riley tucked the lizard back beneath her chin and gave her hair a tousle. Almost there, he thought, his heart pounding. Almost done...

"Mr. Riley, could I kiss you g'night?"

Such a wee, small voice to strike such terror into his grown-man's heart. Barely breathing, not allowing himself to think at all, he bent down...and felt the warm little arms encircle his neck...the soft, cool touch, like a kitten's nose or the petals of a flower against his cheek. Oh, Lord, he couldn't endure any more, couldn't hold her a moment longer; the trembling had already begun.

He gave her a quick squeeze, touched his lips to her forehead and rose, vibrating like an out-of-balance top. "Okay," he said, "g'night, now," and the words felt like sandpaper in his throat.

As he moved away to their singsong duet of "G'night, Mr. Riley," his eyes sought Summer like homing beacons. And found her in the doorway, leaning against the frame as she'd leaned against the one in his study, with her arms folded across her waist. Watching him. And if he'd expected to see a thank-you, a glow of warmth and appreciation in her eyes, he'd have been sorely disappointed. She looked as if her heart was breaking.

Riley had had the nightmare before, so he knew when he woke in the clammy darkness, wrapped in a familiar spiderweb of dread, that there would be no more sleep for him that night. A glance at the clock-radio on his nightstand told him there was at least an hour or two until dawn. So he'd do as he always did at these times, go downstairs, get himself something to drink, a book to read...maybe take another crack at deciphering that computer setup manual. He'd have to be careful not to disturb anyone—and please, God, let the dog be sleeping!—but just to be on the safe side, he put on his robe and belted it securely before opening his bedroom door and tiptoeing like a cat burglar into the hallway.

Once downstairs, he could see a faint light coming from the kitchen. Probably Summer had left one on, he thought, in case she or one of the children needed something in the night. It still gave him an odd feeling, that reminder that he was no longer alone in his house. He didn't know whether it was a good feeling or a bad one—just that it was odd.

He found that it was the light above the stove that was burning. He didn't turn on any more—didn't need even that much to get a glass out of the cupboard and fill it with water from the bottle in the refrigerator, so often had he done those things before under these circumstances. But as he was about to leave the room, his hackles suddenly stirred and prickled with the awareness that he really *wasn't* alone. He checked abruptly, and turned to see what his peripheral vision had barely caught a glimpse of—a lone figure sitting at the table in the morning room with the light from the kitchen gleaming in her blond hair.

"Hey." He changed direction, angling toward her, heart leaping against his throat, water glass in hand. "Couldn't sleep, either, huh?"

And heard her give a soft, embarrassed laugh. "I was afraid to say anything for fear I'd startle you."

He gestured toward the mug she was holding between her hands. "What's that you're drinking? Hot cocoa?"

She shook her head. "Postum—you probably never heard of it."

"Huh—I remember buying it—and you're right, I'd never heard of it. What is it—a coffee-substitute-type thing?"

She examined the contents of her mug critically, as if they were the result of a scientific experiment she'd just conducted. "I guess it can be, if you make it with water. If you make it with milk and sugar, though, it's more like cocoa, only no caffeine. My mother used to make it for us when we were kids.'' She shrugged. "The children like it. It makes a nice nighttime drink. Sort of comforting.''

"Sounds like just the ticket," Riley murmured, taking a sip from his water glass.

"Oh—would you like some? I'll get—'' And she was already half out of her chair.

"No, you won't.'' Riley kept her where she was with a hand on her shoulder and put his water glass on the table. "I'm perfectly able to get it myself. What'd you do, microwave it?''

She gave a quick little nod; he could feel her edginess, a coiled-spring tension in the shoulder beneath his hand. "It works best if you dissolve the stuff in a little boiling water first, then add as much milk and sugar as you want and warm it up to however you like it.''

He nodded. "I think I can handle that.'' He gave her shoulder a gentle squeeze and left her.

As the space between them widened to a more bearable distance, Summer lifted her mug, carefully cradled between her two hands, held it to her lips and took a long swallow, then rested it against her chin and let the fragrant steam, evocative of the security of childhood, warm and comfort her. It would have been nice, she thought, if Postum could somehow warm the cold and still the shivering she still felt deep inside. But it was plain the beverage's healing powers could only reach so far.

She watched Riley over the rim of the mug as he worked at the kitchen counter—shoulders broad and hips narrow underneath the navy silk robe, feet and calves bare and oddly defenseless. He was favoring the bruised one.... She saw his dark head bending low and intent over the mug as he spooned and poured and stirred, noticing the way the hair grew on the back of his neck and fell unevenly over the wound in his scalp.... And like a sneaky wave, a vision surprised her, washed over her and engulfed her...a vision of the way he'd looked last evening, bending down to kiss her children goodnight. *Oh, God, my poor children.* Cold erupted from wells deep inside her to spread the shivers throughout her body. She felt an almost overwhelming desire to cry. Oh, God, please, she prayed silently, don't let them grow fond of him. *Or me, either*... But already she knew it was too late.

She had to blink several times rapidly and sneak deep breaths to restore herself as he came strolling back, taking cautious and judicious sips of his Postum. After giving it a little shrug of at least tentative approval, he said, "Well, that was quite a day yesterday."

And Summer could only think how vital and sexy he looked, with his beard stubble and his hair in rakish disarray— more Rhett Butler this morning than Cinderella's Prince.

She tried to maintain a smile in return, but it collapsed miserably and she had to look away. She felt him come close to her, set his mug on the table. Heard his voice ask softly, "What's the matter?" And felt his fingers in her hair. She drew a long, shuddering breath and then held herself still...very still. And after a few moments that seemed like an eternity, she felt him pull his hand away and sit down.

"Summer?"

"Riley—" she cleared her throat, cleared it again, shook her head, touched her lips with her fingertips...but there was no way to make it sound like anything but what it was...a desperate, desperate plea "—we can't stay here."

One eyebrow rose, confirming the Rhett Butler look. "Why's that?"

"We just can't."

His voice grew softer, almost gentle. "May I ask what brought this on?"

What brought this on? My God—yesterday I almost lost my child! And I almost lost my head—over you, dammit. Over you! She shifted, angry suddenly, and overwhelmed by guilt. "That's obvious, isn't it? We're destroying your life." And she felt slightly foolish, but much more in control when he laughed.

"That's being a bit melodramatic."

"So is that," she replied softly, her eyes sliding upward to the purplish knot on his forehead, clearly visible just above the hairline.

He touched it, shrugged dismissively and leaned back in his chair with one arm resting on the tabletop. Summer recognized the position instantly; it was the one he'd adopted the day he'd interviewed her in his office. A position of relaxed and confident authority. "Well now," he said in the quiet lawyer's drawl she remembered, "maybe this is somethin' we oughta discuss."

A week ago, that calm tone had filled her with hope; now it prodded her temper and her fragile emotions like a tongue on a sore tooth. "There's nothing to discuss," she said flatly. *I came so close yesterday…so close. What if it happens again? I'm afraid I wouldn't be able to resist you.* "We simply cannot impose on you this way. We can't."

She hadn't even finished before Riley grimaced and made an irritable shooing gesture, as if waving off a tormenting insect. "Didn't we have this conversation? I thought we'd covered all this the other night, over at the FBI headquarters."

Her body jerked involuntarily, almost a physical rejection. "I was in a state of shock! I should never have let you convince me. Look—this is insane. Look at the way you live—"

"What? I live a very simple life."

"Oh, yeah, right—you came to pick us up in a tuxedo, for God's sake!"

"Oh, well—"

"And all this—your home…"

He was peering around with exaggerated eagerness, as if looking for a hidden surprise. "What about it?"

Summer knew a stone wall when she saw it. She sat for a moment, breathing quietly to dampen her frustration and restore her customary patience. She knew she was right; she just had to convince him, somehow. Slowly and patiently, she began, "It's beautiful. It's elegant, and classy, and rich—"

"It's got six extra bedrooms.…"

"Hush. I mean it. It's *beautiful,* Riley. You know it is—you've obviously spent considerable time, money and effort making it so. These things—your paintings, the furnishings—even that pool, with all the plants and flowers, are like a little piece of paradise.''

He grinned. ''I'm glad you like it.''

She wanted to hit him. ''Will you *stop* it? I'm serious. It's obvious all this is important to you, as it should be, or else why do you protect it the way you do—all this security?'' When he didn't seem to have a flip answer to that, she took the moment to rein in her emotions, then continued in a calm, reasoning tone, ''And it's just as obvious that a woman with two kids, a dog, a cat and a parrot do *not* exactly fit into this picture, if you see what I mean. We just do not belong here.'' *We can't ever belong here. And if I were foolish enough to fall in love with you...*

He was silent for a long time, regarding her steadily and somehow unnervingly, almost as if he'd read her thoughts. His jaw was propped in a cradle made of the index and little fingers of one hand—another pose she remembered. Finally, in a voice utterly devoid of inflection, he said, ''What is it about me that makes you think 'all this' would be of greater importance to me than the safety and well-being—the *life*— of my client?''

And it was she who was silenced. Suddenly and unmistakably he was her lawyer again, and she felt foolish and ridiculous to have imagined she might ever be anything else to him but a client. Whatever in the world had made her think she could argue with him, anyway? He was the great Riley Grogan, the man who in court had reduced her to the role of brainless bimbo. Right now she felt just as bogged down and trapped as she had on that dreadful day, as he continued to subject her to his hard, unreadable stare. But with one difference. Now, for all his outward appearance of authority, she had the distinct impression that she'd touched a nerve in *him*. That in some unfathomable way she'd even hurt him.

Not yet ready to concede defeat, she looked away and said softly, ''But you have a life. I know you must—or, anyway, you did before we came. Since then—''

He leaned forward suddenly, on the attack, cutting her off, startling her. "What do you know about my life?"

"I told you, I—"

"You checked me out before you hired me." His smile was sardonic. "And tell me, what did you find out? All about my professional reputation and track record, I'm sure. Social gossip. I'm certain you were able to discover that I am unmarried, and that I make the rounds of various Charleston-area social functions, fulfilling my duties as one of the Low Country's most reliable escorts. What else? The fact that I serve on the boards of several charitable organizations? That I am known to be law-abiding, upstanding and trustworthy? Those things would be of particular importance to you, I imagine." He paused and leaned closer to her. "Now, tell me, Mrs. Robey, what do you know about *me?*"

She flinched away from his nearness, cheeks burning, dry-mouthed, and could only mutter, "Obviously—"

He straightened and made a smacking sound with his lips, something else she'd seen him do, she fuzzily recalled, that day in court. "You keep using that word—*obviously.* Now—how can something be obvious if you don't know a person?"

But she wasn't in court, Summer reminded herself, grasping at that like a drowning rat hauling itself aboard a floating twig. And she wasn't a brainless bimbo. And she would not let herself be intimidated again—not even by Riley Grogan. She shook herself mentally and leveled a look at him. "You're right. I don't know you. All I know about you is what I've seen. What you've shown me. I've seen the lawyer—" she gave him a small, sardonic smile of her own "—you do that *extremely* well, thanks for reminding me. I've seen your clothes, your car, your home—"

He made an impatient movement that told her she'd landed another blow, however small. He sat back, frowning, though not at her, and after a moment said in a low, gravelly voice, "I had my reasons for acquiring...all that I've acquired. At one time I suppose it *was* important to me. Things change.

Priorities change…'' And he was silent, gazing at the thinning darkness beyond the windows.

Summer saw the deeper darkness reflected in his eyes and suddenly felt a sadness in him that she didn't understand. Surely not, she thought. Riley Grogan? But he has *everything*.

Sorry now that she'd pushed so far and presumed so much, she said haltingly, ''I think…people see you the way you want them to see you. Maybe, if I don't know you it's because…you really don't want me to.''

''Oh, that's not true.'' But it was an automatic denial, and after a moment he shifted as if the chair had become uncomfortable to him. ''If it is, it's probably because I don't—'' he cleared his throat loudly ''—I don't quite know how.'' And he looked at her, his smile askew. ''Maintaining an image can get to be a habit. A hard one to break.'' In a sudden change of mood, he clasped his hands together on the tabletop and leaned toward her. ''Try me. What would you like to know? Go ahead—ask.''

The intensity of his gaze was like a physical force; bracing herself to meet it seemed to take all her strength. Faintly, she said, ''You'd answer me truthfully?''

He nodded. ''Or not at all.''

But she found that it was hard to think when he looked at her like that—as if, like Mowgli's Kaa, his eyes had the power to mesmerize her. In another moment, she feared, he could if he wished take control of her completely…body, soul and mind.

''Your witness,'' he prompted softly.

It took a great effort, but she managed to wrench herself away from him both physically and mentally, rise and walk to the windows, where with the safety of distance and her back to him, she cleared her throat and ventured, ''Okay…family. Nobody seems to know anything about your family.''

''That's true. That's the way I want it.''

She nodded, waited, and when he said nothing more, turned bravely to look at him. ''Well? Do you have one?''

''Not really.'' He shifted uncomfortably—unaccustomed,

she imagined, to being on the receiving end of probing questions—and finally muttered, "My father died when I was…young."

"I'm sorry," she said softly, but was not ready, yet, to let him go. "What about your mother? Is she alive?" He nodded, but his eyes slid away from hers. She persisted, "Do you…see her?"

His eyes were on the mug in his hands. He raised it to his lips and drained the few drops that were left before he said in a carefully neutral tone, "From time to time."

"Really?" She couldn't have said why that surprised her, or why speaking of it should so obviously unnerve him. But her heart quickened as she asked, "Any brothers or sisters?"

He lowered the mug and now examined it minutely. His lashes were dark curtains across his eyes. "I had a brother," he said at last, again in that voice devoid of all expression. "Younger. He died when I was twelve. He was…about six."

"Oh, God—how awful." And she thought: *Just about Helen's age.* Shame and regret overwhelmed her, squeezed her chest and tightened her throat, so that she whispered through the pain, "I'm so sorry. I mean, I can't even imagine what it would be like. My sisters and I—we were so close. Even to think of losing them…"

From half a room away, Riley saw her eyes fill with tears, and saw in those tears his own escape. Maintaining control of his natural empathy—his gift, his curse—had been challenge enough to him lately, it was true; but it was a battle he waged on a daily basis and was therefore accustomed to. Watching her, he said quietly, "You miss them."

She gave a liquid-sounding laugh, like a hiccup. He watched her lips play through a whole symphony of emotions and was as fascinated as he'd been that first day in his office. She said huskily, "Yeah, I do. And the funny thing is, until last year I didn't even see that much of them. I guess—" she shrugged, drew an uneven breath "—I was too busy. There was my job, my clinic, and then I was married and they weren't, I had kids and they didn't. But then, after Hal left, and I knew I was going to have to start over, and I thought about where I would go.... My parents live in Pensacola Beach, I could have gone there. But when I really thought about it, it was my sister— Mirabella—that I..." her voice broke, surprising her, he thought, and she drew another unsteady breath. "So, I came here. And now—" suddenly her hands were clenched fists and her voice trembled with anger "—I can't even *see* her. I can't even talk to her on the phone. *Now,* when I need her the most. It makes me so *angry.* I feel like—" She broke off with a laugh. "You know what it's like? Remember that day, last winter, when you saw me in court? And the judge threatened to send me to jail? I thought, I can't possibly go to jail—*no way!* And now, here I am—if I'm not in jail, I might as well be!'"

Unexpectedly stung, he forced a smile. "Oh, come on, is it really that bad?"

"Oh," she said quickly, empathetic enough herself to realize how her words might be taken and anxious not to give offense, "not that it isn't a very *nice* jail. You've done everything you could possibly do to make us comfortable—too much." She came toward him, arms folded tightly across her waist in what seemed to him an unconscious effort to contain treacherous emotions. Instead, because of the tension in her, the effect of that determinedly subdued tone and manner was to make her words all the more poignant. "But—my life has been taken from me. Don't you understand? I have no freedom to come and go as I please. I can't go to work, or shopping, or to visit my family or take the kids to McDonald's. If that's not prison, what *is* the definition?"

Her face was stark, strained...the unhappiness in it so distressing to Riley, he finally had to look away. "It's only temporary," he muttered. "Until the bad guys are put away. And the FBI, with all its resources—"

"Can't find one man named Hal Robey!" she broke in, anger and derision thick and hot in her voice. "You know what makes me the maddest? It's that I'm *afraid.* All the time.

Do you know what it's like to live every moment of your life in *fear?*"

He was stunned to hear himself say, "Yes, I do." And felt with the admission, a curious sense of lightening.

Summer's eyebrows rose with surprise. *"You?"* She came back to the table at once and sat, once again close enough to him to touch, as if, he thought, his confession of human frailty made him seem less dangerous to her.

To him, though, the danger seemed incalculable. Shaken by his brush with it, he forced a smile and murmured, "I told you, you don't know me."

But, to his relief, she wasn't listening, focused once again on her own concerns and reassured enough for continued confidences. Gazing at the lightening windows, she said in a musing tone, "Sometimes, you know, I think I'd rather confront the fear. Go out there and face those…those *bastards!* Like— I don't know, set myself up as bait for an FBI sting, or something. *Anything* to get those people caught."

"But," Riley reminded her gently, "you have the children to think about."

"Yes…" He heard her breath escape in a long, slow sigh. "I have the children." Then for a while she was silent, while her whole being seemed to wilt, and grow pensive and sad. When she spoke again it was in a halting half whisper, and he knew without any doubt that she had never spoken those thoughts aloud to a living soul before.

"Sometimes…it seems like I've been in jail all my life—a kind of jail, anyway. Maybe not all my life, but at least since I realized that the man I'd married wasn't ever going to be a partner, and that it was pretty much going to all be up to me— providing for us, you know, raising my children. I've felt…so *damn lonely.*" The last word came from her with rough edges, like torn burlap. "I've felt *trapped,* you know? I feel like I've had no choices. It's like that story of the little boy with his finger in the hole in the dike. Like I'm all alone and trapped by the whole overwhelming responsibility for survival—everyone's…my own, my children's—and that everything I've done has been because I had to, for someone else's sake, never because it was what *I* wanted to do.''

She stopped abruptly, and Riley found himself with a heart full of words he could not—dared not—say. It was a vulnerable, exposed feeling, like a thief caught with his hands full of stolen booty, pinioned in the glare of police spotlights. *Did you ever in your life, Summer Robey, do something just for yourself? Take a cruise? Shop for perfume? Kiss a lover in the rain? Go dancing after midnight? Have an affair with a dashing attorney...?*

The moments ticked away, counted in his heartbeats. He felt his body grow heavy and humid, with rumblings and growlings deep down inside of unacknowledged and unassuaged hungers. What would happen, he wondered, if he touched her now? If he were to reach out, reach across that small distance between them and take her hands...her strong, capable, no-nonsense hands...would he feel them tremble? Hands could tremble, he knew, for many reasons, and so could lips...and bodies. He suddenly knew that he wanted to feel hers tremble—her lips, her body—but for no other reason than desire. Not with cold, exhaustion, nerves or fear. Never with fear—never again with fear! Only desire. For him.

He realized then that it was *he* who was trembling—deep down inside where only he could feel it. Where only he could know. He also knew that while it was desire that made him tremble, there was fear, too. And finally it was the fear that made him back away, tiptoe carefully away from the edge and, instead of touching her, lace his fingers together on the tabletop and lightly say, ''Tell me, Mrs. Robey—if you *could* choose what you wanted to do, what would it be?''

She stared at him, wordless with surprise.

He gestured toward the windows, which, without either of them noticing, the dawn had painted a soft, seashell pink. ''It's Sunday. Say you could do anything you wanted to do today—say I'm a genie, and I'm granting you one wish, just for today—what would it be?''

Summer caught a breath and held it. After the traumas of

the day just past, the night's demons and a conversation fraught with strange undercurrents and unknown tensions, his mood, the question, the sheer lightheartedness of it, were as enchanting and restorative as a rainbow. And in spite of herself, knowing what a fantasy it was, she allowed herself to be drawn into the game, if only for a moment. Closed her eyes and opened her mind and allowed the yearnings to take shape…and color…and then, choosing one, just one, she whispered, "The beach…I'd go to the beach."

"Done!" he said, slapping the table with his palm. "Today we'll go to the beach."

And just like that, the sunlit vision evaporated in the cold rain of reality. She shook her head, fiercely emphatic. "No. No—absolutely not. You've done enough—too much. Seriously." A thought struck her. She sat up straight and fired it back at him. "What would *you* normally do on a Sunday? Whatever it is, I insist you do it—as if we weren't here."

"Okay," said Riley. But she didn't like the gleam in his eyes.

He got up from the table, gathered up his water glass and the two mugs and went into the kitchen. A moment later, Summer heard water running, cupboard doors opening and closing, the subdued rattle of pans. Intrigued, she went to investigate, and was confronted with the mind-boggling vision of Riley Grogan, street-fighting lawyer, tuxedoed man-about-town, dashing rescuer of tree-stranded children, Rhett Butler in a blue silk dressing gown, coolly dumping handfuls of flour into a mixing bowl.

Chapter 11

"What are you doing?" She couldn't seem to take her eyes off his chest, where a careless swipe of his hand had dragged a smudge of flour across one silk lapel and sifted it into the adjacent V of dusky brown skin and crisp black hair. Impossible, she thought, finding herself for the second time in as many days fighting an urge to laugh.

"What am I doing?" He glanced at her, eyebrows aloft. "What does it look like I'm doing? I'm cooking breakfast. Obviously."

"But I can—you don't have to—"

"Ah, but you said I should do what I normally do on a Sunday, so...I normally make breakfast. Beginning with biscuits. Excuse me."

She dodged aside as he reached past her to turn on the oven. "Biscuits. My God," she murmured, her mouth dropping open in awe, "where on earth did you learn to make biscuits?" Captivated, she leaned against the counter. "Your mom teach you?"

His laugh was low and ironic. "No ma'am—just a friend. Hand me that fork, would you?"

She did, and was barely even aware that in doing so her arm had brushed against his. "I have never been able to make biscuits. Mine make excellent hockey pucks."

She watched a smile etch itself into the side of his face beneath the furring of beard stubble. "Ah, but you see, the trick…is to be *quick*." And he turned the bowl upside down, dumped its contents onto the counter and began to knead the floury mixture with light, deft strokes.

And Summer, staring at his fingers, his long, elegant hands, remembering how they'd reminded her of fine, smooth leather, felt a prickling of the nerve endings in her skin, a tightening sensation in her nipples, a tingling heaviness between her thighs. As if it were a lover's touch—as if…*he'd* touched her!—she experienced a wave of purely physical desire such as she hadn't felt in a long, long time.

"Of course—" Riley's voice seemed to purr in her ear "—these would be better with some redeye gravy, but I haven't got any sausage, I don't think…."

She mumbled thickly, "It's just as well we don't. Isn't that what they call heart attack on a plate?"

He clicked his tongue sorrowfully as his hands wielded a biscuit cutter, making tidy circles in the lumpy mass of dough. "Ah, I see you've been thoroughly brainwashed by the Health and Fitness Nazis out in California."

Who are you, Riley Grogan? Summer thought as she gripped the edge of the countertop, shaken by the force of her attraction to him, weak-kneed with reaction. *Every time I think I have you figured out…* She cleared her throat and gave a low, uneven laugh. "Will the real Riley Grogan please stand up?"

He paused in the process of transferring the rounds of dough onto a cookie sheet to throw her a surprised and uncertain smile. "What?"

"I'm having a little trouble with the redeye gravy, if you want to know—it doesn't quite fit your image, does it?"

He gave her a longer look across his shoulder. "The image you have of me, you mean."

She held his gaze. "The image *you* foster."

"True." And his mouth quirked in a Rhett Butler smile.

She couldn't help it. Her breath caught. "So," she said, all but whispering, "Which are you—filet mignon, or biscuits and redeye gravy?"

It seemed an age before he answered, an age in which she searched for answers in his eyes and saw there only the tiny twin reflections of herself. "Both, of course." His voice sounded raspy to her, as if it came from poor-quality speakers. "Most people are."

"Multifaceted, are you?" Had she forgotten to breathe? It seemed so, because without air to support it, her voice suddenly cracked and broke.

A strange, dark chuckle seemed to vibrate through the space between them. "Mrs. Robey—" he touched her nose with a floury finger "—I have facets you haven't begun to explore."

She found herself staring at him, her mouth dry as flour, heart thumping. My God, were they flirting? She wanted to reach for something, anything to hold on to, and discovered to her surprise that she was already gripping the granite countertop with both hands. Thank God, she thought, for that support. But…oh, she thought, how good it would feel—and her whole being ached with yearning—if it were his lean, warm body and not cold, hard stone beneath her hands.

Sounds reached her, like the preliminary rumblings of an avalanche. Familiar sounds…and her mother's instincts responded with the surge of adrenaline she needed to pull herself out of the quicksand. Yes, she thought—that's what it had felt like, those terrible, treacherous woman's desires that came over her lately when she least expected it, so suddenly, so powerfully…like stepping into quicksand, overwhelming, all-consuming, impossible to defend against.

And yet, she must. She *must*. How could she even think such thoughts, when her children were in danger? How dared she feel *desire?* Now—of all times! And for a man whose life held no place for children...

Preceded by muffled bumps and thumps, hers came into the kitchen, David first, rubbing his eyes and yawning, with Beatle scampering at his heels, then Helen, peeking flirtatiously at Riley around the edge of the door.

"Mom?" David mumbled as he shuffled over to her for his good-morning hug. "How come you have white stuff on your nose?"

Summer was scrubbing hastily at her face when Riley turned from the oven with a flourish and declared, "We made biscuits, that's how come. Breakfast in ten minutes. In the meantime, better go get your suits on if you want to go to the beach."

Already jangled by her brush with disaster, she was caught totally off balance, blindsided. All she could do was gasp in delayed reaction, while Helen was hopping up and down and yelling, "Yay! The beach, the beach!" and David screeched, "The beach! Oh, man—really? Honest, Mom?"

"No, Riley—"

"Honest, swear to God." His smile was smug—so very male. "And it's a long drive, so you'd better get crackin'." Ooh...and his calm, authoritative tone *infuriated* her.

While the children thundered out of the kitchen shouting, "Oh boy, the beach!" at the tops of their lungs, Summer turned on Riley, quietly seething. "I told you—" she began.

"Ah-ah—" he stopped her there with upraised finger and eyebrows "—a deal's a deal."

"A deal?" She frowned. "But, I don't—"

"You told me, as I recall, to do exactly what I normally do on Sundays—which I am doing. And unless you'd prefer to stay home, Mrs. Robey, I suggest you go and get into your beach duds." And he touched her with his finger, first between her brows, then her nose, thereby restoring the flour she'd just so energetically disposed of.

"Oh, *cool,*" cried David. "A real drawbridge!"

"That's the Intracoastal Waterway," Riley informed him,

pointing while David leaned over his shoulder to watch the mast of a sailboat glide lazily past. "If you wanted to, you could sail all the way from the Florida Keys to New York Harbor."

"I'd like to do that sometime," David said wistfully. "Do you think—" Summer's heart skipped a beat, but he broke it off and scrambled over to the other side of the car in time to catch a glimpse of the boat as it emerged from beneath the bridge.

"Are we almost there?" Helen whined. She had little interest in bridges and boats. The numerous squashed turtles along the roadside had kept her entertained for most of the trip, but she was disappointed she hadn't seen alligators.

"Almost." Summer glanced at Riley, who nodded his confirmation just as the drawbridge barrier rose and the cars in front of them began moving again. "Buckle up," she reminded the children, and settled back to watch the blue ribbon of waterway and green tidal marshes slide past far below. On the other side of the canal, the highway dropped down to arrow across seemingly endless expanses of wetlands, wound through dunes and congested beach towns and over bridges that tied the coastal islands together like beads on a chain.

"It's so different," she said at one point, unable quite to prevent a sigh, or deny her inner disappointment. "From California beaches, I mean."

"Really?" Riley glanced at her. "How so?"

"You may not believe it, but in California, the whole West Coast, there are places—lots of places, even close to the cities—where there aren't any houses, where you can stand on a cliff and look out across the ocean, it seems like, all the way to China. And where the mountains come down to meet the sea, the waves crash on the rocks, and there are tide pools, and pelicans and sea lions, and hardly any people…and you can drive right along the edge of the ocean and watch the sun sink into the water…. Here, you'd hardly even know the ocean was there, because of all the houses."

He nodded, and after a moment said softly, "There are very few wild beaches left on the East Coast, but I do happen to know of one." And he smiled a dark and secret smile.

Intrigued and strangely comforted, Summer settled back to enjoy the rest of the drive. But she could sense in Riley a kind of edgy excitement, along with a certain melancholy that she didn't understand. She kept stealing glances at him under the pretense of sightseeing, and was mystified by the little knot of tension she could see working beneath the edges of his smile.

He turned off the highway, finally, onto a paved road that zigzagged past towns and churches and fishing shacks, then through wetlands and woodlands where blue herons rose with a great beating of wings to the safety of ancient trees, and Spanish moss hung like remnants of tattered curtains over dark, mysterious pools. Eventually, he turned off that road, too, onto a gravel track that wound through woods so deep and dense the Spanish moss swished against the roof of the car, and the only sounds were the cries of birds and the crunch of their tires on the gravel. Even the children seemed to have been awed into silence, just a little too nervous, Summer thought, to risk a question.

"We're here—everybody out," said Riley at last, halting the car in a grassy clearing. "End of the road."

And indeed it was. Ahead through the trees, Summer could see blue sky, the green of marsh grass, the glint of sun on water. She could see a house, too, at the edge of the marshes, a small wood frame house with wide porches and a faintly ramshackle look about it in spite of what appeared to be a fresh coat of paint. After seeing to the unloading of the car and making sure everyone had everything they were supposed to have, however, Riley struck off, not toward the house, but along a footpath that led past it to a long wooden jetty, which angled off across the marsh to where a tiny fishing shack sat on the edge of a landing jutting into a broad inlet.

The children were delighted with the jetty. Liking the way their footsteps sounded on the wooden planks, they stomped along it with restored confidence, running on ahead until their noise brought a man out of the fishing shack to investigate. He was a tall man, thin but muscular and slightly bent, and wore overalls and a light-colored, short-sleeved shirt. He had a frosting of white whiskers on his weathered face and a bald head that shone like polished walnut. Seeing him, both children froze like guilty miscreants and waited for the grown-ups to catch up.

With one hand on David's shoulder and the other on Helen's head to steady them on the narrow jetty, Riley stepped between and then past them. Summer, moving up behind the children, saw the old man's face blossom with his smile.

"Hey you, boy," he called out, in thickened, lilting cadences that were unfamiliar and difficult to understand.

"Hey, Brasher," Riley called back as he went to meet him.

After a moment Summer followed, herding the now-shy and tongue-tied children, and was in time to see the two men clasp each other's arms with the restrained affection of old, old friends. She could see them talking, see nodding heads and gesturing hands, hear the murmur of conversation she couldn't quite make out. As she drew closer, though, she heard clearly the words *boat, island* and *tide*. And last and unmistakably: *hurricane*.

"What's this about a hurricane?" she asked as she and the children joined the two men, with a smile to take away the rudeness of the interruption.

"Brasher, here, says we're gonna have one," Riley drawled as he turned and with a casual sweep of his arm made them part of his company. And as she listened to him make the introductions, Summer felt a prickling behind her eyes and an ache in her throat, because she realized that with that single gesture, Riley had made them sound more like a couple, and with her children, a family unit, than she ever had in all the twelve years of her marriage.

The black man's name, she learned, was Brasher Kemp, and she liked his smile, the feel of his warm, leathery hand, the look of honest appraisal in his wise old eyes. She liked the way he took each of her children's hands in his two big ones and bowed over them as he repeated their names with great solemnity.

"A hurricane?" said Summer, using a hand to shade her eyes from the bright sunshine while she scanned the pale summery sky, the typically hazy and undefined horizon. "Oh, surely not any time soon."

"Not today, for sure," said Brasher, his eyes twinkling. "Today be good beach weather."

"What's a hurry-cane?" Helen asked, squirming with uncharacteristic shyness.

David snorted and rolled his eyes, clearly mortified by his sister's ignorance, but Brasher put his hands on his knees and stooped down so that his face was nearly on her level. "That'sa bi-ig ba-ad storm, little missy," he said in his thick, deep voice, in that strange-sounding cadence. "Wind howls like ten thousand demons, an' the air turns to water, an' waves come roll ovah the land—blow down trees an' blow 'way houses an' blow all the boats up on the shore. Hurricane comes, you don' wanna be down here, child." He straightened with one gnarled hand on Helen's soft curls to wink at Riley. "But don' you worry, this boy here been through the hurricane, he'll take good care of you. He knows what to do. You be safe with him. You go on to the island now, have a good time on the beach. Be a good day for the beach. Been some nice shells this summer...." He threw them a wave as he walked back up the jetty toward the house.

"Island?" Summer asked in a low voice as Riley ushered them through the fishing shanty and onto the landing. "We're going to an island?"

He answered her with a nod, his focus on getting them all into the small wooden rowboat equipped with an outboard motor that was tied up to the landing. He felt curiously detached as he lowered their gear into it, then climbed down and braced himself with feet planted wide apart in the bottom of the boat and one hand on the ladder, but he knew it was a protective kind of withdrawal, a shield against vulnerability.

"Okay, David, you're next...there you go. Life jackets are

under the seat in the bow—that's the pointed end. Put one on
and get one for your sister while you're at it." Then came
Helen, her mother handing her halfway down the ladder, Riley
lifting her the rest of the way. And it was Summer's turn. He
tried not to watch her as she came down the ladder…first those
long, tanned legs of hers right at his eye level, then that fanny,
nicely rounded and firm in blue denim shorts…but his
breathing quickened, anyway, and his body stirred with natural
and unavoidable responses. When he put his hands on her
waist to steady her into the boat, he knew he had to pass her
on and release her quickly—too quickly, almost as if he'd
found touching her unpleasant—or he would be in grave danger of lingering too long and giving himself away.

"Do you row?" Summer asked him as he was stowing the
oars out of the way in the bottom of the boat. Her voice was
casual, if slightly breathless, but when he glanced up at her he
saw that her eyes were focused on his arms and shoulders,
and with a look that gave him a sudden and rather adolescent
urge to take off his shirt and flex his muscles.

"I do when the tide is right," he said, turning his concentration upon the outboard motor instead. "It's less intrusive,
and—" now he couldn't resist acknowledging that feminine
appraisal with a frankly masculine grin "—I like the exercise." He was inordinately pleased at the blush that spread
across her cheeks. And even more pleased that she did not
look away, but instead held his gaze with an acknowledgment
of her own, clear and plain as the light in her sky-blue eyes.

It took all his willpower, that time, to turn away from her
and back to the motor. And when he had it started up and
throttled down to a throbbing growl, he was well aware that
the vibration he felt inside did not come from the engine.

He cast off the line and headed the boat into the channel
on a course he'd followed countless times before—and yet
now it seemed different to him somehow, as if he were seeing
everything for the first time. What would she think, he wondered, if she knew she was the first living soul he'd ever taken
to his island? What did *he* think?

Once again the veil of detachment settled around him, protecting him. He did not want to think.

"Is it really an island?" Summer wasn't sure why she was whispering. Riley had cut the engine as they approached so that they drifted into a tree-shaded inlet with the oars and the tide, and there was something a little intimidating, almost sacred in the silence, like being inside a church. The only sounds were the hum of insects, an occasional birdcall, and the shushing of waves on the sand. "And no one lives here?" she asked when he'd replied to her first question with a nod. "No one at all?"

"No—and no one ever will." There was something grim about his smile.

"Are you sure it's all right for us to be here?" She was whispering again; she'd seen several Private Property—No Trespassing signs already, posted on the dunes and tacked to the trunks of trees.

For a few minutes he said nothing while he nudged the boat's bow up to a wooded embankment, jumped out and nudged the line to a small tree stump, then pulled the stern in close to the bank and held it so that the children could easily hop from boat to shore. But when it was Summer's turn, he offered his hand to steady her and said for her alone, with that same enigmatic little smile, "It's all right—I know the owner."

"Brasher?"

He shook his head, the smile darkening. "Brasher takes care of it—chases away trespassers and poachers and such. But he doesn't own the island. Not anymore."

Understanding came as they walked along a barely discernible pathway between banks of scrubby vegetation, and she gave a small gasp. "*You* do. You own this island, don't you?" He nodded reluctantly, as if it was something to be ashamed of. "Oh, my God—it's really yours? All of it?" The idea that someone could own an island seemed incredible to her, the

most impressive of all the impressive things she knew abou
Riley Grogan.

But he shrugged, and once again a look of discomfor
crossed his face. "I hold the deed, but I don't consider that
own the island. I think of myself as...more of a guardian—
like Brasher." He was quiet for a few moments, watching the
children run ahead between seagrass-tufted dunes, then said i
a soft, almost musing voice, "It was deeded to Brasher's great
grandmama after the War—that's the Civil War, of course—
by her former master, who was also Brasher's great
granddaddy. That was on his daddy's side. Brasher was raise
in Jamaica where his mother's people were. I don't believe
anybody ever actually lived on the island. I used to come here
when I was a child. It was...kind of a refuge for me, I guess
you might say." His lips flicked briefly with that dark, bitter
smile. "Then a few years back, Brasher's kinfolk got to figh
tin' over whether or not to sell out to the developers that'
been circling around like buzzards for years, half thinkin' they
ought to take the money and the other half wantin' to keep i
wild like it is. Anyway, I got wind of it and...I had a few
assets I felt I could live without, and the upshot of it is, I wa
able to make Brasher and his family an offer they could al
live with. First thing I did was take the necessary steps to
ensure that the island will never be developed, no matter wha
happens to me. That's one hundred per cent guaranteed."

They had come through the last of the dunes, and suddenly
there it was, a pristine expanse of sand stretching away from
the inlet to a distant point far to the right—to the south. A
glistening sheet still wet from the retreating tide, it reflecte
the silvery blue of the summer sky and made mirror-like im
ages of the stilt-legged birds that pecked and played tag in the
lacy froth of the gently rolling waves. Riley checked suddenly
his brow furrowed with concern and his eyes on the children
who were already far down the beach, dancing and chasing
each other barefoot through the shallow surf, their cries and
laughter carried back on the warm sea breeze. "Are they—"

Summer laughed. "Don't worry about them—they've been coming to the beach since they were babies."

Riley nodded and started forward again, reaching for her hand in such a natural way that it would have seemed unnatural not to give it to him.

Natural, yes...but so were lightning, and electricity, and fire. Her hand tingled where it met his; heat raced up her arm and flooded her body; her heartbeat quickened. With a mumbled "Just a minute..." she slipped out of her shoes, one by one, then scooped them up in her free hand while he waited. "Thanks..." Breathless, she straightened, and she could feel his eyes on her, narrowed with a puzzling frown.

"Someday," he said on an exhalation as they walked on, leaving their own footprints beside the children's smaller ones, "I imagine this will be the only wild beach left on the southeastern coast."

"It's beautiful." But Summer felt a heaviness inside, a yearning ache behind her smile. She could go no farther but instead halted and raked her hair back from her face and lifted it to the sun and the breeze in an almost defiant gesture, as if by sheer will she could hold the loneliness at bay.

"I sense a 'but' in there," said Riley softly. She glanced at him in surprise and guilt, wondering how he knew.

She took a deep breath and shook her hair free, letting the warm wind have it—and to hell, she thought, with the frizzies. "It's funny," she said with an attempt at a laugh, "but it reminds me of the desert—the Mojave Desert, you know?— where I grew up."

He looked at her with curiosity in his smile. "That is funny—our beach reminds you of your desert? How so?"

She tried another laugh that failed, then gave it up and walked along in silence for a time, smiling at her bare feet making footprints in the wet sand and thinking, How is it people smile most determinedly when they are trying hardest not to cry? But Riley didn't press her—again, she wondered how he knew—and after a while, when she felt quiet enough inside, she lifted her eyes to the horizon and said softly, "My sister Evie used to say it gave her a case of 'the wild lonelies.' The desert, I mean. It's beautiful, you know, in a wild sort of way, and there are things about it I still miss—the huge, endless vistas, the way the colors change from day to day, hour to hour. You know, the desert never looks the same way twice—the flowers in the springtime…the enormity of the sky. But it can suck the life out of you, too. And the hope. Evie always says the desert is a great place to be *from.* I'd have to agree with her about that, but about the loneliness, I guess I never really knew what she meant until…''

"Until now?'' She nodded, and once more felt his look, this one more penetrating than curious. "What about this place makes you feel lonely?''

She shook her head but found it easy enough to answer him—too easy. If this keeps up, she thought, I will have no secrets left! "I don't know why, really—the openness, maybe. The quiet…the wind…the marshes. And yes, it does make me feel lonely.''

Riley was silent for a long time, and she was afraid she might have wounded him somehow—as if she were inappreciative of his generosity in bringing her to his special place, for she knew that was what it was. But again he surprised her when after a while he said in a voice as quiet as hers had been, "Or…maybe it's not that the place makes you *feel* lonely, so much as it makes you *know* you are. There's an…absence of distraction out here. Nothing to hide behind. No shelter, no choice but to confront who you are…all the things that are inside you—the thoughts and feelings, the hopes and dreams, the lies and truths. As beautiful as it is, this place can do that to you.'' And then it was his time for introspective silence and hers for patient waiting, before he drew a deep breath and murmured, "And beautiful as it is, like your sister said, it's a great place to be from.''

She threw him a quick, startled look, surprised not as much by the revelation, which she'd already begun to suspect, as by the fact that he'd shared it with her. "You are from here then?''

"Well, not from *here* here, but…around here, yeah, I am."
And his smile grew enigmatic once more. "As I said, this island has sheltered me more than once. Brasher taught me how to drift in on the tide when I was still too small to row very far. He taught me how to fish for crabs…taught me a lot of things, Brasher did."

"Is he the one?" Summer asked, casting him a sly, sideways glance.

"The one…what?"

"The one who taught you to make biscuits."

And he laughed out loud and didn't answer her. Instead, they walked together, holding hands like lovers, trading surreptitious glances and hiding them in discoveries of shells and sand dollars. Summer understood that they had each come as close to admitting to loneliness as the constraints of pride and personality would allow, and she was certain Riley knew it, too. She felt a trembling inside that was not of fear or exhaustion or excitement or desire, but more like the wobbliness of a vulnerable newborn creature, standing for the first time on uncertain legs and gazing at the world in wide-eyed wonder. The world seemed miraculous to her, and all things new.

And when she found a whole and perfect sand dollar, showing it to him with a cry of delight, he cupped his hands around hers and gazed down into her eyes as if it were *she* who were the treasure. She felt it not only possible but even somehow inevitable that he would kiss her…simply the culmination of something that had begun at that moment when he'd first taken her hand.

He whispered something she couldn't hear for the rushing in her own ears. She felt his warm breath on her lips, and her own breathing ceased. Her body rocked with the force of her beating heart. Incomprehensible tears pricked her eyes.

I will remember this moment, she thought. I will remember his kiss, whether it is the first and the last, or the first of ten thousand more. *I will remember this place, this day, this moment…this kiss.* And treasure it, like the rare and perfect sand dollar she held pressed against her breasts, against her heart pressed between their bodies as his mouth covered hers.

Time stopped, and the world retreated. She felt nothing— not even the mischievous waves that ran in to tickle her feet and then run away again—except the warm, firm pressure of his lips, the raw silk texture of his skin. Heard nothing—not the wind, the shushing of the waves, the high, bright calls of seabirds—except the singing of his name inside her head, and the rush and thunder of her heartbeat, like the noise of a storm.

And then, too soon, she felt him pull away, gently, reluctantly, and the world rushed in like the waves around her feet. She felt the shifting of the sand underfoot, the cooling breath of the wind, and in the distance, like the cries of seabirds, the children's voices calling to them.

How glad she was then that Riley's back was toward the children! As it was, shielded by his body, she had barely time to step back, brush the telltale evidence of his kiss from her lips with trembling fingers before they were there, David first, breathless and excited, yelling, "Mom! Mr. Riley! Come see what we found—it's something really weird. Hurry up! Come on—come *on*..."

And then they had to run to investigate, Summer on legs she wasn't sure would carry her, far down the beach and around the point, the children hopping and dancing and urging them on.

"There!" David's voice was a whisper of awe as he halted and pointed. "What in the world *is* it? I never saw such a thing, did you?"

"Yes, as a matter of fact I have," said Riley, as with a wink for Summer he took each child by the hand and moved close to the strange markings in the sand. "What this is is a sea turtle's track. A mother sea turtle—most likely a loggerhead— came in last night to lay her eggs. This right here is the track she made when she went back to the water. Her nest should be...right up here somewhere...."

With the children following, silent and tense with awe, Riley led the way up the beach to a spot above the high-water mark just where the dunes began, where the sand had been recently disturbed. "Yeah—here it is, right here. See, she digs out a hole in the sand with her hind feet, and then she lays her eggs—dozens of 'em. They look sort of like Ping-Pong balls—" Helen giggled "—and then she covers 'em up and drags herself back down to the water and swims away. Then, in about two months the eggs hatch, and the baby turtles have to dig their way out of the nest and make their own way down to the water."

"I saw that on Discovery Channel," said David solemnly, his eyes round. "Most of 'em get eaten up before they even get there. By birds and stuff."

Helen gave a cry of outrage. "I won't let 'em get eaten! I'll kill those ol' birds—I *will*."

"Oh, dear," Summer said to Riley in an undertone, "we aren't going to hear the end of this. Isn't there anything we can do?"

He nodded as he rose to his feet, brushing sand from his knees. "I'll tell Brasher about this nest. He'll mark it, put wire barriers over it to protect the eggs from predators. He'll date it, too, and try to be on hand when they hatch, but it's hard to figure exactly when that'll be." He gave a sigh as he looked past her, his eyes following the track of the turtle to the water's edge. "The cards are stacked against 'em—that's one of the reasons I wanted to protect this place. There are so few places left where they can come ashore. They'll lay offshore, you know, waiting until it's safe—any loud noises, voices or lights will scare them off."

"What about the hurricane?" Summer asked in a low voice, not wanting to give the children something else to worry about. "You said one was coming. Can this nest survive?"

Riley shrugged. "Who knows?" He looked down then at the sand dollar she still held in her hand. "When it comes to the forces of nature, there's only so much we can do. The rest is mostly a matter of luck." Just for a moment, and with a strange bleakness in his eyes, he curled his own and her fingers around the sand dollar and held it, protecting it as though it were a precious jewel.

It was a magical day, and over too soon. After their discovery of the turtle's nest, the children swam and played in the warm surf while Summer hunted in vain for another unbroken sand dollar and Riley kept a watchful eye on the sky. There was an edginess about him now, vibrations of awareness that she sensed had nothing to do with her. *It's the weather,* she thought; *he's worried about what Brasher told him.* So perhaps it was true, then, in spite of all the evidence to the contrary, that they were in for a bad storm.

They ate the sandwiches they'd brought, but by early afternoon, with thunderheads piling up on the horizon, Riley loaded everyone into the boat and they headed back across the channel and motored up the narrow inlet to Brasher's landing. Brasher wasn't anywhere around when they arrived, but while Summer was coaxing her cranky and tired-out, waterlogged and sun-sated children into the car, Riley quietly excused himself and went off by himself, following a barely discernible footpath to the little house at the edge of the marsh.

He's gone to find Brasher, she told herself, *to tell him about the turtle's nest.*

But—she didn't mean to watch, she really didn't—it wasn't Brasher who came out on the ramshackle porch to meet him. Instead it was a young black woman, tall and slender with close-cropped hair, who greeted Riley with a warm hug and the unmistakable ease of an old and close association. Something knotted inside Summer's chest, and she tried to look away. It was none of her business, she knew. *It wasn't.* One kiss, no matter how magical, did not make it so. But she watched, anyway, while Riley and the woman talked for what seemed like a long time but was probably only minutes, then went together into the house.

It was a long time before they came out again—ten minutes at least, or even fifteen. Summer tried to distract her mind with her children and their beachcombing haul, mediating arguments about whose treasures were prettiest or most numerous, but her senses would not be distracted; they were tuned to the slightest movement, the faintest sound from the house at the edge of the marsh. And so it was that, even though she didn't want to be, she was watching when Riley and the young woman emerged from the house to stand once more on the porch, talking together, heads bowed and arms folded. Even from that distance Summer could see that the tension had gone out of him, that there was a heaviness about him now...a certain sadness. And how, she wondered, deriding herself, did she feel she knew him well enough to know that?

With a tightness in her throat, she watched Riley take something from his pocket—it could only have been money—and give it to the woman, then leave her and stride across the porch and down the steps without a backward glance.

When he joined them again, the heaviness came with him, and a mood of melancholy and secrecy that banished the day's magic as completely as a thunderstorm can turn the day to night.

Chapter 12

All the way home Riley berated himself without mercy. What had he been *thinking* of? For the last week behaving like a horny adolescent with his brains in his boxers, allowing his lust for a woman to lead him so far astray that he'd lost sight of who he was, who she was, and even more unforgivably, the fact that there were very probably the lives of two innocent children at stake. He couldn't recall ever having behaved so badly, even when he *was* a horny adolescent.

There was no excuse for his actions—none at all. He could have no future with this woman. She'd said it herself: she didn't belong in his life. She didn't *fit*. How could she possibly? God knows he was not cut out to be a father, much less a stepfather! And with this woman anything short of full commitment would be unthinkable. Unforgivable.

What had he been thinking of? Summer Robey was his client. He was responsible for her safety. What could have possessed him to kiss her?

It was Monday morning before the truth finally hit him. It came while he was shaving, staring at his reflection in his bathroom mirror, the image repeated in the mirrored wall behind him over and over to infinity. His image…

Ah yes, his image. There he was, eyeball to eyeball with the Riley Grogan he'd so carefully crafted, honed and polished and placed on display before the world, and in his mind, in his heart and soul, the *real* Riley Grogan was whispering, *You're a fraud, Grogan. The truth is, all that lofty rationalization about ethics and moral responsibility and all—it's nothin' but hooey, that's what it is, just a bunch of hooey to hide the fact that you're scared to death somebody's gonna find out what a fraud you are. You're afraid, Grogan. Afraid…*

So, needless to say, he wasn't in the best humor when he walked into his office later that morning. For one thing, his sore foot was giving him trouble, it being the first occasion he'd had to put on a pair of dress shoes since stabbing himself in the instep with a pair of hedge clippers. And naturally, it was the first thing his secretary took notice of when he stopped by her desk for his messages. She glanced up at him, covered the telephone receiver with her hand and sang out, "Hey, what'd you do to your foot?"

"What happened to 'Good morning, Mr. Grogan, how was your weekend?' " he said sourly.

"Good morning, Mr. Grogan, how was your weekend? What did you do to your foot?"

"I kicked a door. Who's that on the phone?"

"It's your old buddy—Jake Redfield. Want me to take a message?"

In spite of himself, his heart gave a lurch. Please, Lord, let this be good news. Maybe, he thought, while he was spending his weekend cutting hedges, rescuing tots from trees and groping his client on the beach, the FBI had managed to find Hal Robey, bring down the syndicate and lock up all the bad guys so everybody could go home. Uh-uh. "No," he said, frowning, "I'll take it. Put it through to my office."

"Tom Denby's waitin' for you in there."

"That's okay. Anything else of interest?"

"Couple things…" Hands busy with the phone, Danell

jerked her head toward the tray on the corner of her desk. So
since Riley had to look down in order to gather up the message
slips that had collected there, naturally the next thing he hear
was "Hey, what'd you do to your head?"

"None of your business," he growled as he shuffled
through the pile. He picked up his briefcase and started down
the hallway.

"Bumped into a door, I bet..."

In his office, Riley closed the door behind him and said
"Mornin'" to Tom, who was sitting in the client's chair with
one ankle propped on the opposite knee reading a Stephen
King paperback. The investigator dog-eared the page and
closed the book, even though Riley checked him with a hand
gesture while he went to pick up his phone.

"Agent Redfield," he said crisply, making eye contact with
Tom Denby as he hitched his backside onto a corner of his
desk, "what can I do for you?"

The FBI agent gave a mirthless snort. "I think you know
the answer to that. Mrs. Robey ready to talk to us yet?"

"Depends," Riley drawled. "You arrested the people responsible for burnin' down her house yet?"

There was a pause, during which he could almost hear the
FBI man counting to ten. Then, in that patented bureau monotone, Redfield said, "As a matter of fact, we may have gotten
a little bit of a break in that regard."

"You have?" Riley glanced at his investigator, who had
lifted his briefcase onto his knees and was snapping it open.

There was a long pause; clearly, sharing information with
an attorney—the enemy—wasn't something the FBI enjoyed
doing. Finally Redfield said, "We have reason to believe he
may have been in contact with his wife's parents."

Riley's eyebrows shot up. "Hal Robey? What reason? Did
he or didn't he?"

Another pause. Then, on a resigned exhalation, Redfield
explained, "This past weekend, Mrs. Robey's mother received
a call from someone claiming to be from her daughters' high
school class reunion committee, requesting information as to

how they might be reached. Mrs. Robey's mother didn't recognize the voice—said it may even have been a woman—but that doesn't mean anything. It's possible Robey could have disguised his voice or had someone else make the call for him.''

"What makes you think it was Robey?'' Riley held up a finger to forestall Tom Denby, who ignored it and leaned over to hand him several sheets of paper with what looked to be photocopied credit card receipts on them. He took them, stared at them.

In his ear, Redfield's voice was saying, "We've been monitoring credit card activity on Robey's known aliases. Over the weekend we had a hit—a Motel 6 on Interstate 10 in Pensacola, Florida.''

Riley swore, dragged a hand through his hair. Winced. He frowned, his mind in high gear, chewing it all over. "Mrs. Robey's parents live in Pensacola Beach.''

"Uh-huh…''

"All right, so he's looking for her.'' Riley was silent for a moment, listening to the sound of his own breathing. "You're thinking when he doesn't find his wife at the address and phone number he's got, he'll get in touch with the sisters next.''

"If he hasn't already. From what I understand, the only one reachable is the one here in Georgia. He's gonna be careful about it—he knows he's a target.'' Redfield paused, then said very quietly, "What we're thinking is, when and if he does, if we're not already too late, we'd like to make his next move a little easier for him.''

Riley sat still for about three beats, then came up off the desk as if somebody'd shot him in the butt with a BB gun. "No. Lure him in, you mean—using Summer as bait. Are you out of your mind? No. Absolutely not. I can't allow it.''

"You can't *allow* it?'' Redfield's voice had gone soft. "You mean, *advise,* don't you? In the final analysis, isn't the decision up to Mrs. Robey?''

"Dammit, Redfield, the woman's got two kids!''

"I know she does—and you can't keep them locked away forever, now, can you?"

Riley said nothing. His skin felt itchy and hot, but there was a cold, sick feeling in his stomach. *If I'm not in jail, I migh as well be....*

"Look—" Redfield exhaled gustily in his ear "—you know as well as I do, if the bad guys want her badly enough, soone or later they're going to find a way to get to her. You wan to live with that? You want her and those kids to live with that?" Riley said nothing; his eyes were following Tom Denby as the investigator paced at a polite distance, fidgeting with things in his pockets. The FBI man continued, almost gently "They might be on Robey's trail right now. He could be lead ing 'em right to her. If they get the chance to use the wife and kids to leverage Robey, they won't hesitate for one minute and you and I both know it. Robey's gonna find her, the bad guys are gonna find Robey, and who knows who's gonna find who first? Isn't it better to have us be the ones writing the script? And if it gives us a chance to clear this thing up, once and for all..." The agent's voice had taken on a curious vi bration, and Riley remembered suddenly what Summer had said about Captain Ahab and Moby Dick.

Then Redfield paused, and Riley could almost hear him fighting down his demons. Finally, once more back in the classic feds monotone, he murmured, "At least let us talk to her. That's all we ask."

Sometimes, you know, I think I'd rather confront the fear Go out there and face those...those bastards! Like—I don' know, set myself up as bait for an FBI sting, or something Anything to get those people caught.

"I'll talk to her," Riley said heavily. But he already knew what her answer would be. "I'll get back to you."

He cradled the phone and sat for a moment, staring at it Then he straightened and looked at Tom Denby, who had turned from the window and was regarding him with a small waiting smile. Denby was a stocky, nondescript man with thin ning hair and nondescript glasses, the kind of man who would be easy to overlook in a crowd. But a man whose eyes and ears missed nothing, and the one man Riley wanted at his back in a brawl.

"Tom," he said on an exhalation, "I'm gonna have to ask you to be on standby for a while."

"I gathered." The investigator nodded toward the phone. "That was the feds?"

"That was the feds." Riley smiled, but he felt dark and cold inside. "And I'm afraid we might not be working on quite the same agenda, if you know what I mean. We have…different priorities."

"I hear ya," said Denby softly. "Just tell me what you want me to do."

"You don't have to do this," Riley said in an undertone as he ushered Summer and the children into his office the following afternoon. "Please keep that in mind—you are not obligated to do anything they ask you to do. Do you understand?" She sure should understand, he thought; he'd told her that often enough in the past twenty-four hours. Emphasized it, with silent gnashing of teeth, knowing how futile it was.

As he'd feared, she'd jumped on the idea of using herself as bait in an FBI trap the instant he'd mentioned it to her. Far from being nervous or apprehensive, the notion of putting herself in jeopardy in order to bring about an end to her present state of fear and uncertainty seemed to have ignited something inside her—something fierce and purposeful. He could see it in the light that gleamed in her eyes, in the lift of her chin and the set of her shoulders. Feel it in the excitement and tension that seemed to emanate from her like a field of electrical energy. For the first time, he saw and understood just how strong and brave she really was, this woman he'd once allowed to be judged an airhead and a bimbo. Understood that for all her gentleness and nurturing heart, Summer Robey was a woman to be reckoned with, and an adversary to be feared.

And she'd never looked more beautiful to him. Maybe it was because of the way she was dressed, which was the way he'd always pictured her, in a dress of soft, sunshine yellow with buttons all down the front, a scooped neckline and belted waist, her hair falling to her shoulders in gleaming golden waves, or it could be that new inner fire, or simply a change in his own perceptions. Whatever it was, he couldn't seem to keep from looking at her. And whenever he did, his heart would begin to pound.

"I'll be fine," Summer said in a quiet voice just for him, and at the same time with a radiant smile for Danell, who responded with a syrupy, "How're you, Mrs. Robey, nice to see you again."

"They here yet?" Riley asked in a muttered undertone.

"Waitin' in your office." She leaned across her desktop, braced on her forearms, to smile at the children. "Hey…who's this we got here?"

"David, Helen," said Summer, "say hello to Mrs….uh—"

"Johnson—but y'all can call me Danell if you want to, okay?" The children both nodded; apparently overcome with awe, they were expressing it in their own individual ways— David in round-eyed silence, Helen antsy and primed for battle.

"It'd probably be better if they stayed out here," Riley said, frowning. "Danell, do you think you could—"

"Oh, sure—no problem." She shooed them off with a wave of her hand and a toothy grin for the children. "We'll be fine—won't we, hon? Hey, you guys like to draw pictures?"

Riley murmured, "Thanks," and put his hand on Summer's waist, his heart already beating like a trip-hammer.

"Can I watch you work the computer?" he heard David ask shyly as he ushered Summer into the hallway.

And his secretary answered, "Well, sure, I guess you can if you want to. How 'bout you, ladybug? Hey, that is a *very* pretty dress you're wearing."

And Helen's response, in a tone of uncharacteristic sweetness: "Uh-huh—Mr. Riley bought it for me. He bought us lots of stuff—books…even one about dinosaurs. An' you know what else…?"

Riley closed his eyes and gave an inaudible sigh as he opened his office door and waved Summer in ahead of him. Oh, Lord. Danell was never going to let him hear the end of this.

The feds had gone. The outlines of the plan to trap and capture Hal Robey were in place; all that remained was the phone call that would set it in motion. Summer looked drained but resolved; Riley felt as if he'd spent a week in court. He felt exhausted, but wired, too, a mood he normally might soothe with a quiet evening in feminine company…an elegant dinner…good wine…soft music…. He tried putting Summer into that picture, but it just wouldn't work, somehow. Somehow he'd known it wouldn't. No matter how lovely she was in that yellow dress and high-heeled shoes, she was always going to be more at home in blue jeans and sneakers.

In his secretary's office, they found David jammed in between Danell's knees and the computer, avidly click-clicking away with the mouse. When she heard them come in, Danell threw a look over her shoulder long enough to say indignantly, "Hey, did you know there are card games on here?" And then, turning back to David, she said, "There you go—red nine on that black ten right there. See it?"

"Is Helen—"

Danell jerked her head toward the waiting room. "She's out there paperin' the place with pictures of dinosaurs on sticky notes."

"Could I please use the rest room?" Summer murmured.

"Sure," Riley said. "Down the hall on the left." While she excused herself, Danell surrendered her chair to David and came around her desk. Riley saw the look in her eye and held up a hand. "Don't even start."

"Don't tell me don't start," she huffed in a whisper. "That woman and those kids been *livin'* with you."

"Oh, hell." He scrubbed a hand over his eyes and whispered back, "It's not what you think."

"Hey—you don't even *know* what I think." He looked at

her then and saw that she had a sparkle in her eyes and a big grin on her face—clearly tickled to death.

"Hush, Danell—you know she's not my type."

"Uh-huh."

"Seriously—you've known me *how* many years now? How many women have I been out with in that time? Now, tell me—have you ever known me, even once, to date a woman who had kids?"

She didn't say anything, just nailed him with one of her looks. Riley rolled his eyes; he knew he wasn't off the hook yet. Sure enough, Danell folded her arms, moved in close and poked him in the chest with one of her inch-long silver-blue fingernails. "Now, you tell *me* somethin'. If all those women you been datin' all these years were your *type*— how come you never married any of 'em? Hmm? Tell me that."

Riley just looked at her. He'd have come up with an answer for her, though; he was sure he would have, except that right then Summer came back into the room, looking like she'd just washed her face and brushed her hair. Looking as fresh and lovely as a field full of daffodils. And his words, his breath, and it felt like his whole beating heart, somehow wound up stuck in his throat. "Ready?" he asked in a garbled croak.

She nodded and said breathlessly, "Mrs. Johnson, thank you so much," but her eyes were on Riley's face.

And he couldn't take his eyes away from hers. He thought, Why not? At least…dinner? And he was seeing her sitting across the table from him, candlelight shining in her eyes and in her hair.

"Can we go now?" Helen whined, shuffling in from the waiting room. "I'm hungry."

"Yes, honey, we're going." And Summer turned her face away from him, reaching out to pull her child against her in a one-armed hug, leaving him feeling strangely off balance and bereft, as if something precious had been wrenched from his grasp. "Do either of you need to use the rest room before we leave?" That was directed at the children, of course.

"Uh-uh," said Helen with a decisive shake of her head, and

David elaborated without looking away from the monitor, "We just went."

"Why don't I take you out for dinner?" Riley said to Summer, ignoring Danell's smirk. He was still thinking of nice restaurants—one of Charleston's less touristy seafood places, perhaps. Somewhere the children wouldn't be *too* out of place…

"Pizza!" yelled Helen, doing her bunny-hop thing, and David looked up long enough to echo, "Yeah, pizza! Can we, Mom? We haven't had pizza in a long time. Please?"

Riley's vision of a romantic dinner vanished like a puff of smoke.

"There's a very nice pizza place right down the road— would you like me to call and make you a reservation?" Danell purred with a perfectly straight face.

Riley looked pointedly at his watch, then said with a pained grimace, "Danell, it's past quittin' time—don't you have someplace you need to go?"

"Yessir, boss—" she shut off the computer's monitor to David's yelp of disappointment "—I am goin' home to mah man an' mah kids." She made two syllables out of both "man" and "kids," which she could do when she chose to lay the Southern molasses on thick. She swooped down to collect her pocketbook from under her desk and slung it over her shoulder. "Hey—I'm serious about that pizza place. Down the road to the left, 'bout a mile on your right. Poppa Joe's." She gave them a wave, and Riley a wink. "Y'all have a nice evenin', now."

"It was nice of you to do this," Summer said an hour or so later as she dropped a crust onto the pizza platter with a small, replete sigh. "They've had a good time." Her eyes were on the children as she said it; they were across the room in an alcove that held a dozen or so video games, and she could see David's head jerking as he worked the controls, and Helen's head bobbing up and down beside him as she watched.

She didn't want to look at Riley; she didn't have to know how uncomfortable he was in these surroundings. His look of abject misery was like a black storm cloud on the horizon—enough to cast an uneasy pall on the picnic, but not enough to cancel it. She almost felt sorry for him—the suave and elegant Riley Grogan, brought to this. Pizza and video games! What next? *Almost.* To her surprise, what she did feel was annoyance. Even anger. Like a mild undercurrent of electricity running just beneath her skin.

"It's all right," she said, unable to keep that little burr of irritation out of her voice, "the effects aren't permanent, you know."

He came back from the dark place where he'd been with a small start and a puzzled "What?"

"This place...us...our life-style. It won't rub off on you—unless you wanted it to, I suppose—which I'm sure you don't. Once this is all cleared up and we're out of your life, you'll have no trouble at all going back to the life you're used to."

He shifted uncomfortably, but didn't smile or deny. Instead he held her eyes with a long, dark look and said quietly, "I'd rather not talk about my life right now, if you don't mind." Then, in abrupt reversal of that, he looked down, released a long, audible breath. "It's just that sometimes places... things...remind me of places I've been in my life...places I'd just as soon not be reminded of. Do you understand?"

Summer nodded, the anger tremors inside her becoming something else—tension...awareness...anticipation. But she didn't want to let it go. "A pizza place?" she murmured, smiling a little, letting him see the compassion—and a little of the sadness—in her heart. "Can that be so bad a memory?"

And then he smiled, too, finally. "Not the place—the time. Reminds me of when I was in college, if you want to know the truth." The smile slipped sideways and he abandoned it in a swallow of beer. "My college days were a time of—" he searched for a word and found it "—struggle. Not the best time of my life. Nor the worst." He laughed suddenly. "Even the music's the same." And he tilted his head, listening to the song—an old one of Olivia Newton-John's that had just come on the jukebox.

Summer sat up straight. "I remember that. It's from the movie *Grease*. I was in high school when that came out." She began to sing softly, and after a moment, he did, too. Then they both stumbled over the lyrics and stopped at the same time, laughing together.

"Hey," said Riley suddenly, "would you like to dance?"

She blinked and said, "What?"

"Dance. You know—man, woman, step-together, one-two-three…"

Dance? Oh, God, thought Summer. *I will not think of Cinderella…I will not!* She felt an overwhelming desire to laugh, but there was no room in her chest for anything except her rapidly beating heart. She made a small, desperate sound. "I—I don't think they do that here."

He looked around. "Don't see why not—there's plenty of room." It was true; at that hour on a weeknight the place was nearly empty. He slid off the end of the bench, braced his hands on the table and leaned close to her. His voice, when he spoke, was low and held a current of urgency. "Come on, Mrs. Robey, dance with me." And he tilted his head and smiled with heart-melting charm. "You know, I was gonna take you out on the town, after that ordeal this afternoon, but…well, that seemed a little impractical under the circumstances. So this looks like the only opportunity I'm gonna have. Dance with me."

Why do you want me to? It was on the tip of her tongue to ask him that. But she was too afraid of the answer. And it was on the tip of her tongue to say yes. She wanted to—oh, how she wanted to. But her tongue, her whole body felt heavy, weighed down by the wash of memories of all the times and ways he'd touched her, heart, soul and body…of Cinderella's Prince, Rhett in a blue silk dressing gown, and a wounded hero with her child in his arms…of his hands enclosing hers around a perfect sand dollar, the feel of his mouth on hers.

Her lips had felt swollen, hot, on fire, that day. Now she felt like that all over.

"Could *I* dance?" It was Helen, who had come without either of them noticing. She was standing at Riley's elbow, smiling up at him and squirming with unwonted shyness, winsome as a kitten, and as irresistible.

For a moment longer his eyes clung to Summer's, burning with a strange, wild light. Then he dragged them from her and in one graceful motion, straightened, turned and swept Helen's small hands into his. "Can you...? Sure you can." He bowed low over their clasped hands, making her giggle. "Miss Helen, may I please have this dance?"

Helen wriggled, almost overcome with shyness, pushed her tongue into the side of her cheek and finally mumbled, blushing rose-pink, "But...I don't know how."

"Ah," said Riley. He thought about it. "Okay, I think I have it." He winked at Summer as he led his diminutive partner to the open space next to the jukebox. "I think I saw this on a television commercial once...okay, missy, stand on my feet—that's right, put your feet right...there."

And he carefully guided Helen's Marvin the Martian sneakers onto the tops of his polished leather dress shoes, wincing only slightly as her weight settled onto his injured instep. Then, with a grace and ceremony worthy of a palace ballroom, he danced the utterly dazzled little girl around and around while Olivia Newton-John sang sweetly of hopeless devotion, and Summer, watching, pressed her hand over her mouth and struggled with all her strength to hold back tears.

Oh, God, what have I done? They've fallen in love with him. And so have I.

The song ended, the music stopped. Helen immediately cried, "More! I want to do it again! Please, Mr. Riley, can we?"

But he shook his head and said firmly, "Nope—now it's your mother's turn. Here, tell you what—" he fished a coin out of his pocket and gave it to her "—you put this in the jukebox. Yeah, right there, like that. We'll find that song again…okay, here it is. Now." And then he was beside Summer, and her hand was warm in his grasp. She felt herself rising, standing up on legs that felt hollow, fragile as blown glass.

"You're trembling, Mrs. Robey," he said softly as his arms came around her and his hand pressed warm and strong against her back. "Why is that?"

She tried to laugh. "It's been a long time since I've danced."

"I was sure it had been."

There was a strange timbre in his voice that made her shiver even more, and her voice was bumpy as she said, "What if I've forgotten how?" In her high-heeled sandals she was almost as tall as he was; his finely chiseled lips were on a level with her eyes.

He smiled, and the movement drew her hungry gaze. "Would you like to stand on my feet?"

"I'm wearing heels," she said with a husky chortle. "You'd be crippled for life."

He laughed and said, "I doubt that." But she thought, No, it is I who will be crippled. After this, when we leave here, how will I—how will *we* ever forget you? After you, Riley Grogan, what man can there ever be…for me?

When he checked suddenly in the middle of the song, she gave a small, almost guilty start, as if he'd walked in on her private thoughts. But his hand had gone to his side and was pushing back his jacket to unhook a beeper from the waistband of his slacks.

"Oops," he said, glancing at it, "I'm going to have to see about this. Do you mind?" It was a formality, of course; she shook her head. Riley was looking around for a pay phone.

"Back there, I think," she murmured, pointing. "Behind the video games." He nodded, muttered his thanks and went off to find it, weaving his way among long wooden tables, while Summer went back to their table and Helen, who awaited her with smiles and eyes that sparkled with delicious feminine conspiracy.

I guess it's like that with lawyers, too, she thought, remembering that she'd summoned hers in the middle of a black-tie affair. Remembering, too, the times when she'd still had her own veterinary clinic and had so often been beeped in the middle of family outings to tend to some pet emergency or other. The children were used to hurried endings. Thinking of that, remembering that she'd once had a life, and a good one, long before Hal's desertion, crime syndicates, the FBI and Riley Grogan, helped to restore her equilibrium, calm her panic, and quiet her soul. She would have a life again, someday. After all this. After Riley Grogan. *For the children's sake, I must.*

She had just settled onto the bench and gathered her daughter against her side in a one-armed hug when Riley came back to the table, steering David along with a hand on the back of his neck. His face was grim, and his eyes held a hard, steely glitter.

"I'm afraid we're going to have to cut this short," he said quietly. "We need to get home—now."

Summer was already on her feet, her heart pounding. "What is it? It can't be—" He shook his head, glancing at the children. "Okay, guys, clean-up time," Summer said briskly, picking up his cue. "David, you take the trays. Helen, you gather up the trash. Hurry up—chop-chop."

While they were thus occupied, Riley moved close to her and spoke in a low voice, for her ears alone. "That was the police. My security monitoring service called them. Somebody tried to break into the house this afternoon."

Chapter 13

The phone rang while Mirabella was giving Amy Jo her bath. Since Jimmy Joe was out on a cross-country haul and J.J. was spending the night at his friend Rocky's house, she had no choice but to let it ring until the machine picked it up. And then it was a hang-up after all. She really hated that.

It rang again while she was getting Amy Jo settled down, reading her her bedtime story and tucking her in for the night, and there was no way she was going to let a phone call interrupt that! Especially a phone call from somebody who didn't even have the courtesy to leave a message.

Consequently, when it rang for the third time just as she was sitting down to the computer to work on the plans for Blue Star Lines new company offices, she was a wee bit short-tempered and out of sorts.

"Yes!" she barked. And then, slowly, she said, "Yes, this is Mirabella Starr." For some reason the voice on the other end of the line, though polite as could be, made a chill go down her spine.

"Mrs. Starr, this is Special Agent Jake Redfield, with the Federal Bureau of Investigation. I'd like to ask you—"

"The FBI?" Mirabella's first impulse was to laugh. For some reason, instead, she asked very quietly, "Is this a joke?" And her heart had already begun to beat faster.

"No, ma'am, this isn't a joke. This concerns—"

"It's my sister, isn't it? Which one? Oh, God, it's Evie, isn't it? I knew something was wrong—I *knew* it."

"Ma'am—calm down, please. Ma'am, this does concern your sister, Summer Robey—"

"Oh, God—"

"Your sister's fine, Mrs. Starr. However, we would like to ask you for your help in resolving a matter that concerns her."

"A matter—hey, wait just a minute," Mirabella cried, relief restoring her naturally bossy and forthright nature, "how do I know this isn't some kind of joke? Just because you *say* you're with the FBI—"

A sigh interrupted her. "Mrs. Starr, here's what I want you to do, okay? I want you to hang up, and then dial long distance information for Savannah. Ask for the number for the FBI. When they answer, I want you to ask for Special Agent Redfield—would you do that for me, please?"

Mirabella gulped and gave a grudging "Okay." There was a distant "click."

She had to look up the area code for Savannah. But a few minutes later she was listening to a flat male voice droning, "Federal Bureau of Investigation," while fear fluttered in her stomach and icy sweat beaded like dew on her forehead. She had to unstick her tongue from the roof of her mouth in order to ask for Special Agent Redfield, but a moment later heard the chillingly neutral voice saying, "Thank you for calling me back, Mrs. Starr. Are we okay now? All squared away?"

Well, you needn't be *quite* so polite, Mirabella thought testily. After all, you can't just trust people nowadays, can you? She cleared her throat and said crisply, "Yes, thank you. Now, you say this concerns my sister Summer? Is she in some kind of trouble?" *Oh, God, I knew it. I knew it.*

"Not at all," Agent Redfield said smoothly. "But what we'd like you to do, if you wouldn't mind, if anyone should call you or contact you asking about where they can get ahold—"

"Hal! This is about him, isn't it? That no-good ex-husband of hers—I knew it!"

"If *anyone* contacts you, Mrs. Starr—anyone at all—asking about your sister, I'd like you to give them this address that I'm about to give you. Got a pencil? Okay, good—then I'd like you to call me immediately. If you can't reach me here, I'm going to give you my beeper number. Call me anytime, day or night, understand?"

"Yes, of course," said Mirabella impatiently; she disliked being asked if she understood. Did they think she was mentally deficient? She frowned at the numbers she'd written on the message pad beside the phone. "Agent Redfield, did you by any chance try to call me earlier this evening? Twice?"

"No, ma'am, I didn't. Just the one time. Why?"

"Nothing. Just had a couple of hang-ups on my machine, is all. I thought—well. Never mind…" She let her voice trail off as shifting patterns of light and shadow glanced off the kitchen windows and slid across the walls of her office. Someone—a car—was turning into her driveway. At this time of night? Jimmy Joe wasn't due back until tomorrow.

"Just be sure and call the minute—"

"Yes—would you hold on for just one second, please?" The hand that gripped the phone had become slippery with sweat. She was suddenly aware that, except for her baby daughter sleeping in her crib upstairs, she was alone in the house. Alone, and surrounded by uninhabited darkness. The phone in her hand had become a lifeline.

"Mrs. Starr? Everything okay there?"

"Just a minute—someone's coming." She tried not to sound breathless; she really didn't want the FBI man to think she was afraid, especially if it turned out to be nothing. With the cordless phone pressed tightly against her ear, she tiptoed through the darkened living room and peered out across the front porch. Her heart pounded as she watched an unfamiliar car pull in and park beneath the oak trees at the edge of the lawn. Lights and motor were turned off. There was a long and suspense-filled pause…and then the door opened, briefly—too briefly—illuminating the driver inside. Mirabella's breath caught.

"Mrs. Starr? You okay?"

The car door closed, and a lone figure started toward her, walking with purpose, angling across the grass. She gasped, "Oh, my God—"

"Mrs. Starr?"

"It's okay, it's okay." She was laughing, maybe half crying, too. "I have to go now. It's my sister—she just arrived. My *other* sister—*Evie.* Agent Redfield, I'll call if I hear anything—I will, I promise. But I have to go now. Bye!" She punched the disconnect button and threw open the front door. "Oh, my God—Evie!" She flew across the porch and down the steps. "I can't believe this—you have no idea—where on earth did you come from?" And then she was enveloped in her older sister's arms, and in the warmth of her throaty chuckle.

"Hey, Bell—wow, this is some reception. Sorry I missed the big anniversary celebration."

"Never mind—I'm just so glad you're here. You have no idea…but what are you doing here? I thought you were in Las Vegas."

Her sister dismissed that with an airy wave. "Oh, I was. Now I'm on my way to Savannah, actually. Gotta meet my crew there day after tomorrow. That should give us a day or two to get set up—"

"Set up for what? You're filming in *Savannah?* What's in Savannah?"

"The hurricane, of course! Don't you watch television? Hurricane Angela's supposed to be on course to make landfall somewhere between Savannah and Charleston in the next couple of days—nobody knows for sure, of course. But hey—

wherever and whenever it hits, I plan to be there right in the middle of it.''

Mirabella gave her head a shake, already feeling overwhelmed. Evie had that effect on people. "You could at least have called—"

Her sister waved that aside as well. "Oh, God, I've been so busy. Just swamped—you have no idea. Besides—" she gave a cackle of laughter "—this news just had to be delivered in person.''

"News? What news?" Mirabella paused, frowning suspiciously, only to be spun around and gripped by both arms as her sister, taller by a head, bent in an exuberant crouch and resoundingly kissed her cheek.

"You'll never guess—never, in a million years." She paused, and in the light spilling from the kitchen windows, Mirabella could see her eyes light with excitement.

"What?" she breathed, already caught up in it herself. "Tell me!"

"You'll never believe it, Bell, after all these years! I never thought it would happen, but it has—I'm getting married!''

The police were finally leaving. Summer stood in her children's bedroom and watched the lights of the patrol car grow smaller down the curving lane and wink out beneath the canopy of live oaks. Behind her all was quiet. The children were in bed, though probably not yet fully asleep, with Beatle nestled alert and on guard on David's pillow, for a change, instead of snuggled down with the covers tucked up to her chin.

Downstairs, Cleo—whom they had found backed into a corner of her cage with her wings upraised like a gargoyle, screaming "Get out, get out!"—was brooding and muttering beneath her night cover, and Peggy Sue, pacified with a quarter can of water-packed albacore tuna, had stopped pacing and growling in front of the morning-room windows. Beyond the windows, lightning bugs winked, insects screeched and frogs resumed their interrupted love songs. Out there, the air was hot and oppressively still. Inside the air-conditioned house, Summer hugged herself and shivered.

A cup of hot Postum, she thought; that's what I need. It had been a roller-coaster kind of a day. She felt tense and on edge. Her skin felt sensitized, as if all her hair were standing on end. Maybe something sweet and warm would soothe her.

She had just reached the top of the stairs and was starting down when she heard Riley come in. She hesitated, thinking he might go straight to his study, but instead he came on through the kitchen and into the hallway, turned and started up the stairs. Took two steps, looked up and saw her, and halted, one hand on the banister rail.

Two steps down from the top she waited, then said softly, "I saw them leave. Is everything all right?"

He made a restless movement, something between a nod and a shrug. "They think it was probably just some kids— climbed the fence just to see what was on the other side." His eyes remained on her as he climbed two more steps. "How 'bout you? Everyone okay in here? The animals seemed pretty upset."

She descended two more steps, waved a hand and gave a low laugh. "They're fine. They were definitely spooked, but that could just as well have been because of all the strange people tromping around out there with flashlights."

He shook his head and, as he came up several more steps, said dryly, "With those three around, who needs a security system?"

Summer had no reply to that. She continued on down the stairs, sliding one hand along the rail, her heart beating like a trip-hammer. She didn't look at Riley as he came up to meet her, closer...and closer. But she could feel him. It was as if he'd brought the outside in with him—the heat and humidity, the heaviness and tension—so that the warm summer night seemed to rise as he did, and engulf her like a fog.

They met somewhere just below the landing, and as they drew even Summer said in a stifled voice, "With any luck you won't have to put up with us much longer." His hand shot out and caught her by the arm, and she gave a little gasp. She had no choice but to stop then; he wouldn't let her continue. But she still wouldn't look at him. There was so much tension in his fingers...in his voice. She couldn't bear to see his face.

But she couldn't bear the silence, either. She licked her lips and said with a tight laugh, "Don't try to tell me you aren't going to be glad when this is all over and everything's back to normal again. Just think—you'll have the place to yourself...peace and quiet...."

"For God's sake, what kind of man do you think I am?" His voice sounded scratchy, but oddly thickened, too. His fingers gripped her arm like steel bands, urging her to turn and face him.

But she resisted, and instead turned her head and looked at him along her shoulder. "One who lives alone," she said softly.

He made an impatient sound. "I live alone. That doesn't mean I prefer to *be* alone."

She didn't answer, and the silence between them sang with tension. She wanted to cover her ears and run.

He broke it finally with a whisper, one so soft it was like the brush of an owl's wings on the night wind. "Don't pretend you don't know what's been happening to us." And her small, distressed cry was like the sound the mouse makes in that final instant she knows she's been caught. Ruthlessly he continued, "Don't pretend, Summer. Don't *lie*. The other day, on the beach..."

She felt a sob rising in her throat, but swallowed it and whispered, "You kissed me—that's all."

"Do you have any idea how many times I've wanted to, before and since?" She shook her head, meaning many things. But his fingers on her arm...the pressure was inexorable. She could feel herself weakening. "Tonight, when we danced...you were trembling."

"I was nervous...."

"You're trembling now."

So was he. And how did she know that? Because somehow, unbeknown to her, the same arm he held so tightly had bent at the elbow and her hand had found its way to his waist, where it rested now, palm flat against the pulsating warmth of his belly.

"You're trembling…don't deny it."

"I won't…I can't—"

"Nervous?"

"No…" she whispered as his mouth came down to meet hers. "I can't—"

The breadth of a whisper away from her lips, he paused. "Can't what?"

"Can't do this," she gasped. And she could already feel his mouth, and the kiss she couldn't allow to happen. She could taste him—his breath was in her mouth, his heat and energy already part of her, already inside her, running through her veins. "No matter how much I want to." Her lips twisted, she'd never known such pain. She felt engulfed by it…made hopeless and exhausted by it…like a starving person denied all hope of food. "I have…the children…"

He made a sound so full of frustration and sorrow she wondered if he might be feeling the same pain, or at least understood hers. For the space of a few dozen heartbeats neither of them spoke, while the truths they couldn't bring themselves to utter vibrated in the hairbreadth that was left between them. *Yes, the children, Riley. We both know there is no place in your life for my children.*

"Just once in your life," he grated as he released her, the warmth of his exhalation settling on her face like a veil, "just once…have you ever done anything…that was just for *you?*"

She shook her head, half numb now with loss and regret, and mumbled, "When you become a parent…" One step above her he paused to look back. His head was high, and she could see his eyes glittering down at her through the curtains of his lashes. She swallowed in a futile attempt to ease her aching throat and finished in a whisper, "You forfeit the luxury of thinking only of yourself." And then it was she who turned and continued down the stairs on legs she couldn't feel, knowing his eyes would follow her all the way.

Sheer will carried her as far as the kitchen, but she didn't stop at the refrigerator or the cupboards as she'd planned. It would take a lot more than a cup of warm Postum to soothe her now. Instead, she wobbled on through and into the morning room, where she pulled out a chair, sank into it and laid her head down on the table, pillowed on her folded arms, the way nursery school children do during rest time. After a time, Peggy Sue came padding in, climbed up the trailing skirt of the yellow dress and into Summer's lap, and the gentle rhythm of her kneading paws and ratchety purr became like an anesthetic to her mind, blocking out thought.

Riley knew he wouldn't sleep. And of the several alternatives available to him, he knew the only one that carried with it any real hope of surcease for the turmoil inside him was to swim himself to a state of exhaustion. He seldom swam these days; it wasn't often that he found himself in need of that distraction. His pool was more decorative than functional, designed more to feed the senses and relax the mind than exercise the body. But there were still occasionally nights, like this one, when some new stress drove him to the water as old demons once had, and he would find in the humid darkness, in the caress of warm water on his naked body, in the churning of his arms and legs and the burning in his lungs...in the memory of nights when those things had meant actual physical, not just mental, escape, a strange comfort.

He'd been at it for a while—had no idea how long, or what time it was—when he felt the crawling sensation along his spine that told him he had company. He halted and sank in midstroke, heart pounding more with adrenaline than exertion, then surfaced cautiously, eyes first, like a cruising gator. And just barely did get his nose and mouth out of the water before his gasp of shock would have had him inhaling half the pool.

It was Summer. She was standing there on the deck near the shallow end, a pale, almost ghostly form with her golden hair, golden skin and the yellow dress lit to a silvery glow by the house security lights.

He growled, ''What're you tryin' to do, scare me to death? Damn near...'' But his voice faded to nothing as she unbuckled her belt and let it drop to the flagstones near her bare feet.

Now her fingers were on the topmost button of the long row of buttons that ran from chest to hem down the front of the dress. Very slowly, Riley let his feet sink to the bottom of the pool. His mind was full of thoughts and questions, all of them zooming around and flaming out like bugs in an electric zapper, none of them living long enough to give rise to coherent speech. In that bemused state he watched her hands...her strong, nurturing hands...work their way down that row of buttons to a point several inches below her waist...watched her slip her arms from the sleeves, then skim the dress down over her hips and let it fall in a creamy puddle around her feet, leaving her standing before him in a pair of the panties he'd bought for her...and nothing more. And then those, too, were peeled off, rolled down, abandoned like an old chrysalis....

He wondered if he could be dreaming, hallucinating—some fever of the brain, perhaps, a by-product of the fire in his loins. But no—his heart was pounding too hard, rocking the water where it lapped against his sternum. He could feel his blood surging through his body, feel himself growing hot and hard. Barely breathing, he watched her move away from the puddle of her clothing and step over the edge of the pool, her legs long and graceful, one foot reaching for that first step down into the water, slender arms extended out to her sides just a little for balance. Her body was like sculpted marble in the dim light. He'd never seen anything so lovely. A modern-day Venus, he thought, rendered by the hand of an Old Master.

And then she was in the water and moving toward him, the dark water sluicing over her breasts like oil. Incredibly, he felt her hands on the sides of his waist, her touch cooler than the water—felt them slide around him, fan across the ridges of muscle that cushioned his spine, then down over his buttocks.

A bolt of desire shot through him, so intense it was like pain. His eyes closed of their own volition, and he groaned aloud. He opened his mouth, wanting to ask her—meaning to ask her—what in the hell this was all about, and did she have any idea what she was doing to him! But his arms were full of her, his hands—both hands—were tangled in her hair, and his mouth was filled with her mouth...her lips...her tongue. Standing in water up to his middle, he felt as if he were being consumed by flames.

This was madness...insanity. He knew she'd been right to stop him, there on the stairs, right to remind him of all the reasons they shouldn't do this. He knew that, and surely she did, too. But though he knew it he didn't care. There was a wildness in him—yes, and she'd called it *the wild lonelies!*—that he remembered from long, long ago. A terrible emptiness. She—this woman in his arms—could fill it; he knew that, too, in the very depths of his soul. And yet the slippery friction of her body against his, and the panting heat of her mouth, seemed only to taunt and torment him, while his mind screamed *Yes! But not like this...not like this!*

The sound she made when he tore his mouth from hers was like a sob. With his fingers tangled in her hair he held her head ruthlessly still, upturned so he could look into her face as he demanded in a harsh, guttural cry, *"Why?* What... is...*this?"*

She answered him the same way, her head thrown back and defiant, while her eyes glittered with a fierce, pale light. "This is for me. For *me!"* She shook her head free of his grasp. "It came to me that I've been too proud to admit—" she was panting, out of breath, as if she'd been swimming long and hard "—that it wasn't the children I was protecting...it was *me.*" Her laughter was like moonlight on water—it touched only the surface. "My kids aren't going to be hurt by this— how can they be? They'll never know. I'll find the right man for them—for *us*— someday. I'll find someone who'll be the father to them they deserve...*need.*"

"My God, Summer—" It was torn from him, a groan of anguish.

"No, I will—I *must*." Her hands slid up his back and pressed against his shoulder blades with a strength that shamed him for all the times he'd thought her vulnerable and weak. "And when I do, the only one who'll ever know about this…about us…is me. *I'm* the one that has to live with it. I'm the only one who can be hurt. So…this is for me."

No—not the only one! "God, Summer…" He felt the emptiness yawning before him, felt as though she were the only thing keeping him from being swallowed by it. Like an animal in a trap, pain-racked and dazed, he growled, "What if I don't want to let you go? Maybe—"

She stopped him there with a shake of her head and a finger touched gently to his lips. "My children deserve more than just to be taken on as part of my…baggage. It's okay, I understand. I don't expect happily ever after. This is enough—for as long as I'm here, okay? *It's enough…*" The last was a whisper, rough as sandpaper. And so were the words that followed. "Please, Riley…just close your eyes and…kiss me."

He'd never felt so conflicted, so torn. He was on fire with passion, but there was a heaviness inside him; he trembled with fury, but ached with tenderness. Never in all his life had he wanted a woman as much as he wanted this one, but the thought of taking her made him feel one good breath away from crying. He wanted to lift his head and cry out from the depths of his soul, scream to the heavens his rage at fate, which had given him his demons, the demons that would not let him give her all she deserved, and take from her what he needed.

Instead, he simply did as she asked, and kissed her.

And in the end, for that moment at least, it was what he needed; she was a healer, after all.

He held her tightly at first, taking her mouth with a savagery that was more a product of frustration than of passion, plunging his tongue deep, with a growl in his throat, lungs burning and his heart exploding in primitive rhythms. And she gave it back and more, but with a little chuckle of pleasure that for some reason delighted him. It rolled up from her throat, passed from her mouth into his, rippled down into his chest, and he gave her back its echo.

He drew back a little, and she brought her hands to the back of his neck, swirled her tongue over his lips and then between, opening to him, inviting him in, deeper...deeper. She was all warmth and generosity, her body lush and humid even in the coolness of the water. Her femininity seemed to surround him like a sultry summer night; she was the air he breathed; he absorbed her through the pores of his skin. He wondered whether he'd ever really made love to a woman before...whether all the experiences he'd had before had only been leading him to this...preparing him for this. For *this* woman.

He slipped his arms under her buttocks and lifted her—or did he only suggest, and she come without hesitation? He didn't know for certain—the water made it such an effortless thing. Her legs parted and slid around his hips and he nested himself in her warm and giving softness...just nestled there, hot and aching with his need. And groaned with the sweet agony of it, knowing it was a need that must not be filled. Not yet...

He walked with her to the shallow water, still plundering her mouth with a hunger that only seemed to grow more insatiable with every kiss. The air cooled on their bodies, raising shivers and goose bumps and hardening her nipples so that they abraded his chest like pebbles. He wanted them in his mouth with an intensity he could *taste,* sharp and edgy as brass on his tongue. But not yet. Not yet...

She made a small growling sound of protest when he lowered her to the steps, uncoiled her legs and arms from around him and tore his mouth from hers, until he muttered, "Sorry...but before this goes any further, there's something I have to do."

She opened her mouth to say something, to protest, and he could see the struggle play out across her expressive face—frustration warring against gratitude. Then she nodded her acceptance. He kissed her once more, lingeringly, promising...asking patience. Then he snatched up the towel he'd left on the deck, knotted it carelessly around his hips and left her there.

He wasn't gone long; it only seemed like forever to her. She'd been afraid that the fever that had driven her to do this insane, this aberrant thing might cool before he came back, but she'd underestimated the intensity of her hunger for him. Her whole body vibrated with it. She waited for him, sitting on the steps, half submerged in the tepid water, rocked by the rhythm of her own life forces and counting the seconds of his absence in the slow drumbeat of the pulses that throbbed in her swollen, secret places.

When he came it was almost without a sound, but she'd have needed none to know he was there; every nerve in her body sprang joyfully to life, humming with excitement. Languid with arousal, her breath heavy in her throat, she tilted her head and watched him as he dropped the towel on the flagstones and stepped into the pool. She couldn't see his face; his body was a dark sculpture silhouetted against the house lights. Like a phantom, she thought. My phantom lover. And somehow that made it easier, to think of him as something not quite real. Not a real man but a fantasy...a dream that would vanish in the light of reality. Or like Cinderella's Prince, at the stroke of midnight.

She felt him ease in behind her on the step, felt his legs slide around her so that the silky unsheathed hardness of him nestled in the cleft of her buttocks. She sighed and would have arched back against him, but unexpectedly, almost roughly, he pushed her forward, gathered her hair in his hand and thrust it aside, baring her vulnerable neck. He lowered his mouth to her nape, savagely demanding, raking her tender skin with his teeth, marking her there with his sucking, staking his claim on her in that most primitive and elemental way so that she gasped at the surprise, the raw sexuality of it. Then she began to whimper as desire exploded inside her with such force it frightened her.

She was on the edge of panic when, with a gentling sigh, e abruptly leaned back and drew her with him so that she lay n her back on top of him, completely open and exposed to is sensitive hands…his long, questing fingers. Exposed and ulnerable…bewildered at the flood of feeling that had all but wamped her. Trembling. The warm, humid night air cooled 1e water on her naked body, raising goose bumps and hard-ning her nipples until they hurt.

"This is for you. Just for you." The words were a whisper f warm breath against her ear. She felt his hands warming er breasts, and then the pressure of his fingers on her tight, :hing nipples. A shaft of pure need, bright and sharp as pain, rrowed through her belly and deep into her core, and she rched her back and uttered a high, thin, panting cry as she 1rned her head, frantically seeking him. His head came down, locking light and thought. As his mouth angled across hers, wallowing up her cry with a masculine growl of satisfaction nd encouragement, his hands swept down over her ribs and elly, and the friction of his fingers rubbing on her chilled skin 1ade her burn, but *inside*. His hands cradled her hips, slipped own and under the backs of her thighs, lifted and drew them part. She'd never felt so utterly vulnerable, so exposed…so aked and helpless.

Do you trust me?

Where had they come from, those words? Were they a re-1inder or a plea?

Trust me. A great shudder passed through her body. With 1motion swelling inside her like a tsunami, she lifted her arms igh above her head, thus opening herself to him even more, 1aking of herself an offering, totally without restriction or 2straint. She reached blindly for him, found his shoulders and 1en his neck, clung to him and whimpered as his fingers :roked her, soothed her, parted her, pushed into her yielding oftness…and then withdrew…slid inside her again, gently at rst, then deeper, deeper…until she felt as if he touched the ery center of her being. It was then that she felt herself com-1g apart, as though her physical self was separating into its

individual atoms and then merging with all the bright electric
impulses that made up her emotional self…her soul, her *b*
ing… so that it was no longer possible to distinguish one fro
the other. Her physical self and her emotional self were on
and somehow she knew that neither would ever be the sam
again. She held on to him, to Riley, the man who had brough
her to this, dazed and sobbing partly with rage, partly wi
rapture, and with hopelessness, too. And fear. And she though
What have you done to me? I trusted you. And you've show
me heaven, knowing I can never have it. Knowing this is ju
a fantasy that must end at the stroke of midnight…

It was later, much later, when Riley carried her to the nea
est chaise and laid her gently, tenderly down. He ached s
exquisitely, the pressure inside him was so intense he fear
he would explode before he'd even had a chance to savor th
feel of her feminine softness around him. He was surprise
then, and humbled, too, when he felt her body enfold hir
almost immediately swell and heat and quicken to his urge
rhythms, and finally, one last time and even as his own bod
tightened and trembled, then seemed to break apart in tot
devastation, he heard her small, wild cry and felt her bod
pulsing with his, drawing him out, nurturing his r
lease…healing, even then.

They lay together in the aftermath, bathed in the warm, so
night, lulled by the soothing music of the water, stroking eac
other with lazy, sated fingers. Riley couldn't remember ev
having felt so relaxed in his life before. Or so…he realize
with a shock that the word he was looking for was *happy*. H
felt dazed with happiness, dizzy with it…awed by it, as if he'
spent his entire life up to this point under clouds and w:
seeing the sun for the first time. When Summer sighed and s
up, stretching and combing her hair back with her fingers, k
felt bereft, even though he knew and understood that the
couldn't have stayed where they were.

"Come upstairs with me," he whispered, drawing his fi
gers lightly down her spine. But when she looked at him wi
longing and shook her head, he understood that, too.

So he sighed and drew her down for one more lingering kiss. And when she'd pulled away from him and turned to pick up her dress from where she'd left it in a puddle like melted butter on the deck, and her fingers were deft and hurried on the buttons, he gently and wryly teased her, saying, "What's your hurry? Do we turn into pumpkins at the stroke of midnight?"

He didn't understand what made her burst into ironic and pain-filled laughter.

Chapter 14

The next three days were a time of waiting. Hurricane Angela, now a category-three storm, wobbled her way through the Atlantic, gathering strength. She would only grow more powerful the longer she vacillated, drawing energy from the warm ocean waters. Storm flags were up all along the coast from Savannah to the Outer Banks, with the National Guard positioned to help with the evacuations, if necessary. The weather stayed overcast, hot and oppressive.

While the Southeast waited to see what Hurricane Angela would do, Riley and Summer waited for a phone call. The trap had been set; now all they could do was wait and see if the quarry they sought would take the bait.

To Riley, the atmosphere in his house seemed to have turned as gray and heavy as the weather, sultry with unvoiced passion and weighed down by the awareness that regardless of the outcome of the FBI's ''sting,'' there could be no happy-ever-after outcome for what had begun between himself and Summer. Once the threat to her and her children had been eliminated, by whatever means, she would leave his life forever; she was adamant about that. And he was left on the horns of a terrible dilemma, knowing that the circumstances that would give her back her life would, in effect, take away his.

Because he was in love with her. Of that he was no longer in any doubt. The thought of his life beyond her leaving loomed like the vast emptiness he'd known all his life, and felt sometimes now even as he held her in his arms.

Sometimes when he looked at her, when he looked at the children…when Helen squinched up her face in that imp-look she got just before she bopped him on the nose with one of her pile-driver kisses, or when David looked up from the computer at him with that sudden brightening of joy that erased the pleat of worry between his eyes…then he'd teeter on the brink, thinking, *Maybe…maybe I could.* But each time, the fear drove him back from the edge.

Meanwhile, the schedule of their days had reverted to that awkward time right after she and the children had first come to stay with him, when she'd been avoiding him and doing her best to keep the kids and animals out of his way as well. But at night, after the children were asleep and the house was quiet, she would come to him as he swam, dropping her clothing on the flagstones and slipping silently into the pool and into his arms. She would not sleep with him, nor share his bed, nor any other bed in his house, no matter how briefly; but in the warm, dark, womblike water, it seemed she could allow herself to shed the constraints of motherhood and revel in the primitive joy of simply being a woman.

They made love in and out of the water and in every imaginable way, with the fervent abandon of wartime lovers, knowing it could all end tomorrow with the ringing of a telephone.

Midway through Friday morning Danell beeped Riley out of a conference with a client. Because he knew she wouldn't do such a thing unless it was urgent, his heart gave a lurch and accelerated as he went to meet her in the hallway.

"Who is it?" His voice sounded like a truckload of gravel. Danell shrugged and said with a frown, "Sounds like one of those guys on the commercials, you know—'Don' worry, be happy'. Hey—he *swore* you'd want to talk to him. Man, he better be right. Said it was personal—''

"It's okay," Riley passed her with a reassuring touch on her arm and headed for his office. He picked up the phone, gripped it hard. "Hey, Brasher, what's up?"

"They say we got to go now," the deep musical voice answered without preamble. "Say the hurricane be here by tonight." There was a pause and an apologetic sigh. "Well…she's pretty upset, you know…doesn't want to go."

"Oh, Lord." Riley closed his eyes and rubbed his forehead hard with his fingertips.

"Well…she's scared, you know." Brasher's chuckle sounded almost tender. "She's kickin' up a fuss pretty good, too." There was a pause, and then in a voice as gentle and inexorable as the tide, he said, "Boy, you know you're the only one can quiet her down…make her go. You bettah come now. She'll listen to you."

Riley nodded, though there was no one there to see. He felt as though a lead weight had settled on his heart. "I'll be there," he said finally. "As soon as I can."

He broke the connection and sat for a moment frowning at the windows, at skies that matched his mood. Then he went and stuck his head around the corner into Danell's office. "Give me five minutes to wrap this up," he said, indicating the conference room. "Cancel the rest of the day, and then go on home and batten down the hatches. You got plenty of milk, bread and flashlight batteries?"

Danell rolled her eyes at him. Like him, she lived far enough from the coast not to have to worry about tidal surges and such, and when the last big hurricane—Hugo—had come through Charleston she'd been in high school somewhere in Alabama. She didn't really have any idea what they might be in for.

It took him three times longer than normal to get home. Although the Charleston area hadn't been given the official order to evacuate, the tourists and the faint of heart—those who remembered Hugo all too well—were already heading out. At the last minute he stopped in at the Wal-Mart where he'd lately become a regular customer and picked up milk, some lanterns, a portable radio and a good supply of batteries, just in case. The lines were long there, too.

Even with all that, it was early enough that when he pulled into his driveway, Summer met him at the door, sure something must be up. Her face was pale and set, but her eyes were bright and battle-ready.

"Have you heard? Did they call?"

Resisting a powerful desire to gather her into his arms and shelter her, he shook his head and moved past her to set his shopping bags on the island countertop. He could hear the children's shouts and laughter out by the pool.

"Something's come up," he said quietly as he put the gallon jugs of milk in the refrigerator, closed the door, wadded up the plastic bags and tossed them under the sink. "I'm gonna have to go and take care of something." He heard her little gasp of dismay and steeled himself against it.

"These are for you," he continued, keeping his tone matter-of-fact, not letting himself look at Summer's face as he calmly spread the radio, flashlights and batteries he'd bought out on the counter. "In case I don't get back…in case the power goes out—as you know it can." His mouth twisted, more a quirk than a smile. He took a breath, then headed for the stairs, jerking at his tie and talking as he went. She followed him silently. "If it does, the security system for the house has a battery-powered backup that should last for a couple hours—power's never been out for more than an hour or so at the most, so you should be okay. Let's see…there's bottled water in the cupboards, and you can use what's in the pool for washing and flushing and such.…"

He turned into his bedroom, and she stopped in the doorway and leaned against the frame. He could feel her watching him as he undressed, tossed his jacket, shirt and tie on the bed, then sat down on it to take off his shoes. His movements were jerky with anger—not at her, although she couldn't know that.

How could she know he felt guilty for leaving her, resentful for having to, and defensive because of it? He strode into his dressing room wearing only trousers, footsteps heavy with his anger, resentment and guilt.

"They're evacuating the islands," he called back to her as he rummaged for Dockers and windbreaker, polo shirt and athletic shoes. "I've got to go and help somebody…somebody I'm responsible for."

"Is it Brasher?" Summer asked, though she didn't want to.

For a moment there was silence, and then quietly from the depths of the closet, he replied, "Yeah, Brasher's one…"

"And the woman…the one I saw you talking to?" Oh, she wished she hadn't said that! She'd tried not to, felt miserable the moment she did, but somehow it just wouldn't be denied. Too late to contain the words, she stood dumbly with her hand clamped over her mouth and watched Riley come slowly around the corner from the dressing room, carrying his shoes in one hand and holding his pants together at the waist with the other. Neither Rhett nor Prince nor hero now, but just a man, an ordinary man with a life and secrets she couldn't share.

He came across the room, his face hard, his eyes shielded from her, and sat down on the bed. She watched him as he methodically peeled off one dress sock, put on a cotton athletic sock and then the shoe. Watched him repeat it with the other foot. Finally, with both feet once more on the floor, he rested his forearms on his knees and raised his face to hers. What she saw in his eyes shocked her. There was no anger there at all, but only a deep, incomprehensible sadness.

She muttered a stricken, "I'm sorry—"

He shook his head, stopping her there. And then said, in a slow, careful way, as if every word pained him, "Her name is Modeen Kemp—the woman you saw me talking to. She's Brasher's granddaughter. She's a licensed practical nurse, and I pay her to take care of…someone…for me." He paused and looked away, but she saw his throat move and suddenly knew how he was aching. And *her* throat, *her* chest, every part of her ached for him. "That someone," he said harshly, "is my mother."

Though she'd already guessed by then, she made a tiny, involuntary cry. She would have gone to him, but he held her back with a look. "You asked me if my mother was alive, and if I ever saw her, and I told you yes. What I didn't tell you was that she has no idea who I am."

"Alzheimer's?" Summer whispered.

There was no humor whatsoever in his smile. "Among other things—in recent years, anyway. The alcohol had done its work long before that."

Once again she whispered, "I'm sorry." But he had already risen and turned away with a shrug, his face cold.

"She's happiest on the marshes with Brasher and Modeen, and she'll stay there as long as they can care for her. Sometimes she gets hard to manage—when she's upset…scared. I've got to go and help get her moved, settled down in a strange place—"

"I understand," Summer murmured. "Don't worry about us—we'll be fine."

In the doorway he paused and looked down at her for a long, silent moment, then enfolded her in his arms and held her the way he'd held and comforted her when they'd discovered Helen in the tree. Only this time she knew beyond any doubt that it was he who drew comfort from her.

And when he had gone, she went on standing there hugging herself and aching inside, thinking, My God, Riley—what's wrong? What else is it that you're not telling me?

Because what she'd seen in the depths of his eyes and felt in the tremors deep within him was as unmistakble as it was bewildering. Why should so strong and capable a man know *fear?*

Mirabella was frustrated. And when she finally succeeded in getting through to Special Agent Redfield on the telephone number he'd given her, he sounded just as frustrated as she was, maybe more so.

"I've been trying to reach you all day," she said accusingly. "The circuits have been busy."

"It's this damned hurricane," Redfield growled, then apologized for his language with a sigh. "First they had us ready to evacuate, then they changed their minds, said it looks like it's gonna miss Savannah, after all. It's complete chaos around here...." All of a sudden it seemed to occur to him who he was talking to, and Mirabella could almost feel the electricity coming through the line. "What've you got? You've heard?"

"Well, I *think* so...." But in spite of her caution, she couldn't keep a thrill of excitement out of her voice. "He *said* he was from Summer's class reunion committee. His voice was kind of muffled—you know, like he was talking through cloth? But it was Hal—I *know* it."

"And you gave him the address?"

"Of course," Mirabella said impatiently, "I did exactly what you told me."

"Okay...okay...." It was an exhalation, almost a sigh. Then, brisk once more, he said, "Okay, thanks very much, Mrs. Starr. Let me know if you hear from anyone else—same procedure, okay? We'll be in touch."

And he broke the connection before Mirabella could tell him she hadn't had any luck getting through to Summer's number, either. As a result, she felt more frustrated than ever. And more afraid.

"She be fine now." Brasher's fingers, gnarled as twigs, briefly touched the lined and haggard face of the woman asleep in the hotel bed. Her sallow skin hung loose over the bones of her skull; gray hair with touches of rusty gold, like tarnish, lay sparse on her blue-veined temples; a snore issued from between thin lips sunken over empty gums, the teeth for which were on the nightstand beside her, submerged in a hotel water glass. "Let her sleep...."

Modeen, who was sitting on the bed taking her patient's pulse, looked up at Riley and nodded. "It's just a mild sedative. She'll sleep now, tomorrow probably be a little bit more isoriented than usual, but once she gets back in her own place, she'll be okay.'' She stood up, coiled the blood-pressure cuff that had been lying across her lap and put it in the medical bag on the other bed, closed it, then went into the bathroom and closed the door.

"She was beautiful once,'' said Brasher softly. Tender and sad, his eyes rested on the woman's gaunt face. "When she was a girl. You know, she had so many dreams.''

Riley said nothing. He felt no connection to the woman in the bed at all. He felt nothing. His heart was like stone. "Well,'' he said, "I guess I'd better be getting back.''

Brasher nodded. "You go on home now. Your mama be fine. Best you go now, take care of your woman…those nice kids.''

Riley made an involuntary movement of denial that involved his whole body. "She's not my woman,'' he said on an exhalation as he twirled his windbreaker over one shoulder. "Wish she could be, but…'' He shook his head and walked to the door. "It's never gonna happen.'' He took a deeper breath trying to make room for his heart—still a stone, but too big now for his chest.

"Boy, what you mean by that?'' Brasher threw a look toward the bathroom door, then came over and caught Riley by the wrist.

Riley shrugged and looked past him, looking for escape. "Oh, you know…she's got the children—''

"That's what's holdin' you back? What's the matter with you, boy? Those kids, they *need* you—you tell me you don't see that? That boy, his eyes, they follow you ever' where you go, 'bout eat you alive. That little girl, she just want a daddy to love her, you can tell that by lookin'.''

"They need a father. They don't need me.'' Now Riley's face felt like stone, and his voice sounded like it. He opened the door, but Brasher followed him through it and into the deserted hotel hallway.

"Boy,'' the older man said in a wondering tone, "I know what you're thinkin'. You thinkin' you gonna be like *her?*''

He jerked his head toward the room they'd just left. "Lil your daddy was?"

Riley flinched. He said harshly, "I can't risk that possibi ity."

For a few moments Brasher didn't say anything, just gaze at the floor, his hands hooked in the straps of his overalls. Ar for some reason, instead of walking off and leaving him ther Riley found himself waiting, while tension hummed behir his eyeballs and through his molars and vibrated in the pit his belly. Finally, the old man lifted his head and looked n at him, but dreamily into the distance beyond his shoulder.

"Remember," he said softly, "that time the big storm con through—you were a little boy, 'bout ten—an' afterward w went out to the island—"

Riley nodded. He caught a sharp, edgy breath. "And w found the osprey on the beach. I remember. It had been injure in the storm and couldn't fly."

"No, boy—he only *thought* he was injured. He only *thoug* he couldn't fly." Brasher chuckled low in his chest. "Poor o osprey so battered and beat-up in the storm, he too scared fly. He just sittin' there on the beach, too scared to move."

"I walked right up to him," Riley said slowly. "I was goin to put my jacket over him so we could take him home…fi him up. But before I could, he started to flap his wings an hop, trying to get away. And then he just…flew away."

Brasher shook his head, his body jerking with silent laugl ter. "Just needed a strong-enough incentive to make him tr Found out he wasn't as banged up as he thought he was. Fa is, he was *fine.*" He stopped chuckling and gave Riley a sid ways look. "That woman, you know, she got the healer touch."

Riley gave a laugh of surprise. "How'd you know that?

Brasher shrugged. "See it in her eyes…her hands, too. O yeah, she got the touch." His smile broadened. "Maybe she *meant,* boy—" he pointed toward the ceiling "—you eve think 'bout that? Maybe she meant to heal *you.*"

Riley laughed again, this time with a growing sense of ligh

ness and hope. He said with a smile of irony, "I told her once I was the doctor that was going to take care of *her*."

It was then that his beeper went off.

Summer had never liked wind. She'd grown up in the desert where the winds blew so incessantly they molded the trees and shrubs to their will. She'd lived in a part of the Los Angeles Basin where the Santa Ana winds blew down the valleys and through the passes with enough force to toss tractor-trailer rigs like toys, hot and dry enough to suck every last drop of moisture from plants and people alike. She didn't mind rain, even in torrents, and actually found thunder and lightning sort of exciting. But wind to her seemed like something *alive,* like a raging beast trying to get to her where she cowered inside her pitiful shelter. When the wind blew hard, she felt small and helpless, and afraid.

But she couldn't let the children know that. For them she had to be strong, confident and brave. Even when the power went out early on, and they couldn't make popcorn or watch videos as they had during the big thunderstorm, she stayed cheerful, making an adventure out of it. Instead of popcorn, they made peanut-butter-and-jelly sandwiches by flashlight, took them upstairs—along with a huge bowlful of grapes—where, as before, everyone including Beatle climbed into Summer's bed. No one was going to be doing any sleeping, not with the wind screaming like someone being tortured, and things snapping and crashing and thumping around outside. So, instead of watching videos, Summer read while David held the flashlight. They'd finished *The Black Stallion* and were well into *The Black Stallion Returns* by now. Summer kept the portable radio on the nightstand, tuned to the emergency station but turned down low.

Once, after a particularly loud crash that made the windows rattle and the bed shake, Helen crept closer against Summer's side and said in a small, frightened voice, "Mommy, is this the hurry-cane?"

Summer put an arm around her and hugged her. "Sure i:
Remember what Brasher said? 'It's a bi-ig ba-ad storm.'"

Helen giggled, then instantly looked as if she might cry
"He said Riley would take care of us, but he's not here
Mommy, when is Riley comin' home?"

"Soon," said Summer firmly. "He'll be here soon. Hey—
you know what? I'm tired of reading. Why don't we sing fo
a while? How about, 'Jingle Bells, Batman Smells—'"

"Mom!"

"Well, okay, then how 'bout, 'On top of Old Smo-o-key
all covered with fleas...'"

They were singing that, all the verses they could remember
as well as some *really* silly ones they made up on the spur o
the moment, when suddenly Summer went very still.

David stopped singing and gasped, "What?"

"Hush," she said, giving him a squeeze. "Listen..."

"It's quiet!"

"Does that mean the hurry-cane is over?"

"No, dummy, it's the *eye.* That means it's only *half* over."

"David, please don't call your sister a dummy—how woul(
you like it if I called *you* a dummy?" But she said it in ;
teasing way, tussling playfully with both children, a surefir
way to start a roughhouse. But before it could get under way
Beatle went "Wuf!" and jumped down off the bed.

"Riley's home!" Helen said with a little gasp of joy.

But Summer said, "Hush," and her arms tightened aroun(
both of her children. She hadn't heard a car drive in or a doo
open. And Beatle's tail wasn't wagging. Instead, from her tin
throat came a low but unmistakable growl.

"Mom—"

"Shush!"

At that moment, from downstairs there came a terribl(
screech. A panic-stricken *"Get out, get out, get out!"* Then ;
splintering crash. And finally...silence. Dead silence.

But Summer knew. Someone was in the house.

Riley was on his cell phone shouting at the top of his lungs
trying to make himself heard above the roar of wind and rai

and the futile slap of his windshield wipers. Somewhere out there in that chaos of fallen trees and blowing shingles and whipping power lines he knew Jake Redfield was doing the same.

"I can't get through," he bellowed. "It's flooded here. I'm gonna have to try another way. Dammit, can't you do something? Send a damn helicopter!"

"Are you out of your mind?" Well, that came through clearly enough. But then Riley heard, "Best I can...police...emergency band..." and then nothing but static.

He swore, and in a gesture of rage and futility, hurled the phone onto the passenger seat. His lungs burned with cold fire, as if he'd been running. Like a nightmare—*his* nightmare. From out of his past, from the distant echoes of memory, he felt it—the icy paralysis of fear.

He wasn't going to be in time. He'd left them unprotected, knowing that even then the syndicate thugs might be closing in. If they'd taken the FBI's bait, picked up Hal Robey's trail, if they came for Summer and the children now, in this...and why wouldn't they? It was the best possible moment. Power and phones were out, roads blocked, Jake and his agents cut off, the local police helpless to respond even if the security alarm did sound. Dammit, they were alone...helpless.

He wasn't going to be able to save them. Dear God, he raged, *Why?* Why did he always seem destined to fail those he loved most?

He had only one hope left. Tom Denby. Please, God, he prayed, let him be there, even in this. *Please, God, let him be in time.*

"Shh—not a sound," Summer whispered. With one arm around each of her children, she herded them, tiptoeing, out of her room and into the dark hallway. She'd turned off her flashlight, figuring the one advantage she had was that she knew the layout of the house better than any intruder would.

"Where's Beatle?" David hissed. "Mom—"

"Shh! I'll find her. Never mind that now. Come on—i here." As quietly as she could, she led them across the ha and into the room where they'd discovered Helen in the mag nolia tree. "Quick—under the bed. Stay there and *don't move* And not a sound, do you understand me? No matter wha happens. *Not one sound.*" For once there was no argument no squabbling. Just silence. Summer watched her childre wriggle under the edge of the canopy bed, then smoothed th spread and left them there. Left the room and closed the doo soundlessly behind her.

Out in the hallway she stood for a moment, listening. He heart was pounding, but her head was clear. As she weighe the flashlight in her hand, she knew what she had to do. was obvious to her that the FBI wasn't coming, at least not i time; all their carefully laid plans had been blown apart by th hurricane. No one was going to come and rescue her. She wa on her own. The flashlight was the only weapon she had, an it wasn't enough. Her best hope was to get outside. If it wa just a burglar she'd heard, taking advantage of the storm an the power outage, let him ransack the place. He could tak whatever he wanted—he wasn't going to find the children. it was Hal—please, God, let it be Hal—he'd make himsel known and then she could talk to him, convince him to tur himself in. And if it wasn't Hal or a burglar...if it was th same thugs who had burned her house...well, then she'd dra them out after her, make them chase her, like a mother lar pretending a broken wing. They'd probably catch her, bu she'd convince them the children were somewhere else, some where safe. Then...

Beyond that she didn't dare think. First, she had to get pas whoever it was...get outside. *But where were they?* Sh couldn't hear anything!

And then Beatle began to bark. Furiously, viciously, growl ing and snarling the way she did when she was shaking an mauling one of her practice "kills." Summer heard mut ters...swearing. A muffled shout. A soft but dreadful *thud*. sharp, shrill cry.

"Oh, no," she whimpered. "Oh, Beatle—" She lunged for the stairs, her heart racing.

And stopped, stifling her sobs with her hand. No—she couldn't go to pieces now. She had to stay calm. Keep her head. Brushing tears from her cheeks, she crept silently toward the stairs.

Someone was coming up the stairs.

Summer dropped down into a crouch in the shadow of the banister, and as she did, felt something brush past her face. Something silent as a breeze or a puff of smoke. Or a cat's tail. *Oh, God—Peggy Sue!* Once more she clamped a hand over her mouth and held her breath, this time to stifle a hiccup of half-hysterical laughter. It was almost too much—no doubt about it, the cat was heading down the stairs. Completely unperturbed by either storm or strangers, parading right down the middle as if she owned them, as she always did. And the intruder was coming up. Somewhere, the two were going to have to meet. And, of course, only *one* could see in the dark....

No sooner had the thought formed in her mind than there came an outraged feline screech, followed by a muffled cry and then a whole series of bumps, thumps and clatters. Almost the moment they began Summer was on her feet and running as soundlessly as she could down the stairs, counting on the racket to cover any noises she did make. Near the bottom she halted, warned by some primitive sense. No help for it—she had to risk turning on the flashlight, just for a second. Just for an instant—but it was enough to reveal what she had already suspected. And though she had been prepared, she couldn't stop the sharp intake of her breath.

A man lay sprawled on the floor at the foot of the stairs— not dead, or even, she feared, badly injured; he was already beginning to move and groan a little. She couldn't see his face, but she knew it wasn't Hal—too big and broad to be Hal. And there was no doubt in her mind about what she needed to do. Leaning over the man and gripping the flashlight upraised like a club, she switched it on once more.

But before she had time to bring it down on the dazed man's

head, or even cry out, someone grabbed her from behind
knocking the flashlight out of her hand. She could hear i
rolling across the tile floor as a powerful arm clamped acros
her throat, cutting off her air supply. She struggled, kicking a
her assailant's legs and making contact at least once. She hear
a satisfying grunt of pain and a vicious snarl. "Do that agaii
and I'll break your neck."

She believed that, so she stopped struggling. And in th
sudden stillness a voice came quietly from the darkness nea
the door to Riley's study. "It's me you want. Let her go."

Hal!

The pressure on her windpipe eased, and her body dragge
in air in a shuddering, convulsive gasp. There was a roarin
in her ears. Fighting to remain conscious, Summer heard gar
bled bits of conversation: "*…is it, Robey?*" "*Haven't got…*"
"*Tell…kill her.*"

Her head cleared just as a flashlight beam slashed throug
the darkness, pinioning the figure of a man…the man Summe
had been married to for twelve years, the man she had onc
loved. Her children's father. He looked strangely unchanged
she thought. His smile was as charming as ever.

"What's that you got there?" the man holding Summe
growled.

Still smiling, Hal held up a package wrapped in bright pa
per. "This? Just some presents for my kids."

"Yeah? Let's see it." A hand moved into Summer's lin
of vision—a hand holding a gun.

What happened next happened so fast, she was never sur
of the exact sequence. And yet, some things seemed in slov
motion: The package and Hal's hand moving in a short down
ward arc. The gun flying out of the man's hand. Hal's scream
"*Run!*"

Then she was running, through the dark kitchen, throug
the mudroom and out into a chaos of howling wind and driv
ing rain. The eye of the hurricane had passed; the storm wa
on them again in its full force and fury, the noise so intens
she couldn't hear her own sobs. She ran instinctively, dow

the driveway and into the lane, heading toward the gate. Around her trees lashed and groaned like tormented souls. She couldn't tell what was happening behind her—shouts, running footsteps, even gunshots were swallowed up in the storm.

Something—someone—grabbed her from out of the darkness. She struggled, half-mindless with terror, screaming, scratching and biting like a wild animal, until a voice growled in her ear, "Hey—take it easy! You're safe now—you're safe!"

Safe. That word punched through the wall of her terror and she went slack, letting herself be half dragged, half carried into the comparative shelter of the trees, just as footsteps splattered through the water rushing down the brick drive, and indistinguishable shapes flashed by them in the thinning darkness.

When they had passed, the man holding Summer gasped, "Sorry I was late—had to ram through the damn gate...leave my car down there in the lane. Trees down."

"Who...are...you?" Summer asked through chattering teeth.

"Name's Denby, ma'am. I work for Mr. Grogan. I was supposed to watch out for you and the kids...sure hope he don't fire me, lettin' this—"

"My children!" And she was running again, back toward the house, running with her heart in her throat and her lungs on fire, deaf to the pleas of her rescuer to wait—wait for him to check things out! But she was driven by something more compelling than fear.

Into the house she went, soaked to the skin, water streaming down her face and into her eyes. Up the stairs and down the hallway, needing no light to see the way. Calling her children's names, she threw open the door of their hiding place and dropped to the floor beside the canopy bed.

"David? Helen? Hey, you can come— *Oh...God...*" The cry tore through her, ripping her apart, a cry of utter devastation.

Her children weren't there. They were gone. *Gone...*

* * *

Riley had some bad moments during that seemingly endless drive home through the height of the hurricane—such as narrowly avoiding a head-on collision with a couple of suicidal idiots, one a four-by-four of some kind, the other a big dark sedan, both heading the other way like bats out of hell. Then finding his gate broken in, and a little farther up the lane, coming upon Tom Denby's car abandoned with its hood buried in a fallen tree. But nothing—not all the worst moments of his life put together—could have compared with the moment when he burst through the wide-open doors of his house and heard that terrible cry. He'd heard something like it once before, the day they'd found Helen in the tree, but this was worse. A thousand times worse.

He didn't even remember how he got up the stairs and down the hallway to that bedroom doorway. But somehow he was standing in it, frozen there, and his eyes were on Summer as she stood silhouetted against the lightening windows. She stood like a pillar, too stunned even to cry as the windows crashed open and two small figures, like storm-drenched fledglings, crept over the sill and ran to their mother's side.

"We were gonna climb down the tree and run for help," he heard David explain, gasping for breath. "I know you told us to stay here and don't move, but then we heard the noises—"

And then Riley was across the room and he couldn't get them gathered into his arms fast enough. He was shaking so hard he felt as though he'd break apart, as if the only things holding him together were their arms, their laughter, their joyous shouts of "Oh, God—Riley!" "Hey, it's Mr. Riley!" "Riley's home!"

Yes, he was. At long last, he was home.

It was David who pulled away first. While Riley closed and latched the window, he drew a hand across his nose, sniffed and said, "Mom, Beatle's dead, isn't she?" But he wasn't crying; his voice was quiet and brave. "I heard. Those men— they killed her, didn't they?"

Summer lifted her eyes from her son's face to Riley's. Hers

was pale and glistening with raindrops in the graying light; dawn was breaking, even in the midst of the hurricane. "She tried to defend us," she said brokenly. "I don't know… I don't know about any of them. They gave the alarm. And Peggy Sue tripped one guy and made him fall down the stairs. But I haven't heard anything since. I just don't know.…"

"Let's not jump to conclusions," Riley said with a confidence he didn't feel. "It's getting light. We'll find them…won't we, guys?" As the two children gazed up at him with trusting eyes, he took them each by the hand and, with a long look at Summer, led the way downstairs. Please, God, he thought, no matter what happens…don't let me let them down.

But somehow, he didn't think he would. Ever again.

Downstairs they found that Tom Denby had already checked out and buttoned up the place and lit the battery-powered lanterns he'd found in the kitchen. With their help and the slowly growing daylight, they quickly located Cleo. The little gray parrot was pacing back and forth along the tops of the living room draperies, muttering and swearing, "Stupid…dog…" and staring with baleful yellow eyes at the cat Peggy Sue, who was stretched out on the back of the sofa just below her like a panther on a tree limb, placidly twitching her tail.

"My God," Summer breathed, laughing weakly with relief, "how did she get up there? I didn't think she could fly."

"Maybe," said Riley, laughing, too, "she just didn't have enough incentive."

"Mom! Mom, come quick!" David's shout brought them into the central hallway at a dead run. "I found her! I found Beatle! She's not dead! Quick, Mom—she's hurt.…"

The little dog was lying on the rug just inside Riley's study, whimpering softly. She didn't try to get up, but when David knelt beside her, she lifted her head and licked his face.

"Quick—" Summer was already down on her knees beside the dog "—get me a blanket—towels, a pillow, anything—go on, David, hurry!" As David jumped up and ran for the stairs, her hands were moving gently and expertly over the little animal's shivering body. When he'd gone, she looked up at Riley and said gravely, "She's badly hurt. She needs a vet."

"You're a vet," he reminded her, balancing on the balls of his feet beside her, his hand on the back of her neck.

She shook her head. "She needs a hospital—X-rays. Her leg's broken, for sure. She could have an injured spine, internal injuries—"

"We'll go," Riley promised. "As soon as the storm's over." He didn't stop to ask himself how they'd get there through all the storm debris; he knew he'd find a way somehow.

When Jake Redfield arrived a short time later, Riley and Summer were in Riley's big bed, fully clothed with the two sleeping children curled like kittens against their sides. Beatle lay on a pillow on Summer's lap cocooned in blankets, also sleeping, shivering and whimpering only fitfully now. Summer was much encouraged by that. With the immediate threat of severe shock seemingly over, she felt the little dog's prospects for a full recovery were good.

"Brave little Beatle," she whispered, gently stroking the dog's glossy black hide. "My hero..."

Riley's arms tightened around her and he started to say something, but before he could the FBI agent knocked softly and stuck his head through the open door.

"Sorry," he said in a low voice as his eyes swept dispassionately over the bed and its occupants. "Your man Denby let me in—told me to come on up. Thought you'd like to know..." His dark, exhausted eyes came to rest on Summer. "Your husband's vehicle has been found, Mrs. Robey. In the river just west of here—witnesses tell us he drove off a washed-out bridge. According to those same witnesses, the car that was chasing him saw it happen and stopped in time. Then turned around and took off. I don't think they'll be back." He paused, then said stiffly, "For what it's worth, I'm sorry." His eyes were dark with frustrated fury.

Summer nodded and mumbled through the ache in her throat, "He saved us, you know. In the end..."

Redfield nodded, frowning. "Yeah...well... What I can't figure out is what brought him back here in the first place. Why was it so important for him to find you?" He shrugged, though the speculation remained in his eyes. "Guess we'll never know that now." He turned to leave, then abruptly came back and handed her a small package wrapped in brightly colored paper. "Oh—Denby asked me to give you this. Said he found it downstairs in the hallway—looks like it might belong to one of your kids."

Summer took the package and held it. "This is why," she said thickly as a tear rolled down her cheek. "Hal brought this for the kids. He said he'd come to see them. He'd brought them a present. This..."

Redfield had come closer, moving stiffly, suddenly alert as a wolf smelling prey. "Ma'am—if you wouldn't mind opening that?"

"Oh—sure." She tore off the paper with unsteady fingers and pounding heart, then relaxed with a sigh of exasperation. "Oh, Hal... I swear to God, he never changes." She held up several shrink-wrapped packages. "He always does this. Computer games—look at this. Most of them completely inappropriate for a child. Amazon Rangers! Doctor Death! What on earth was he thinking?" She sighed and began wrapping the games back in their festive paper. "Oh, well...I guess I'll just have to hide these, like I did the last batch."

Redfield turned away, his shoulders sagging with disappointment. At the door he paused and looked back. "Mrs. Robey, you know it was your husband they wanted, not you or the kids. You were just leverage. Now they know he's dead, they'd have no more reason to harm you. Looks like you're perfectly free to go now."

After the FBI man left there was silence, filled only with the sounds of sleeping dog and children and the rain and slowly dying wind. Summer could feel her heart pounding against Riley's arms where they crisscrossed her chest. She closed her eyes and tears oozed between them. I must not cry, she thought. I must not let him know.

And then she felt a shudder go through his body, and his breath gusted in her hair. "I can't do it," he said in a ragged voice. "I can't let you go."

"Riley..." she began, brokenly. But his arms tightened around her. He lowered his face to her ear, to the side of her face, and to her astonishment she felt the coolness of tears on *his* cheek.

"I mean, all of you—you, them, the animals—all of you. I want you to stay here with me. Please."

She said nothing for a long time, crying silently. When she could, she whispered, "Why?"

"Why?" He repeated it in an incredulous, broken voice. "Because I love you. Surely you must know that."

She nodded, crying harder. "Of course. And I love you. And we both know it's not enough. Not for me. Not for us. What's changed? You didn't want—"

"I was *afraid*." The word as he whispered it was so bleak it chilled her. "And then...I almost lost you. All of you. And that's when I knew there was something I was afraid of even more...."

"But *why?* Riley, what is it about us—the children—that scares you so much? I've watched you with them. You're wonderful. They adore you. I don't understand."

Again there was silence, and she felt his body tense against hers, as if he were gathering strength. Then, with his face pressed tightly against hers, he sighed and began in a slow, careful voice, "I told you my father died when I was twelve. What I didn't tell you was that he died in prison. He was murdered while serving time for manslaughter." He paused, then softly explained, "Other inmates don't like child-killers much."

Summer had gasped, but he went on before she could ask. "The child he killed was my brother. He beat him to death two weeks before his sixth birthday." She made a wounded sound. He held her more closely, rocking her, asking her to let him finish it. "My father was a brutal man. I learned early on to stay out of his way when he'd been drinking, which was most of the time. My mother…found her own means of escape. My brother wasn't so lucky. He wasn't big enough, strong enough…to get away, and my mother wasn't strong enough to protect him. My father hated him, I think, because he always believed he wasn't his child. He could have been right—I don't know.…

"I knew when he came home that day it was going to be bad. When he started in on Rusty I took off—ran to Brasher's to get help. Brasher called the police, and then we both ran back to our place, but we were too late. When we got there, my father was passed out drunk on the bed. My mother was sitting on the couch, holding my little brother in her arms, rocking him. Singing to him." He paused, then said softly, "She'd always been an alcoholic. But she was never sane after that. I left before the police came." His voice was flat. "Never went back."

"My God…" Summer was shaking so hard she could barely speak. "And you think— My God, Riley, you don't— you *can't* believe you'd ever be like them…that you'd even be capable—"

"I made a vow," he said, his voice hard as stone, "that I'd never give myself the opportunity to find out. I couldn't take the chance. Whatever the evil that was in them, it would die with me."

"Riley Grogan," she said fiercely, twisting in his arms to take his face between her hands, "you are the strongest, most self-assured man I've ever met. So strong I thought you didn't need anything or anybody—certainly didn't need *me!* And strong men do not hurt those who are weaker than they are! They don't. You couldn't *possibly* harm a child. Surely you know that!"

"I do now," he growled. "Maybe deep down I always did, but I needed—" he grabbed a breath as if it were pure oxygen "—someone to make me believe it. I needed—" He broke off and caught her hands, pressed them one at a time to his mouth. It seemed a long time before he drew a shuddering breath and murmured, "You have a healer's hands, Mrs. Robey. Did you know that? I do need you. I need you to heal me...." And the words flowed through her fingers like balm.

"I'll be happy to—" her voice was ragged, torn between laughter and tears of exasperation "—if you'll just please stop calling me Mrs. Robey."

"I will—I promise." Then he cleared his throat and continued in an endearingly stiff and formal tone, "I would much prefer, as soon as it can be arranged, to call you Mrs. Grogan."

There was a bemused pause; then in a voice soft with dawning wonder, Summer said, "All right."

"David—wake up, wake up," Helen whispered. "Hurry— you're gonna miss it! Mommy's kissin' Mr. Riley!"

Jake Redfield stood in the early morning fog and watched the uniformed sheriff's deputy stride toward him. Behind him on the banks of the river, other men, some wearing diving gear, were gathered around the shrouded body of a man.

"Fingerprints will have to confirm it," the deputy said as he drew near. "But it's Robey, all right. Everything matches."

"He have anything on him?" Redfield asked. *Like a computer disk, maybe?*

The deputy shook his head. "Wallet, several different I.D.s, a little cash, not much. Sorry..."

Redfield turned without a word and walked back to his car.

*　　*　　*　　*　　*

INTIMATE MOMENTS®
Silhouette®

invites you to Go West, dear reader, to

Cameron, Utah

for the conclusion of Margaret Watson's exhilarating miniseries.

September 1999
The Marriage Protection Program...IM #951

Janie Murphy knew she was Deputy Ben Jackson's *only* hope for gaining custody of orphaned Rafael. But Janie thought Ben would understand her refusal when he learned about her past. Instead, he proposed an irresistible trade—her hand for his protection. And suddenly Janie's heart faced the greatest risk of all....

Available at your favorite retail outlet.

And if you want to uncover more of this small town's secrets, don't miss...

The Fugitive Bride (Intimate Moments #920) April 1999
Cowboy with a Badge (Intimate Moments #904) January 1999
For the Children (Intimate Moments #886) October 1998
Rodeo Man (Intimate Moments #873) August 1998

Silhouette®

Looking For More Romance?

Visit Romance.net

Look us up on-line at: http://www.romance.net

Check in daily for these and other exciting features:

Hot off the press

View all current titles, and purchase them on-line.

What do the stars have in store for you?

Horoscope

Hot deals

Exclusive offers available only at Romance.net

Plus, don't miss our interactive quizzes, contests and bonus gifts.

PWEB

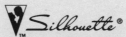

"Fascinating—you'll want to take
this home!"
—Marie Ferrarella

"Each page is filled with a brand-new
surprise."
—Suzanne Brockmann

"Makes reading a new and joyous
experience all over again."
—Tara Taylor Quinn

See what all your favorite authors
are talking about.

Coming October 1999 to a retail store near you.